BEST CANADIAN STORIES 2017

BEST CANADIAN STORIES

2017

JOHN METCALF

EDITOR

BIBLIOASIS
WINDSOR, ONTARIO

FIRST EDITION

ISBN 978-1-77196-206-3 (Hardcover)
ISBN 978-1-77196-204-9 (Trade Paper)
ISBN 978-1-77196-205-6 (eBook)
ISSN 0703-9476

Edited by John Metcalf
Copy-edited by Emily Donaldson
Typeset and designed by Chris Andrechek

Canada Council
for the Arts

Conseil des Arts
du Canada

ONTARIO ARTS COUNCIL
CONSEIL DES ARTS DE L'ONTARIO
an Ontario government agency
un organisme du gouvernement de l'Ontario

Canada ▌▪▌ Ontario
Ontario Media Development
Corporation

Published with the generous assistance of the Canada Council for the Arts, which last year invested $153 million to bring the arts to Canadians throughout the country, and the financial support of the Government of Canada. Biblioasis also acknowledges the support of the Ontario Arts Council (OAC), an agency of the Government of Ontario, which last year funded 1,709 individual artists and 1,078 organizations in 204 communities across Ontario, for a total of $52.1 million, and the contribution of the Government of Ontario through the Ontario Book Publishing Tax Credit and the Ontario Media Development Corporation.

PRINTED AND BOUND IN CANADA

CONTENTS

INTRODUCTION

JOHN METCALF

*B*EST *CANADIAN STORIES 2017* is the forty-seventh volume to appear in this uninterrupted series, which began in 1971. The first forty-six volumes were published by Oberon Press, which has now ceased operations as a publisher. By arrangement with Oberon, Biblioasis has assumed the *Best Canadian* title and is carrying on the tradition.

In 1971, David Helwig and Tom Marshall edited a story anthology for Oberon entitled *Fourteen Stories High.* Helwig's aim in starting the anthology was to provide an outlet for new, previously unpublished work, such outlets being then few in number.

"...[P]robably the real reason that the book happened just then," he wrote to me, "was that my unspoken, even unarticulated, motto in those days—and it was more or less everyone's motto—was 'Why not?' There was a powerful irrational presupposition that anything was possible and probably fun."

We believe the anthology to be of great importance for readers and writers. It alerts readers to unfamiliar names and to forthcoming books and, cumulatively, shapes possible new ways of seeing and feeling. For writers, it is a benchmark, a recognition that their work is now being read, watched, and given imprimatur by their community, that it is being commended nationally to an audience wider and more diverse than that reached by "little mags."

In another letter, David Helwig wrote: "Yes I think that such anthologies are important to writers and audiences. Especially annuals. They present something with substance and variety, offer a home for the very exciting story someone wants to write. I think the Oberon anthology has achieved that. It is an institution—we need institutions—and embodies my sense that there must be something regular and careful and caring, alongside your sense that the story is of infinite importance and must be polished and cherished. Yes, damn it, I think it was worth the effort, arriving every year like a secular Christmas."

Years later, when I was talking to him about *Fourteen Stories High*, he said that Tom Marshall and he had divided responsibilities more or less in half, Tom insisting on experimental, non-naturalistic stories while his own choices had been more traditional. At the time, David was still in England finishing a postgraduate degree; he wrote to Norman Levine and Mordecai Richler to ask for stories. Richler said he couldn't afford to give away a story, but Norman Levine sent him "In Quebec City."

Helwig wanted Marshall as co-editor "to have company, support, the presence of a second mind and thus, probably, more variety." When Tom Marshall dropped out of the project to concentrate on his own writing and David was faced with editing the second volume, now to be called *New Canadian Stories*, he chose as co-editor a Kingston friend, Joan Harcourt. He wrote to me of her: "I chose Joan Harcourt because she was nearby and pleasant and intelligent and well read. She had worked as a writer and editor for *Peace News* in London. I didn't think of the job as requiring brilliance."

In the same letter, talking of *Fourteen*, he said: "I think the Marian Engel story has real originality, though it's perhaps a bit slight. And the Don Bailey wears all its sins on its sleeve, awkwardness, lack of polish, but my god the people do sit up and live. You want perfection or nothing. I know nothing but imperfection."

In another letter he wrote: "I'll do my best to answer your questions, though I think that they are based on your story, your myth, if you like, of the development of the Canadian story, and like any story it is neither right nor wrong, but is a way of shaping the past into some kind of coherence, while there are other kinds of coherence to be found by other people. However there is probably a significant area of overlap between my story and your story. Perhaps it all comes down to the word 'best,' which rises large in your vocabulary and is more or less banned from mine. They don't call me an agnostic for nothing."

Sprinkled among these letters, dating from 2009 and 2013, are other statements that caused the eyebrow to rise.

"I never took the job of selection as a deeply serious matter."

"I was aware of the Martha Foley annual [*Best American Stories*] but never looked at it, I didn't think of stories as a specialized field..."

"I have never had your sense that stories are a special form."

"I just wanted to produce intelligent, readable collections, with maybe a surprise here and there."

David's account of the genesis of the anthology can be found on pages 138–141 of his autobiography, *The Names of Things*.

His co-editorship with Joan Harcourt lasted until 1975, when he resigned to take up hectic work for the CBC. He instigated my succession. I inherited from him both title and Joan Harcourt. Joan and I co-edited the 1976 and 1977 volumes of *New Canadian Stories*. I described the anthology's earliest years in *An Aesthetic Underground: A Literary Memoir*.

The policy of the series when I took over was to publish previously unpublished work. Helwig had started the series with the intention of providing another outlet for new work and new writers. Joan Harcourt and I were receiving manuscripts by the hundred. Nearly all were atrocious. I was soon driven to begging friends for unpublished stories—and at that, I wasn't getting the cream because Oberon could not afford to match the payments offered by some of the magazines, nominal though such payments were. (An entire genre in Canadian literature was shaped by the fact that some publications paid as much as a hundred dollars for a story, others far less, or nothing.) It dawned on me slowly that we were in direct competition with the literary magazines for a very small crop of good work. There was not much point in this and I began to get restless with the whole policy and purpose of the series.

Although Joan and I got on well together, I began to hanker after the idea of a fresh co-editor, someone not quite so *nice* as Joan, someone harsher in judgement. I felt I needed to work with someone who really knew short fiction, who lived and breathed it as I did. I wanted someone who would understand style and elegance and who would be repelled by socially acceptable *themes*. I decided on Clark Blaise. Joan resigned by mutual agreement in 1977 and I persuaded Michael Macklem, Oberon's publisher, to change both the title and policy of the anthology.

The title was now to be *Best Canadian Stories* and the policy was to concentrate on republishing the best stories from the literary magazines. I had wanted an outright policy of republication only, but Macklem argued that such a policy would be bad PR and would result in reviewers berating Oberon for closing off yet another publishing outlet. Under pressure, I agreed that we would continue to read and consider unsolicited manuscripts.

Joan Harcourt, in her farewell foreword to the 1978 book, said:

> I learned some things during my stint as co-editor of *New* (now *Best*) *Canadian Stories*, many of them small, some that I didn't want to know, but learn I did. Mostly I learned that this country is full of people shrouded in arctic light, trapped in their Canadian loneliness, sometimes writing badly about it, sometimes well, occasionally brilliantly. Probably I've read as many stories typed on kitchen tables in efficiency apartments and in echoing old houses in small towns as has anyone in the country. Some of the writers whose stories I read cut slightly ridiculous figures, but they were fighting the battle the best way they knew. Courage is where you find it, and I do dignify them with the title "writer" even when the stories were less than good: they had a faith and that's more important than the product. ·
>
> I think I learned that there is little real fiction in Canada. What we have instead are personal histories with the names changed and the facts slightly bent . . . The large run of the stories we received presented carefully crafted reliquaries, little boxes

in which were enshrined little memories. Some of these reliquaries were elaborately enamelled, but mostly they were simple, sturdy constructions.

This extract from her introduction illustrates what I meant when I said that Joan was *nice*. I found the "simple, sturdy constructions" far less "carefully crafted" than she did.

(Mavis Gallant, in a letter, described them disdainfully as "pallid little 'I' stories" though *she* was talking about the ones we'd *selected*.)

It is with Joan's first paragraph that I am in violent disagreement.

"...they had a faith and that's more important than the product."

Although Joan is saying this of *inadequate* writers, it's an attitude that has condoned and fostered the mediocrity of all Canadian writing from its beginnings to the present.

When I was a child and aunts for my birthday gave me socks, my mother used to say to my disgruntled little self, "It's the thought that counts." I considered this argument but it seemed to me that what I was left with was, inescapably, *socks*.

My desire to change the title and direction of *New Canadian Stories* was prompted by a belief that "product" was more important than "faith."

I was tired of socks.

As I grew into the job I was able to see that, by presenting what I considered the best, I was promoting one kind of writing and suppressing another. I was deliberately suppressing, I came to realize, Joan Harcourt's "simple, sturdy constructions." I wasn't interested in "personal histories with the names changed." I was interested in sparkling language, in play, in glorious rhetoric. I was also promoting a fiction that was looking outwards for its models and its energy. The direction of that gaze was inevitably the United States. I set out to change the concept and shape of what a story is and how it should be read.

In the introduction to *New Canadian Stories 1976* I wrote: "Starting next year, in frank emulation of Martha Foley's *Best American Stories*, Oberon's anthology will be entitled *77: Best Canadian Stories*." This statement was not happily received in the seething nationalistic miasma of the time. Martha Foley was the editor David "had never looked at." A brief account of the history of the American anthology is necessary. This was the series I was "emulating"; its achievement was a vision I hoped to attain.

The American *Best Short Stories* began in 1915 under the editorship of Edward J. O'Brien, a weirdly awful young poet from Boston. The anthology continued under O'Brien's editorship until his death, in 1941. He was succeeded by his friend and disciple, Martha Foley, who edited from 1941 until her death, in 1977. From that point on, a different editor every year was invited to create the volumes, drawing on long-lists of stories culled from the magazines by seasoned professional editors, first Shannon Ravenel, then Katrina Kenison, currently Heidi Pitlor.

Reading the first seven years of O'Brien's anthology is dispiriting; the writing is tedious where not moribund, though O'Brien claimed in his introductions to the 1915 and 1916 volumes that American stories "may fairly claim a sustained superiority as different in kind as in quality from the tale of *conte* of other literatures" and that he was "driven to the conclusion that we were developing a new literary form."

I've written in *The Canadian Short Story* that for those first seven years he was either lying or whistling Dixie. But by 1922–23 he had recognized Sherwood Anderson, Scott Fitzgerald, Conrad Aikin, Ring Lardner, and Ernest Hemingway.

(His verse was dreadful but he could recognize the poetry in prose like a deadeye.)

I wrote of the beginnings of modernism in the States, "By 1922, we see a splendid cavalcade beginning to assemble, horses tossing their heads, bits jingling, brocade and silk in the sun, an almost ceremonial coming-together, a cavalcade that O'Brien *had imagined into being."*

That's me being fanciful and wistful about a glittering past but it also captures the way I felt about the possibilities of our Oberon johnny-come-lately book, about how, starting fifty-six years later, I too, might be able to *imagine into being* a glittering present.

If the early years of the *Best American* anthology were cropping barren ground, *Best Canadian* from its early years was stellar. In 1976, the hinge year between *New* and *Best*, the anthology published—mainly through personal connections—Clark Blaise, Hugh Hood, Norman Levine, Leon Rooke, Elizabeth Spencer, and Audrey Thomas.

> 1978: Hugh Hood, Alice Munro, Elizabeth Spencer
> 1980: Mavis Gallant, Alice Munro, Guy Vanderhaeghe
> 1981: Clark Blaise, Mavis Gallant, Norman Levine, Alice
> Munro, and a fledgling Linda Svendsen.

The history of the editing and co-editing of the Oberon book is as follows:

Fourteen Stories High 1971 David Helwig and Tom Marshall
New Canadian Stories 72–75 David Helwig and Joan Harcourt

New Canadian/Best 76–77 Joan Harcourt and John Metcalf
Best Canadian Stories 78–80 Clark Blaise and John Metcalf
Best Canadian Stories 81–82 John Metcalf and Leon Rooke

With the change of name from *New* to *Best* in 1971 I had wanted an outright policy of republication, but Michael Macklem, the publisher, argued against. Under pressure, I agreed to consider unsolicited manuscripts.

Though at the time I cursed Macklem, few actually readable-beyond-a-paragraph unsolicited manuscripts arrived. Later, I was to be grateful for this Get Out of Jail card he'd forced on me because some years produce a meagre crop. It was sometimes impossible to find ten good stories in the magazines in a given year. In meagre years, it is actually essential for the editor to have access to previously unpublished work. Most writers experienced enough to be editors will have a network of fellow writers to approach.

The following numbers illuminate the Canadian situation.

In 1915, E.J. O'Brien consulted 45 magazines and republished stories from 18.

In 1971, Martha Foley consulted 118 magazines and republished from 19.

In 2012, Heidi Pitlor, the long-listed initial editor, consulted 230 magazines, whittled down her final selection to 120 finalists from which Tom Perrotta, the guest editor, selected 20.

In the same year, 2012, I consulted 17 magazines for *Best Canadian* and published 10 stories, 7 from magazines, three unsolicited.

The number of Canadian magazines is shrinking further; this trend will likely be countered by the growth of internet magazines such as Doug Glover's splendid *Numéro Cinq* though I must confess that I'm sufficiently antiquated as to still believe in the magic of print and paper.

The tiny number of literary magazines in Canada is not the only problem; magazines reflect their editors. Magazines run by collectives or boards tend to be pallid; magazines bearing the impress of strong literary personalities tend to be more dependable. During my years of editing, *The Fiddlehead* has always been interesting and under the editorships of Kent Thompson and, more recently, under Mark Jarman, a force. As also *The New Quarterly* under Kim Jernigan. *Event* is unusually dependable. *Prism* wanders in the wilderness and *Malahat* has lost much of its authority since Connie Rooke's death. *Walrus Magazine* blazed to brief editorial glory under Nick Mount until its board namby-pambied him out of his role in the name of "family values."

To return to the history of Oberon's *Best*.

Best Canadian Stories 1983–86 David Helwig and Sandra Martin

I was alarmed to read Sandra Martin's introduction to the 1984 volume, which read, in part: "It is worth noting that five of the twelve stories in this year's anthology are previously unpublished. Next year we hope it will be possible to *increase this number...*" [italics added]

No! No! I wanted to scream from the sidelines.

She went on to say: "... our first priority was to publish stories that were written to be read rather than merely to be admired, or even envied. We wanted stories that would expand the traditional narrative framework without sacrificing artistry or technique."

Populist twaddle! I wanted to yell from the sidelines.
Culture as Meals on Wheels.
Yet again.

Best Canadian Stories 1987–1994 David Helwig and Maggie Helwig
Best Canadian Stories 1995 David Helwig
Best Canadian Stories 1996–2006 Douglas Glover
Best Canadian Stories 2007–2017 John Metcalf

When Dan Wells and I were first discussing this and
future volumes, I said I wanted to edit this bridge volume between the two publishing houses for sentimen-
tal reasons, but I urged on him, for future volumes, the
American model of having a different guest editor annu-
ally. It has worked well in the States with guest editors
such as Stanley Elkin, John Updike, Raymond Carver,
Ann Beattie, Richard Ford, Lorrie Moore, Salman
Rushdie, E. Annie Proulx, Margaret Atwood, Tobias
Wolff, etc. A spread of sensibilities.

This suggestion brought up in its wake the idea of a series editor: a preliminary reader who would cull from the
magazines a long list from which the guest editor would
select. Dan proposed that I should be the *éminence grise*.

I'd been rather startled at what David Helwig had written in a letter about the selection process:

"Leap to a new subject, working with Maggie: for
some years when Sandra and I were editing together
Maggie did the initial reading of the magazines. I wasn't
going to read them all and she had good taste, and, being
my daughter, attitudes sufficiently like mine. When we
edited together we were usually quite quick to decide,
neither of us too proud for a little last minute horse-trad-
ing. The only thing I remember as a possible mistake was

a story about necrophilia by Barbara Gowdy. Maggie liked it, but I was all come over priggish."

(Odd coincidence, but I'd also rejected that Gowdy story from an anthology. I was less priggish than puzzled, the mechanics of it, he, it, not being able to, well, rise to the occasion. Best not to think about it, I thought.)

Dilshad Engineer, Oberon's first editor, told me that Douglas Glover, during his ten-year editorship, had also baulked at reading all the magazines and had operated, in part, on the strength of a long-list she'd supplied.

I'm very fond of Dilshad, but I'm sure our literary tastes do not exactly overlap. I might apply to Maggie Helwig for theological info, she now being an Anglican priest, but I'm less respectful of her literary authority. As for Sandra Martin, her (coded) aspirations for the story suggest a direction I've been opposing for decades. None of the three is a Shannon Ravenel or Heidi Pitlor.

So the more I thought about this preliminary cull business, this *éminence grise* approach to editing, the more I felt we'd be heading in the wrong direction. Unlike the Americans, we didn't have 230 magazines to consult; we didn't have thirty. I wanted our guest editors to be inside the world of the magazines, to make their judgements against the background of the awful, the tedious, the merely competent, the possibly promising, the *maybe...* and all judged against the achievement of whatever personal pantheon the editor had, over the years, constructed.

In meagre years, I'd expect them to draw on their network of friends and acquaintances for unpublished work. I wanted each editor to feel that the book they put their name to would be, within reason, an expression of their own understanding and appreciation of the story form. I'd expect them to act responsibly towards the tradition yet at the same time connect with work so original that it was, in the now, difficult perhaps for the rest of us to "see." I wanted each editor to feel proud of the book bearing their name. That commitment, that pride, was best fostered, I decided, by my absence.

This volume is my farewell. If I can bequeath anything to incoming editors, it would be excitement at the prospect before them.

My own beginnings were a long time ago and now I feel rather like the narrator in Norman Levine's story "We All Begin in a Little Magazine," but I can remember how wildly excited I was when I was first published in a magazine. I told everyone I met as casually as my delight allowed.

"Congratulations!" they said. *"Prism?"*

And I was forced to admit that, no, it *wasn't* available on newsstands. Or at libraries. Or anywhere, really. And the years passed with my friends asking how you spelled *Wascana Review* and was *Tamarack* as in the tree—until that day arrived when five stories were published in *New Canadian Writing 1969*. The fact that the book wasn't widely available in grocery stores, nor, truth be told, in bookstores, didn't bother me a bit. It was a *book*—or at least, a third of a book—and the effect on me was tonic. With that publication, I started to allow myself to think of myself as a writer; I was, in my own eyes, no longer a high-school teacher with delusions of grandeur but a published author whose book was, if you went to a hell of a lot of trouble, available.

The rewards were immediate. They were not, needless to say, financial. The most immediate reward was that I started writing even harder than before and soon had a book that was wholly mine—*The Lady Who Sold Furniture.*

Some of that excitement still lingers.

When I asked David Helwig what his years of editing the anthology had meant to him, he replied in a letter:

> So you want me to think about the past. "Don't look back. Something may be gaining on you," as Satchell Paige is said to have said. I do like looking back over the tables of contents and noting their range, but I have no intention of looking back to do autopsies. What's done is done. Some careers were helped a teeny tiny bit, and people read some stories. The void forgives us all. I like to have published almost everyone, but as for a general philosophy, I think variety meant more to me perhaps than to you, and beyond that a resonant story is a resonant story.

Again.

"I would not have claimed to ever have mapped any-thing—except that by publishing a lot of readable stories, the books provided pencil and paper for other people to scribble out instructions for reaching their new place of residence."

I couldn't disagree more. When, shuddering, I think back to Joan Harcourt's "simple, sturdy constructions" and "personal histories with the names changed" and "carefully crafted reliquaries, little boxes in which we were enshrined little memories" and then I think of the sophisticated up-roar of the short stories of Leon Rooke, Keath Fraser, Clark Blaise, Terry Griggs, Steve Heighton, Caroline Adderson, Alice Munro, Annabel Lyon, Linda Svendsen, Mavis Gallant, Diane Schoemperlen, Alex MacLeod... an endless cavalcade stretching back now nearly fifty years, then I think we've not merely mapped the coastlines of the genre, and mapped them extensively, we've landed men on the moon.

When David Helwig bade gruff farewell to the series in 1995, his gruffness shielding his gentle heart, his final sentence read:

"Remains only to tip my hat and go."

Having now edited eighteen volumes of *Best Canadian Stories*, I also tip my hat—to our readers, and, gratefully, to the six writers in this year's anthology who are at the outset of careers.

Lisa Alward

Frankie Barnet

Paige Cooper

David Huebert

Beverley Shaw

Martha Wilson

Ottawa, 2017

OLD GROWTH

LISA ALWARD

RAY'S REALTOR appears to have nothing on from the waist up. She flashes across the front window of her bungalow as if startled to see them drive into the yard, though Ray did text her from the ferry. Gwyneth glimpses shapely arms, a firm curve of breast.

"Your realtor's topless."

Ray leers across the steering wheel. "Whaaa?"

But it's just a nude T-shirt. Gwyneth can see this plainly now that the realtor has stepped outside in her sock feet and is smiling at them, or rather at Ray. A tall woman in her forties, reasonably slim with bushy blond hair, the top piece pulled back in a faded green scrunchy. No doubt the younger and more attractive of the two agents on the island—Ray would have done his research. Gwyneth would like to make another crack about this, but feels too chastened by the T-shirt.

Anyway, she's too late. Ray has swung open the driver's door and is loping across the grass to give his realtor one of the bear hugs he reserves for small children and pretty women. Gwyneth pushes her own door ajar and extends one sandalled foot, inspecting her toenails in the late morning light. Purple, at her age, really? As she stands and unkinks her shoulders, Ray gives the blond woman a quick kiss near the mouth. Now, the two of them glance over. This could be interesting. Is he going to introduce her as his ex-wife? Or as his friend, his adviser, his financier? Of course, he might just say she's a hitchhiker. This was how he introduced her to his parents all those years ago, and Gwyneth, twenty-four and in love, played along the whole weekend, though they'd actually met tree planting and Ray had gone to the bus station to get her.

"Fern," Ray says, "Gwyneth. Gwyneth, Fern."

Fern smiles limply. Then, brightening, she says to Ray, "Just give me a sec," and turns back to the bungalow, where a pair of hiking boots waits beside a painted chair.

She has a breathy little-girl voice, though on scrutiny looks closer to forty-nine than forty. Gwyneth tries to catch Ray's eye, but he is gazing around his realtor's property— three acres with a vegetable garden, an orchard, and a pen for her horses (Fern gives riding lessons on the side). Gwyneth knows his air of distraction is deliberate, that he's already pulling away from their tenuous connection on the drive up the coast. If she speaks now, he won't hear her, so intent will he be on communing with his realtor. Fern certainly seems flattered, pointing out the different types of apple trees and detailing the contents of the compost heap next to Ray's mud-splattered Focus.

Already, Gwyneth is regretting she's come.

I think I've found it, he announced on the phone. My land. And when she'd said, That's great, Ray, he surprised her by suggesting she drive to the island with him before he made his offer. They could get there and back in a day, and if they missed the last ferry, well, they could sleep in the car, like old times. Classic Ray. Yet he seemed so eager. C'mon,

Gwyn. You can tell me if I'm crazy or not. And when she still hung back, I promise I'll be on my best behaviour. Neither of them mentioned the loan, but that's another reason he would want her to see it, so she'll feel easier giving him the $20,000, and on the phone, perversely, this touched her. Not that she cares which piece of wilderness he buys. She's already made up her mind to loan him the money—for Cam and Jenna, so he'll have something to leave them, especially now that the cottage has finally sold and Ray is tearing through his share. It's your money, Ben had shrugged, but you know what he's like. As for doing a road trip with her ex-husband, he merely rolled his eyes. Maybe you can talk him out of it.

Ray at least was on time for once—early in fact. He appeared preoccupied with a map while she was kissing Ben good-bye on the porch but smirked as she slid in beside him, Honeymoon still not over, I see. Then he buzzed down the driver's window and called out, Don't worry, man. I'll take good care of her. See you in two weeks! So that she had to reach across his skinny lap and shout, Tonight, Ben! See you tonight! As she eased back, she remarked, Still the same old asshole, I see, and Ray gave her a mock salute. But it seemed to relax them both, this allusion to a sexual rivalry that had never really existed—Ray being with Angie still when Gwyneth met Ben.

Still, it felt strange sharing a car with him again. He'd started combing his hair back, she noticed, no doubt to camouflage his bald spot, and the light green hemp shirt he was wearing—short-sleeved with a collar and looking like it could use a little ironing—was one she'd bought a couple of months ago for Cam to give him on Father's Day. In the store, she'd spent a long time fingering it, the fabric stiff like linen but with a hint of softness. So Ray. On the way out of the city, he detoured through a Tim's for coffees, and Gwyneth pulled back his tab and dabbed his jeans with their stack of napkins after he spilled the first sip. When Jenna texted, How's your holiday with Dad? Killed him yet? Gwyneth sent back a smiley face, Not yet. However, it was surprisingly relaxed, like catching up with an old friend. They talked about the kids (how great it was that Cam was finally getting his act together, and who was this new guy of Jenna's anyway?) and also about Ben. (He's a good man, Ray said. Solid. You deserve that, Gwyn.) They even joked about a few of his more harmless flaws—how she still has to remind him about his mother's birthday and the time he drove six hours to his brother's wedding without his suit. Mostly, though, they talked about the land.

The seller, a middle-aged German, would be leaving behind a half-built house, and Ray was debating whether he should finish it or use the lumber for his own cabin in the woods. Why didn't the German finish his house? Gwyneth asked. No idea, Ray grinned. Maybe he got bored, or his marriage fell apart. He had spent much of his summer Googling solar panels, composting toilets, organic gardening. A couple of pals were willing to help him build next year. In the meantime, he was hoping to find someone local (his realtor had a few names) to do the extra clearing he wanted. Then he would be able to quit his job and retire to the island, go off the grid. He looked at her with that intense light gaze, daring her to tear down this new plan. But that was one of the dispensations of being divorced so long: she would not criticize, not anymore. Sounds great, she said. Then thought of the VW bus he'd bought for $500 and left to rust in their driveway, the tree house he was always going to build for the kids, all those rotting boards behind the shed. You're going to love it, Ray enthused, tapping the steering wheel. Wait till you see all the old growth.

Fern won't stop going on about the trees either.

"Wait until you see the old-growth firs on Ray's land," she says, catching Gwyneth's eye in the rearview mirror, as if to signal her to gush as well.

They have switched to the realtor's Outback and Gwyneth is already feeling carsick. Not only is she stuck in the backseat, but Fern keeps taking her hands off the wheel to talk, then jerking the wheel back in place to round another bend. Gwyneth wonders if calling the land Ray's before he's put in an offer is an old real estate trick. Even Ray is doing it now, worrying aloud that the farmer next door to his land might be tapping his maples.

When they first set out from the bungalow, she made a point of asking Fern about herself. The realtor explained that she had been born on the island, as were both her grannies, but that her parents left for the mainland in their teens, only to return with the back-to-the-land movement in the mid-seventies. Up until Fern was eight, they lived on a communal farm with two other families. She was home-schooled but mostly she ran wild in the woods. Ray would like that, Gwyneth reflected. He'd always considered himself a latter-day hippie and often seemed dazed by their mortgage, the kids, his job teaching communications to blasé college students. Fern got along beautifully with the island's other realtor (who made pottery on the side), and, no, she didn't know why the German had abandoned his house. When Gwyneth asked about her horses, she boasted that she'd been riding since she was three. That's a long time, Gwyneth said, but Fern laughed, I'm not that old yet. She kept waiting for Fern to ask a question back. Surely, she must wonder why

Ray brought along this definitely old-already woman with the purple toenails. But Fern seemed no more curious about her than the dusty ostrich ferns lining the ditches.

Gwyneth directs a question now at Ray. "Have you looked into the water supply?"

"Oh, he doesn't need to worry about that. There's good access to groundwater everywhere on the island."

"Gwyneth's partner's a civil engineer," Ray remarks, though he knows full well Ben is a tax lawyer.

"Are you okay?" Fern says into the mirror.

"I'm fine. I just get carsick in the back."

"Well, make sure you tell us if there's anything we can do to make you feel better," she says cheerily, turning back to Ray to chat about his new neighbourhood while Ray surveys the dense bush with childlike wonder.

When she finally pulls over, asserting with an excited flick of the hand, "Here we are!" there's nothing to suggest they are anywhere, certainly no For Sale sign. Fern, however, hops out of the Outback and points to a stick smeared with pink paint on the side of the highway.

"The western marker for your property line, Ray."

Next, she unfurls a survey map that shows how the eight acres begin narrow, then widen near the house before narrowing again for four more acres. Ray, of course, has seen the land before—clearly, this is how he's become so cozy with his realtor—but he frowns at the map and stares vaguely at Fern, as though he's forgotten who she is or why he's here. Gwyneth, who's seen him like this before, guesses he's starting to feel nervous about the prospect of going off-grid for real. Commitment has never been Ray's forte.

Fern doesn't seem to notice and leaps into the ditch. As Ray plunges in after her, he throws Gwyneth a quick backward grimace. "You coming?"

"You bet!"

On the phone, she did think to ask about footwear. Would sandals be okay? Yes, yes, he'd assured her. The German had dug a road in from the highway. But Fern must have decided to take an off-road route.

"You okay?" she calls over her shoulder.

Huge rubbery leaves slap Gwyneth on the face. Bark grit jams beneath her toes. "Just fine."

Up ahead, Ray, who has regained his composure, is tilting his head close to his realtor's as she regales him about the natural attributes of his land. In addition to being a real estate agent and riding instructor, Fern appears to have an exhaustive knowledge of island flora and fauna. She is practically running now, showing off this big-leaf maple and that rare forest flower, noting how interesting it is that a cedar has rooted itself around the stump of a fir. She is quite the nature girl. No doubt she also leads a Brownie troupe on the side. Ray, however, Gwyneth observes with grumpy satisfaction, is even balder than she'd realized.

"Look at this, Ray."

Fern has stopped beside an enormous fallen tree. Someone has chain-sawed it into chunks, the largest spanning almost four feet. She nudges Ray's elbow, beckons Gwyneth.

"See the rings," she says, pointing at the largest chunk. "You can tell how old it is by counting them." Definitely a Brownie troupe.

Now, she's caressing the outer rings with her fingertips, and Gwyneth worries that she might actually count them. Instead, she steps back, her yellow hair grazing Ray's hemp shirt.

"The rings look pretty much the same until you get right up close. Then you can see that some are wider, meaning an easy winter and long growing season, and some thinner, usually a hard winter and shorter growing season."

"Just like relationships," Ray quips, "except the best ones are usually the shortest."

Even Ray seems puzzled by what he's just said. He and Fern are still hovering by the rings, so Gwyneth rests on one of the smaller chunks of sawed tree and flaps her cardigan at the mosquitoes. She's promised herself that she won't think about Angie anymore. But the rings remind her. Once, she watched Ray and Angie standing together like this at a family bonfire—not talking or touching, just standing, and yet the force of their attraction cutting her to pieces. You know he's not monogamous? his own brother had warned her. She knew but married him anyway. What was she thinking? That the two of them were rooted together in some elemental way? That once he had a family he wouldn't stray? Watching Fern try to make sense of his joke about the rings, Gwyneth almost feels sorry for her. It's Ray who turns her into such a bitch—even now when there's nothing between them but their almost-grown children and this loan. Why should she care anymore who he screws around with? She's supposed to be done with all that, starting over fresh with Ben.

But he still gets to her. She should have known this. She did know. All the time they were talking in the car, on the phone as well, she'd been softening, feeling the nearness of the old Ray—the one who kissed her breasts before babies, who was always floating off somewhere but still could somehow make her laugh. Even the wrinkled hemp shirt is a tendril, pulling her back. But she'd been a fool to think he wore it for her.

She heaves herself forward. "Are we anywhere near the road yet?"

"It's just ahead," Fern sings out.

The road is nothing but a grassy track and the house, when it materializes, weirdly narrow with a tin roof that juts so far out the two storeys look in danger of tipping over. Beside it sits a leaf-strewn camper van and, in front, a rusted pickup truck. The scene has a haphazard sleepiness about it, as if the German has merely gone out for supplies and forgotten to come back.

Now that they've reached their destination, Ray seems about to break into a jig. "What do you think?"

"What's with the roof?"

"We think he must have been planning to build two screened-in porches, one on top of the other," Fern says. "That's why the roof's so extended."

"Is that the only door?' Gwyneth points at a large triangular opening on the second floor.

"Oh, no," Fern laughs. "We think that was meant to be the entry to the upper porch. The door's around the side."

Ray and Fern stride ahead, murmuring back and forth, while Gwyneth picks her way through the nails and shards of wood that litter the long grass. She has wrapped her cardigan around her face to keep away the bugs and knows without looking that the purple polish is all chipped now.

Inside the house, Ray is suddenly attentive again, showing her a table of good-quality tools the German has left behind and cautioning her, as they climb the rough stairs to the second floor, to stick to the crossbeams and not stand too close to that triangular hole in the wall. He is especially proud of a curious window that shutters from the inside and can be opened only by pulling across a wooden dowel. This dowel is about a foot long and carved with leaves and flowers. It is the one detail of the house that is truly finished.

"It's beautiful, isn't it?" Fern whispers, fingering a petal, and Ray looks anxiously at Gwyneth.

This appeal is so hapless that she can't at first respond. Instead, she glances over the edge of the gaping triangle, which seems a perfect metaphor for their unfinished marriage. Large flakes of brown paint are starting to drift loose from the cab of the German's truck. Nearby, a plastic tarp clings by blue threads to a pile of mossy lumber. The tarp looks like Ray's faded one-man tent from their tree-planting summer. There's something you need to know, he'd told her that first night she shared it with him. He was older, had hitched to Mexico, was known around the camp for breaking hearts. I've always been a free spirit. I can't help it. I just blow with the wind. Tangled up inside his sleeping bag, with the shadows of the treetops moving above, she hadn't understood, or cared much, what this blowing might mean. She knew only that she wanted to curl herself around his body, so thin and pale in the tent light, and not let go. I think I'm in love with you, he also said, lifting her bangs. And she'd felt sure he meant it, because he looked so surprised.

Gwyneth sighs and faces him again. The German was clearly insane. She can't believe Ray is considering finishing the man's house. It will take him years, if he even manages to stick with it. Really, Ben was right. The idea of his going off-grid is ridiculous—what does Ray know about organic gardening? She watches him toss a screwdriver of the German's from one hand to the other, his pale blue eyes fixed on her, wanting her to say something nice about a dowel. What is she even doing here? He must know she lacks his realtor's breezy confidence that he can pull this off. And if he is concerned about the money, why risk her seeing the land, or for that matter seeing him with Fern? Then it all seems so obvious. He is as stuck as she is. Even now, he can't make a move without turning back to see if she will stop him. Some free spirit—more a tangled kite, twisting in the wind. And for the first time all day, she feels like laughing.

"Nice workmanship," she says at last, and when Fern asks what she thinks of the rest of the house, she smiles sweetly, "I think it has real potential."

Fern wants to take Ray to see the very end of the property. Gwyneth says she is still a little carsick and would rather wait. Against the side of the house, they find her a bench—just a narrow workbench pocked with ant holes, though she insists it's perfect. They both seem to want her permission to leave, Fern asking a couple more times if she's sure she'll be okay. But she smiles and waves them into wilderness. When she can't hear their voices, she lies back on the bench. Ray's trees are shifting overhead as though preparing to uproot themselves and walk away. Not that they can, any more than Ray. She pictures the two of them out on his land, the giant ferns gently stroking their bare arms, not talking so much now. Ray will be watching for a spot where the ground is soft, where he can pull her down. Or maybe Fern, impatient for his touch, will seize his hand and press him against an ancient maple. Let them do it. She wants them to. Let him add another ring. Even if they forget about her, desert her on this bench by the mad German's half-house, it will make no difference. The sun can go down, the air turn chill, the house cave in behind her. She will be here, waiting.

CHERRY SUN

FRANKIE BARNET

YOU COULD tell the animal wasn't interested in mating season, she'd gone to great lengths to make that obvious. But this was a business, and babies were what the people wanted to see. Come spring, teachers, carpenters, musicians, poets, and lawyers visited our zoo, paid twelve-fifty and stared at all the babies. How thrilling, to be in the presence of such fresh life, such big eyes and awkward gaits.

First, there were problems with her hormones, then her temperature. The vet was called in, spread her hide taut then pricked her with his potions. "She'll be fine now," he said, "I've got her all balanced out."

Her name was Nala and she was a capybara. "I know you don't want to do it," I told her, because at this point I was levelling with her. I wasn't feeding her any of the bullshit I saw other keepers feed their animals. To the seals: *But you'll totally outshine the walruses in the afternoon show!* To the Siberian tiger: *Here are some messages from your family in the wild!*

"Although," I told her, "it might not be as important as you think it is. Just because you have sex with a guy doesn't mean it explains everything about you. It's the twenty-first century. You can have sex with whoever you want, it doesn't matter."

We'd all been there, or at least I had. More times than I'd care to admit. Oh, I'd fucked all those guys: the chimpanzee guy, the sloth bear guy, the guy who ran the cafeteria. These days nobody expected you to be in love.

I told her about the guy I had just started seeing, who minded the antelopes. Actually, he had this nervous way about him, a habit of always knowing how much each keeper's animal was worth in parts and then treating them accordingly. "It's not like I'm coming," I told Nala, just to manage any expectation she might have had. "I mean, sometimes it can hurt, he gets pretty rough down there but... well, I could take it as a compliment really, that he needs me so hard like that."

There were seven capybaras, including Raja, the stud. Their pen was a struggling exhibit in the small mammals department, consistently overshadowed by the meerkats. We had given them pretty much anything they could have wanted: lettuce, water, some shrubs for shade, but they remained awful at performing for the visitors. "We all know you're related to the rat," we told them, "but it's nothing to be ashamed of. All of us have shameful aspects to our family history." But those giant vermin were just so stubborn. If we hadn't gotten the idea to throw their food along the viewing window, the animals would hardly have gotten up from chewing their bark at all.

A team of three handled the rodents: a grad student doing her practicum, a recent high school dropout who happened to be related to the mayor, and myself. Like I said, we were struggling. What killed us was that the meerkats were even more like the rat (considering the tail) and yet it didn't seem to bother them as a species at all. The meerkats had *The Lion King* and it had gone to their heads. They were always dancing around, popping out of holes like they'd just discovered new air. I'd seen people actually cheer.

The capybaras were a different story. Generally, what happened was about five minutes after finding out what a capybara was, the novelty was gone. It was a zoo, after all, there were lions, tigers, hot dogs wrapped in bacon.

In the wild, capybaras ate, often slept and copulated in the water. In the zoo, because of our limited resources, we borrowed a plastic tub from the seal guy to induce intimacy. The mares floated, noses up, while Raja tread behind them with his front paws resting on their haunches.

"You ever done it in water?" asked the seal guy, whose condition for lending us the tub was that he was allowed to watch.

"Yeah," I lied, "I've done it everywhere."

Raja was usually good to impregnate two mares a day, three if we pushed him. We needed to have all the mares impregnated that week, before Raja left on a road trip through the midwest to impregnate mares in Calgary, Minnesota, Indianapolis, and Chicago. What we wanted was for the pups to emerge *en masse*: wet, big eyed, and adorable.

But Nala wouldn't fuck him. When we put her in the water, she dove to the bottom of the pool and kicked Raja in the face after he dove after her.

"This is what you have to do," said our superiors, who gave us a demonstration in their executive office using two plush otters from the gift store. Alright, I thought. Simple enough and for a good cause.

Though in real life, when I stood at the edge of the pool holding her front legs and the mayor's niece tugged a rope that harnessed both her back legs, it was much more difficult.

"This is fucked, this is fucked, this so fucked up," muttered the grad student under her breath as the three of us listened to the violent, splashing water.

"Listen," I said to Nala when we had a moment alone. "I know you're nervous. But what you need to understand is that all we want from you is to be happy and healthy. You get to have three babies! Aren't you excited?"

She looked at me.

"Yeah, three of them! How does it feel?" I really was curious, and a little drunk, from the tequila I'd snuck in for lunch.

She buried her head in the dirt, like she was trying to prove that the dirt went all the way down to the earth's core, not that she knew what a core was, not that it wasn't just the cement pool where the dolphins lived, then died, that one record-breaking winter.

"Clarice!" That was the grad student, always on my ass. "Who are you talking to? No cell phones!"

As I stood up, I turned to say one more thing to Nala. "You can't just stop eating," I said. "You've got to start taking better care of yourself." And for a little while, she did.

When a baby was born at the zoo, you could feel it in the air. When a baby was born, everyone was allowed to abandon their posts to watch. We all crowded around the new mother and melted as she licked the afterbirth from her fresh young. Usually one of the small-monkeys girls said something like, "Oh my god I can feel it in my ovaries!" as the elephant guys shifted away from her nervously. A representative from the executive office would come to visit and name the new being with a megaphone. Welcome Simba, welcome Nemo, welcome Pluto, welcome Roo.

What was with the babies in this place? What was with the people lining pits and cages every Saturday afternoon, pointing at shadows thinking it might be a baby? There were babies on billboards, babies on the side of buses. People hung them on their backs like a jacket, or on their fronts like a medallion. They gave them names and picked out clothes for them to wear. A baby had the potential to be anything and anything had the potential to be a baby when you were desperate to see one in the snow leopard's cage.

Five months later, our mares writhed in the dirt and the sacs of their young burst forth, slimy and pungent. We had put Nala through so much, yet watching her with the little ones it became clear we had made the right decision. It was a series of right decisions that led us to this moment. She slurped embryonic sac from their tiny faces. Hers were the smallest and therefore cutest ones. It was beautiful and peaceful, and I felt like I was, too, just by being near them. I swigged some of the tequila I'd hid in my backpack, holding my stomach together as it sizzled. I didn't always drink at work, but when I did it was usually in slim mickeys, which I hid in the waistband of my skirt. I wondered, briefly, how incredible it would feel to be them, somehow all four of them.

The antelope guy, who had lately been acting distant, texted me on his break and I snuck out to meet him in the secluded shadows between Penguin Plunge and the Amphibian house.

He reached his hand under my skirt and found the mickey, laughed and rolled his eyes. "Crazy, crazy, Clarice." He was shaking his head, then unscrewed the cap and took a deep swig without even asking.

"Hey!"

"What?" He looked at me and swigged again, then threw the bottle onto a bench. "I'm going to make it up to you." He started kissing my neck and moving lower.

I wanted him to lick me, more. "Harder," I said, but that wasn't it necessarily. "Slower," but it wasn't that either.

What was meant to happen was that he would lick me all up. My outside disappeared and, for a great flash, I was just my inside. It happened sometimes, like with the sloth bear guy when I said, "Oh god."

With the guy from the cafeteria when I said, "Heeeeeahhhhhhh."

The antelope guy took his penis out, flipped me around, and pushed himself into me. It felt so big at first, but it was just like a shot. Only for a second, then almost nothing.

When we finished the antelope guy said, "Have I ever told you that you have a real 70s bush?" even though he had told me many times.

I walked back to the capybaras feeling loose and fuzzy. The grad student was deep in conversation with the veterinarian. "This better not mean we lose our bonuses!" the mayor's niece said. "I need that bonus!" She stormed past me. The grad student sighed deeply, like a man. What had happened, the veterinarian explained, was that Nala's pups, all three of them, turned out to be dead. They had been dead for some time, he told me, which explained their underdevelopment. "It's actually not uncommon," he said, "when an animal's under stress."

Before I knew it, my shift was over and the zoo was closed. I could have gone home, I could have just left and eaten chips in my room, watching something stupid on TV.

Even though I lived right across the river, it took almost forty-five minutes with the bus over the nearest bridge. Sometimes I joked to myself, just swim. Just swim, I told myself, and on that day, for some reason, I really felt like it. But then what? Show up for dinner completely soaked and say what to my parents?

So I stayed with the capybaras, I sat beside their feeding gate and watched Nala in the setting cherry sun. She was up and walking, which was strange. Weren't there tests? Shouldn't there be tests? I thought. She was walking away from the south wall of the pen.

"So you're pleased with yourself then? So with the babies, that was all just for show?"

She stopped about five feet away from the wall and turned around.

"Well congratulations." I took another swig of the tequila, the last one. "You got rid of your babies, all your babies are dead."

The light was really like grenadine. It washed over Nala and the other capybaras, west of her in the pen, resting quietly and chewing on whatever shit we'd given them to chew on.

I thought about the time I had sex with my humanities teacher in high school. When I got stoned and drove over his lawn. "You're crazy Clarice," he told me. "You're acting crazy!"

"Allan! Allan!" I said. That was his name. Whenever I said it, I made a point to pronounce both the Ls.

Nala had her eyes glued ahead of her, and I watched as she flung herself into motion, sprinting forward headfirst. She bounced off of the wall, landing with a heavy thud on the dirt and straw. Then she got up, paced back, and ran again.

"What are you doing?" I asked Nala. "What are you even doing with your life?"

But she just kept throwing herself against that wall. She threw herself against the wall over and over again, so many times until her tiny body lay still and at the end of the week she was incinerated with her children and several tropical fish.

BEASTS

GRANT BUDAY

ALL THE way down the St Lawrence and across the sea to France I tormented the beast with a bullwhip. For this and other reasons the beast was not content. It was a big one, this beast, seven and a half feet and maybe three hundred pounds, though it lost weight on the voyage because it got seasick. Its ears were small like a bear's, and it had long fingers and toes and dark brown hair all over, except on its flat face, which was as smooth and worn as a leather apron. Its round grey eyes lurked like cave hermits under a heavy brow.

Now it shuffled down the gangplank ahead of me, shackled at the ankles and wrists.

A crowd waited. Children picked their noses and pointed their fingers. Dogs slank and howled. Even the gulls seemed anxious at the sight of the beast, their shrill cries scraping the air.

The beast hesitated at the bottom of the plank and looked back as if reluctant to leave its last connection to its homeland. I sent my whip cracking above its head. What a beautiful thing is a whip! It had taken time to master and I had the scars to show, but now it was like an extension of my hand. The crowd sucked its breath and fell back. The beast, no fool, stepped onto the wharf and clambered into the cage in the cart. I waited just long enough for the people to glimpse the monster, then I threw a tarp over top then climbed up into the seat and shook the reins. The mule clattered off across the planks onto the dirt road toward Saint Nazaire.

Looking back I saw the crowd flooding after us. I spoke over my shoulder to the beast, a habit I'd got into, even though it never answered. "First we tease them, stir them up, get them excited, then they'll be happy to pay for a good look, eh."

Late September and Saint Nazaire seethed with mosquitoes. The riverbank was mud and reeds. Thunder trembled in the distance.

The beast had pulled the canvas aside to get air. I could hear his wheezing so turned and glared. As usual when our eyes met I was uneasy. I gripped my whip threateningly; the beast let the tarp fall back into place.

"Always watching, aren't you. Always looking for your chance. What'll you do with that chance? 'Hello captain sir, s'il vous plait, I wish to return to Quebec?'" I wiped my brow with the back of my hand. "Listen, if we make money. I mean a lot of money. If you make me rich then who knows, maybe I'll pay your way back on a ship. Ça va?"

But the beast said nothing. Maybe he knew I was lying. I brooded. I'd paid too much for him, nearly everything I had. Five years in Quebec and I come back with, well, I was drunk when I bought him.

Saint Nazaire was all flies and dogs. Thistles sprouted from walls. In the near distance stood a castle with round towers. A crowd was waiting, word having flown ahead, so that by the time the crowd behind me caught up there were hundreds pressing in around the cart.

I lifted a corner of the tarp and whispered, "Okay, this is your debut. Do your dance. Remember, what's good for me is good for you."

The beast looked at me.

"Got it?"

Those grey eyes understood. I'd watched him on the ship, seen how he observed and listened and even moved his mouth forming words.

Climbing onto the seat I raised my arms high, like a priest. I felt scared but I felt strong. "Good people! I have returned from the New World where I have seen wonders. Lakes so big they have tides. Rivers so wide you can't see from one bank to the other, white whales and unicorn whales." I lowered my voice to a loud and confiding whisper. "And something else. Something even stranger." I nodded slowly from face to face, allowing time for this fact to sink in. If my gaze lingered longer on the young girls who had uncovered their hair in the heat, can I be blamed? The voyage from Quebec had taken three months. "I have faced dangers. Suffered wounds." I pulled my right sleeve up to show my scars. That these came from scratching a rash I didn't mention. "And I've fought the beast. Tracked him through the northern forest. This creature, this wonder, this nightmare. And now he is here. Look upon him if you dare. See him dance his dance. Five sous. Or the equivalent in wine or cheese or fowl or," and here I smiled, "a kiss or a cuddle."

The fishwives cackled. The men grinned. A port town, salty and raw.

At the tail of the cart I said form a line and held out a basket. It was shaped like a keg-sized acorn with a knobbed cap. A fine piece of Mohawk handiwork, admirably detailed, woven so tight it could hold water. The first coin dropped in. I held the tarp flap open and the man stepped up and ducked under. He stood a moment, a motionless shape underneath. I smiled around at the people. No doubt he was frozen with shock at the sight of this monster dragged from the underworld. The crowd strained. A woman called, "Gaspard! What do you see?" Then this Gaspard he backed out from beneath the tarp. And what did he do, this peasant, this fisherman, this barge man—press his fists to his eyes to block the vision that had seared his heart—no, he shrugged and made a face. "He's not much of a beast."

I shouted, "What do you know of beasts?"

Gaspard shrugged again. A fool, old, bent, balding, eyes like piss, fish scales stuck to his nose. "It just sits."

"Of course he sits! He's had a long voyage! He's tired! Très fatigue!"

"You said he would dance."

"Let me see!" The next man threw his coin into the basket and ducked under the canvas. I gave this Gaspard a shove.

The second man backed out and blew a raspberry. "What kind of beast is it?"

"A hell-beast!"

Two more men pushed forward. Then an old woman. Then a boy. The boy laughed, no, sneered and demanded I return his five sous.

I threw aside the tarp. The beast cowered like a dog, paws over its head. I poked it with my knife. Nothing. Had the bugger gone and died? I peered closer. It was breathing. I could see that much. "Hey! Wakey wakey." The beast opened one eye, studied me, cool, distant, indifferent, then turned its back.

I left Saint Nazaire at sunset. Clouds had closed in and the air was thick and damp and stifling. To the right was the river and to the left the swamp. The road was so deeply rutted that the cart lurched and swayed and I was forced to proceed at a crawl, making me easy prey to the mosquitoes.

"That was not a good start," I told the beast over my shoulder.

It pulled aside the tarp to get some air.

"Listen," I said, "We can make this work. France is the best country in the world. You should thank me. Would you rather be with those Scotchmen?" I'd bought the beast behind a tavern from three Scotchmen and a Micmac. They'd had it chained to a stump. It was night and we stood around the beast drinking screech and holding torches that smoked and stank of grease. I'd studied the monster.

"What's wrong with him?" I'd asked.

"Nothing. He's a good beastie."

"Then why sell?"

"The wife thinks it's cruel."

"How old a beast is it?"

"Hard to say. Mature. He's a mature beast."

"Have you counted its teeth?"

"Don't know that that will yield a reliable figure."

I held the torch up near the beast's face. It regarded me, wary but unflinching. "Does it do tricks?"

"He dances."

I said to the beast, "Dance."

The beast looked at the stars through the branches. Slowly, it raised its arms high and then began to turn and dip, faster and faster until it was whirling, all the while tracing shapes in the air with its arms. It was a nimble beast, I gave it that. I emptied my purse and led it away.

I reached Donges in the morning. It was market day and crowded. I made my speech. This time there would be no peeking at the beast one by one, this time there would be spectacle. The beast would dance. By God it would dance. My whip would make sure of it. I dragged the tarp from the cage then jabbed the bugger in the arse with my knife. It stood. The crowd oohed. I opened the gate and cracked my whip and the beast descended the plank. The people fell back, but the beast stood there, wheezing. It seemed to have caught a bit of a summer ague and its snout dribbled. It raised its shackled wrists and wiped its upper lip.

"Behold the cousin of Grendel!"

With an easy turn of the wrist I sent my whip slithering through the air. It popped above the beast's head. The crowd yipped.

"Dance, beast, dance!"

It stood there.

I cracked the whip at its feet. "Dance!"

It looked away, frowning, as if trying to recall something.

"He's not in the mood," called some wag.

"He needs music!" called another.

To whip its feet made no sense. I whipped it on the arse. It staggered. A line of blood appeared on its haunch. The crowd fell silent then began to mutter.

"Beast!" I waved my arms as if it were a marionette.

It stood with its weight on its good leg and continued to stare off, frowning, as if at a distant memory.

"Someone should take that whip to you!" Others joined in howling me down. A flung stone struck me. Then another. I drove the beast back into the cage and whipped the mule as rocks, sticks, and dirt-clods hailed down on my head. It was an hour before the last of the mob turned back. The beast groaned in the cart.

Two days later we reached Nantes and the results were no better. No one was interested. We moved on. Angers, Tours, Orleans. The same. The weather grew cold and we turned south. Vierzon, Bourges, Chateauroux. Many times word had gone ahead and the crowd cried: "Free the beast!"

On Christmas Day the mule died. I hitched the beast to the cart and he pulled. I gave it a hat and a coat and if people asked I said he was a Muscovite, a Volga barge puller bred to such labour.

On a frozen February morning in Limoges the beast escaped while I was begging before the cathedral. I looked everywhere. Finally I went into the church. I hadn't been in a church since Quebec. I pushed open the door thinking I might nick a candle or a coin. The beast was at the altar, fur hat pressed to its chest, gazing at the crucified Christ. There were a few old men and women murmuring prayers. A sexton shuffled around lighting candles. The beast seemed transfixed by the red-painted wounds that appeared to seep in the flickering light. I approached carefully. It turned and looked at me with something between a smile and a sneer, as if it had made a discovery. I didn't like that, not at all.

In March we reached Ouitron, my home village. It had been raining for days. The beast and I were wet and cold and muddy and a hard wind blew. It was six years since I'd been home. There was the oak where thieves were hung, there was the pillory, and down the side road was the family house. My sister Marthe saw me through the hole that was our window. She opened the door. She was my twin and we'd always fought. Now we hugged. How big her tits had become. Our parents, it seemed, were dead and she was pregnant and her man had run off. She already had three small filthy children and here she was expecting another.

Seeing the beast in its hat and coat by the cart, she asked, "Who's your friend?"

"He's from Muscovy," I said.

We ate porridge and potatoes. That night I fucked Marthe from behind just like old times. In the morning the beast and I left.

In Bordeaux our luck turned. We met Monsieur Le Mayor. He invited the beast and me to his chateaux, for he was interested in all things related to the New World. Monsieur Le Mayor had large eyes, a long nose, a full lower lip. His moustache was trimmed and his beard short. He was bald but for the sides and back. A calm man, a dignified man, an educated man judging by his accent, but not aloof. His gaze was solemn and direct though lines at the corners of his eyes told of an eagerness to laugh. We sat at a table in the garden and ate bread, cheese, olives and drank a fulsome wine.

It was a balmy April afternoon. Vines and shrubs were in flower and bees bobbed and murmured among the blossoms. The beast sat on the grass with its legs out, like a stuffed bear. A pair of mastiffs chained by the kitchen bayed insanely at the sight of the beast until Monsieur Le Mayor told his steward to shut the dogs away in the barn.

"The creature does not run off?" asked Monsieur Le Mayor.

"It goes into churches."

Monsieur Le Mayor's eyebrows arced in fascination. "It is a devout beast!"

This had not occurred to me.

"And the Indians in Quebec," asked Monsieur Le Mayor. "Tell me, how do they dress, what do they smell like, what do they eat? Do they build monuments, make art, have gods and devils?"

"Some say they *are* devils," I said.

Monsieur Le Mayor regarded me with his heavy eyes. Then he grinned the grin of a man who does not want to say what he really thinks. "Just so."

"Is there more cheese?"

Monsieur Le Mayor nodded to his steward, a gaunt old man in a crisp smock, who went off to fetch more cheese.

"It has been a lean winter," I said, dabbing crumbs with my thumb and then eating them.

Monsieur Le Mayor finished his wine and set his glass down with care. It had a long stem and was engraved with shell patterns. He asked, "Monsieur Le Bête will not object if we approach?"

"I can whip him first," I offered.

"No, no."

"Just move slowly," I said.

"Has he bitten anyone?"

"Not yet."

Monsieur Le Mayor raised his forefinger signalling us to listen. He frowned and tilted his head. "Is Monsieur Le Bête… singing?"

The beast sat as before, legs out, arms limp in its lap, but yes, it was humming. "It hums," I said. "A habit it's picked up over the past few weeks. He was supposed to dance," I added.

"Dance!" said Monsieur Le Mayor. "Better and better."

The steward returned with a half wheel of cheddar.

"Will he eat cheese?"

"I have seen him eat deer turds," I said.

Monsieur Le Mayor refilled his glass and directed the steward to bring the cheese. "We will give him a treat."

The beast continued to hum even as it watched our approach.

"Its song suggests Gregorian chant," observed Monsieur Le Mayor. He signalled for the cheese and, squatting on his haunches, offered both the wine and the cheese to the beast.

It ceased humming. Its eyes, rheumy and sunken, looked at the offering, then at Monsieur Le Mayor, and then at me. I thrust my chin meaning: Take it. The beast was hesitant. Though I could see by the action of its nostrils that the cheddar intrigued.

Monsieur Le Mayor turned to me. "Does he communicate?"

"He—it—is an animal."

"Do birds not sing, frogs not croak, dogs not bark?" He addressed the beast. "Bonjour, mon ami. Comment allez-vous?"

The beast considered the man before it. There was that gaze, again, watchful and evaluating. Then it shrugged.

"Avez-vous faim?"

"Un peu." The voice arose as though from a well—wet, distant, remote.

I nearly fell over.

"Mange, mange!" cried Monsieur Le Mayor.

The beast took the wine glass between thumb and forefinger, very delicately, as though it were a daisy, raised it slowly to its snout and—the cheeky bugger!—inhaled. Its eyes closed as if basking in a summer sun. Then it sipped, mulled, sipped more. It followed this with a modest bite of the cheese and chewed slowly. "Bon."

"Bon!" echoed Monsieur Le Mayor, well pleased. He looked to his steward, who fetched the wine jug and refilled the beast's glass. "You sing very well."

"I sing to the bleeding man on the cross."

"And well should we all," agreed Monsieur Le Mayor.

All afternoon Monsieur Le Mayor questioned the beast. It answered warily, in a salty French picked up, so it said, from listening to the sailors on the ship. I had to admit I felt jealous that the beast talked to this man but not me.

When Monsieur Le Mayor asked about its father the beast said that he had drowned.

"And your mother?"

"She died in whelp."

"Do you like the wine?"

It held out its glass for more.

At dusk, swallows skimmed the grass and a flock of starlings shrilled in an oak. Monsieur Le Mayor invited us to spend the night. As he showed me to my room we passed his cabinet of curiosities. It contained shells and bones, what he termed fossils, a shrunken head from Amazonia, a rhinoceros horn, peacock feathers, the beak of an ancient bird big enough to carry off sheep. "And this," said Monsieur Le Mayor proudly, "a bird of paradise." He held in his hands a creature with feathers of indigo and gold, and a curved black beak. It had, however, no feet. "It never lands. It spends its life in the air." This seemed to delight Monsieur Le Mayor.

The bedroom was big. There were tapestries of sword-swinging angels vanquishing demons, maids in castles, high-stepping white horses ridden by armoured knights. I had a bath with hot water and soap, the first in a year. The bed was stuffed with goose down and there was a net of the finest mesh against mosquitoes.

I was exhausted but lay awake. I had never been a good sleeper, and as usual my mind ranged. Quebec had been a flop. Not only had I failed to get rich, I was not on the road to getting there either. Okay, I'd seen a lot, met many people, most of them thieves, and in this way grew rich in experience. But fuck experience; unless, like an alchemist, I could transform it into gold, otherwise it was worthless. Lying in that bed, I went over what I had done in the New World. Cut wood, lugged wood, stacked wood, said yes sir, no sir, right away sir, carried canoes, paddled canoes, caulked canoes, walked, hiked, climbed, plodded, trod, occasionally staggered, and—when required—run. I'd learned a smattering of Anglais, a few phrases in Mohawk and Micmac. I thought of Marthe, who had taught herself to read by studying the Bible. Three children, another on the way, no man, no prospects. At thirteen she'd wanted to enter the nunnery but our father said never, she would stay on the farm and work. Such was papa's plan for me as well. He took me into the field one day and scooped up some soil and squeezed it. Smell, he said. I smelled. That is the earth, my son. Oui, papa, la terre. Work it hard, he said, and it will yield to you. The next morning I ran off, taking my chances, just as I'd taken a chance on the beast.

Sometime before dawn I dropped into a black sleep. What greater mercy is there than sleep, deep and dreamless? If I could be sure that that was what death was like I'd cut my throat now. The old steward shook me awake. He was holding out a mug of coffee, real coffee, rich and strong. It occurred to me that I should have gone to Africa, to Abyssinia, and grown coffee, built a house and found a woman and had a son. Perhaps for this I would stay alive.

On the table was a tray with rolls and cream, a pot of jam and a jug of coffee steaming in the sunlight that poured through the window. I ate and drank everything then ran my thumb around inside the jam pot and sucked it.

The steward brought hot water, soap, and towels. Before closing the door he said that the master awaited my pleasure in the garden.

I found Monsieur Le Mayor doing exercises. Beneath a rose arbour he stretched his arms high overhead then exhaled and bent forward and touched his toes. Inhaling, he thrust one leg back then the other, and, exhaling, lowered himself to the grass. He was wearing green hose and a loose white blouse. Inhaling, he raised his chest and threw back his head while keeping his pelvis on the ground. With another long exhalation he raised his hips into the air and, head down, arms straight, groaned as if delighting in a delicious agony. He then lunged his right leg forward, then his left, stood there a moment touching his toes, and then with a deep in-breath stood up straight and tall and, with a final exhalation, lowered his arms and smiled.

"My friend! I have been saying hello to the sun."

"And how is Old Sol faring?"

"Tip top!"

He motioned me to a bench by a table. On it was a box with a metal lock. The beast was seated on the grass, humming. Beside him was an empty breakfast tray.

"Tell me," began Monsieur Le Mayor placing his hands on the table. "What are your plans?"

I became furtive. "Plans?"

"I perceive by the state of your cart and your couture that you are broke. There is no shame," he added. "It is the way of the world. Fate. Fortune." He shrugged at the mystery of it all. "But I have a proposal."

I maintained a calm visage and waited even as my stomach churned with excitement.

Monsieur Le Mayor turned his hands palm upward signalling the simplicity of his proposal. "I will buy the beast."

I did not react. This took much self control, for I was ecstatic. But I was also suspicious.

"You have concerns," said Monsieur Le Mayor.

I closed my eyes and inclined my head, acknowledging the truth of this. "I ask myself why."

"Why is an excellent question, an eternal question. But there is a more important question, which is What, as in What will you do when you leave here? And another question of equal importance, which is How. That is, How much am I offering?" He opened the box and plucked out a leather pouch and set it on the table. It made a solid sound and the weight of the coins made it spread. It sat there, the size of two fists.

I stared at the money then I looked at the beast.

"Of course," said Monsieur Le Mayor, "you wish to consider." He strolled off some distance, pausing here and there to inhale the blooms of the many flowers.

I weighed the pouch. It had heft. I placed it on the table and clasped my hands behind my head and considered the sky. A bright clear morning. I asked myself what the man saw that I did not.

Monsieur Le Mayor returned.

I made him wait a few minutes more, even though there could be no doubt of my answer, then said, "I accept."

"Just so. Do you wish to bid Monsieur Le Bête adieu?"

I walked slowly across the grass and said, "So, you have improved your lot."

"As have you," said the beast.

We studied each other. What judgement there was in those eyes. No, I would not miss that gaze. Tugging the key to the shackles from the lace around my neck, I tossed it to the ground.

"You can have the cart!" I called to Monsieur Le Mayor as I left.

I hid in the forest and studied the money. There were French, Spanish, and Portuguese coins, both silver and gold, each stamped with a face or a crown and words I could not read for I had not been as diligent a student as Marthe. I sat a long time. I heard the twitter of birds and the buzzing of flies and saw the shadows and sunlight travel their slow course across the forest floor. I thought of Marthe and I thought of my father, and it occurred to me that I would have liked to have seen him one more time, holding this bag of money.

But what was I going to do? I needed a plan. I crept deeper into the forest, away from the road and thieves and tramps. I had to think. Stretching out on my back, I slept. When I woke it was evening and there were mosquitoes and I knew what to do: I would make for Marseille and a ship to Africa, where I would become a coffee planter. I scraped up a hand full of dirt and squeezed it. My father didn't know anything. I dropped the dirt and weighed the coins in my hand. A good price. Monsieur Le Mayor was generous.

At dawn I was on the road. But I didn't get far. When I halted and turned around the sun was scarcely clearing the treetops. By the time I got back to Monsieur Le Mayor's estate it was high and slanting steeply through the oaks. I was hungry and thirsty for bread and coffee, but more than this I was curious. Creeping close I peered through the manicured hedge. There in the garden was Monsieur Le Mayor along with a handsome woman in a white dress, some laughing children, a few servants, and the old steward, all clapping their hands and cheering the beast, who, eyes closed, arms out, danced.

FUNNY HAT

JOWITA BYDLOWSKA

WHEN I could finally stand up, my husband ushered me out of that room.

I was wearing bloody pads. I was numb. Anaesthetic: mind, body.

I wanted to turn around and come and get her. A mistake has been made.

"You're just in shock," he kept saying.

I walked like an elderly person. He grabbed my upper arm gently but firmly, walked me faster.

The hospital was no longer the good place where we used to go, waiting to see her again, growing inside me. In the blurry ultrasound pictures, she was already baby-shaped; her heartbeat was like a techno track; it seemed to go too fast but the ob-gyn assured us this was normal.

I loved the feeling of cold gel spreading on my belly as they looked for her. It wasn't a pleasant feeling but I loved it anyway.

Back then, I felt affection toward the hospital. There were monitors and birthing beds and skilled doctor hands that would get her out of me and I would get to hold her and kiss her tiny, scrunched-up face.

I kissed her tiny, scrunched-up face.

I did get to hold her. Then she was gone.

Afterwards, the hospital looked like prison to me, like Alcatraz.

In the six-level parking lot my husband wandered around trying to find our car. I sat on concrete steps and waited for a text letting me know he'd found it.

I shivered but it wasn't cold. I couldn't stop shivering.

When he walked me to the car, I finally cried; I felt safe locked in the metal can that drove us away from Alcatraz. I saw it disappear in the rear-view mirror and I blamed it for what had happened inside.

My husband's mouth was a tight line; he was concentrating on driving. He sped and passed cars as if we were late for an appointment.

We got home and I went to bed, covered myself in blankets and waited for nothing. Waited for sleep, which came eventually, mercifully, and I didn't have to deal with the sudden vacancy inside my body.

My husband didn't check on me. He woke me up in the evening. He cooked dinner—blobs of food matter in different colours. I put the food in my mouth like a machine.

He was silent the whole time.

It's a crazy thing to despise someone for how they deal with death but there you have it.

After days, weeks, or years in bed, he ordered me to get up. He said I looked like death. He was right: my cheekbones were like knives and the lines around my mouth were deep ridges.

"I don't know how to help you," he said.

"I don't know how to help me."

He said, "Let's go shopping. It'll distract you."

He bought me dresses and stockings.

He bought me shoes.

He dragged me to see a movie about something; I can't remember what and afterwards we went to eat something. I can't remember what. We sat in the restaurant and he said I looked beautiful. Tired but beautiful. I should start wearing more make-up.

"I'm in so much pain," I remember saying.

"Life goes on," he said.

He held my hand and I felt nothing.

"You need to take better care of yourself. You're too beautiful to waste away like that."

I laughed in that restaurant and it wasn't a nice laugh. I laughed like a hysteric. I was a thing he couldn't fix.

On his computer he had a folder with hundreds of pictures of me in different underwear and dresses and shoes he had purchased for me. I was a thing, a doll, and I had to behave like a doll, otherwise he didn't know what to do with me.

Before Before

It wasn't always like that.

After we got married, we flew to Europe where we rented a small Cinquecento to drive from Denmark all the way to Greece. After hours of driving, we'd stop at hotels in cities where we wanted to spend time. Mostly small cities with small hotels with small rooms with big beds. We'd have sex and shower and change and go out to eat. There was always a pretty town square, a restaurant with tiny tables and chairs spilling out onto the sidewalks where we'd drink sparkly wine and eat a dish of the local interpretation of carbs, and the local cheese and fruit for dessert. If it was lunch, we'd stroll around the city following no specific direction, going inside buildings and churches that were open, taking an occasional photo of things that impressed us: a fading fresco, a gargoyle head, weird vegetables, scrawny kittens, dark-haired children running in the streets, backs of other tourist couples holding hands.

Back then my husband wasn't a planner—I was never a planner—and this mutually agreed-on freedom made us feel free; made me feel free. We would walk around holding hands and not talk or we would talk but I don't remember any of the conversations; I just remember the mood and it was light, lots of laughter.

If it was evening, and the city was bigger, we'd try to find a venue that played music. We'd get drunk and dance and kiss as if we'd just met. Sometimes we'd talk to locals or other tourists but sometimes we wouldn't—we wouldn't even talk to each other. This is not an uncommon experience—I'd read books about lovers not having to talk to each other—that's how deep their connection was—and it was happening to us, in real life.

We would go back to our hotel, my hair curling from the moisture that seemed to be ever present the closer we got to the Adriatic. We smelled of sweat and smoke and alcohol and perfume and we would intertwine our legs and arms, our snaking snake bodies between sheets, which would end up on the floor after many rounds of passionate fucking.

The mornings would be pleasantly hungover, two-dimensional with lazy breakfast in bed, always eggs and orange juice. The hotels catered to dumb, careful tourists; you had to go out to get the local food.

We usually didn't stay for more than one night and we would get back into our Cinquecento and drive through smaller country roads—we avoided highways—and stop sometimes to have sex or check out a falling-apart church or eat a meal.

We agreed on the stops; there were never any arguments about not following the plan because there was no plan. There was just point A—Denmark—and B—Greece—and after that a plane back to Canada.

Now

Maggie, Sarah, Lucy, Olive. Helen. Names I like.

(I never named her.)

Olive. I like Olive best. Olive, an actual name, a regular name for a regular girl who would've been alive to begin with and who would inhabit a name as live girls do, give it personality: Maggie loves horses. Lucy is really particular about her hair. Sarah hates apples.

Salty and bitter olives—like the ones my husband and I gorged on in Greece—for Olive.

Sometimes I see her in little girls on playgrounds and she's mine—she has dark hair like my husband's, my big brown eyes—until she squeaks until she squeaks and runs toward some other woman, calling "Mom!"

I shouldn't be bringing it up with my husband any more. If I do, he'll probably say, as he always does, that his company has good insurance. Fifteen hundred dollars in psychological services, Babe. Fifteen sessions at least, maybe more if I can find someone who charges less.

"Olive," I say, and he rolls his eyes.

"I'm not crazy."

He says, "Please. You must stop. You can't go on like this."

"You mean you can't go on like this."

"I can't go on like this, you're right," he says, and we don't talk about it any more because now it's a Sunday morning and it's warm; it's quiet and beautiful outside, and we are still together because I still remember Greece when I look at him.

After lunch, we go out to the newly opened outdoor market in our neighbourhood where you can buy everything—from weird mushrooms to old medals.

We pass stalls like we're in a museum.

In a vegetable stand I buy beets and multicoloured carrots. The carrots and the beets inspire me; they could become a minor creative project. Not a novel but perhaps a stew.

My husband puts his arm around my shoulder, pulls me close to him. When he turns to me his eyes are half moons, happy. I love him in this moment, deeply, fiercely like I used to. It's a flash of light, a promise of summer perhaps, maybe another Greece.

I grab and hold his hand.

His hand is polite in mine, not particularly interested.

I squeeze his hand harder.

People pass us by and look at us and see us. We must be a reassuring image, a manifestation of everything working out in the end.

We let go of each other's hands after my husband sees a stall with hats. He stops, picks out an ugly hat, and puts it on.

It looks awful on him, a disk of straw like a dinner plate someone threw at his head.

"It looks silly. What about your other hats? There are some in the basement."

"They don't fit," he says and adjusts the dinner plate, but it won't stay adjusted; it moves and pops up as if it were planning to fly off.

I try not to comment on his clothing, his fashion choices that upset me, try not to be the bitch laughing at her husband's fumbly attempts at dressing himself. He's not so bad at it—no polyester shirts, no khaki pants. My mother used to do it to my father, used to berate him for his khaki pants, his terrible khakiness.

It was inevitable he would rediscover his self-esteem between the legs of a quiet, clear-eyed girl who didn't give two shits about khaki pants.

My husband blinks at me, "A dinner plate. Funny." He pulls the brim of the hat down, tries to jam it further onto his head. It makes no difference, the hat pops right up.

I say, "Let's see if they have others over there—"

My husband takes out his wallet and gives the hat seller a twenty.

Is this is going to be the deciding moment that I'll talk about in the future? Will it be me saying to a Sangria-drunk table of newly acquainted divorcee girlfriends: "It was when he bought this dweeby little hat."

I've read of people walking out on their spouses over burnt pasta dishes, missing toothpaste caps.

It's never just that, never just an ugly hat, just a missing toothpaste cap.

"No, it looks great," I say, but he walks ahead of me and rests one hand on the hat; holds it down.

It is never just an ugly hat.

He speeds up but I don't catch him.

(Olive.) I walk behind him rolling my daughter's beautiful bitter, salty name in my mouth.

RYAN & IRENE, IRENE & RYAN

PAIGE COOPER

THE DREAM is its own reality, so I can't be sure I'm awake until I walk into the office at eleven fifteen and see who's at reception. My office in the dream—in all the dreams—is the same as my office in life. Sunny, concrete, perfume lifted and dispelled by air conditioning. In the dream the receptionist is a girl who stopped speaking to me in middle school. This morning I am three hours late. I am unshowered, wearing a suit because nothing else was clean. No one wears suits here, not even Moe. But when the elevator doors open it's just an intern sitting behind the desk, so I know I'm awake. Everything is real.

"Morning, Mad," says the intern, smiling.

I frown past her to Vivian, my assistant, who waits like a meerkat in the bullpen. Maybe she stood there all morning, gazing at the elevator doors. No one else glances up from their screens. Coffees are sipped. Keyboards chitter. Viv slides open my office door for me and says, "I moved Irene back to two."

"What did you tell her?"

"That the lawyers were running long. This is nice."

"Good." I put my purse on my desk.

"Balmain?"

"What?"

"Is it Balmain?"

I look down at my lapels. "Is it?"

"Yes, it is," she says.

Moe made me hire a personal shopper once. The woman tested me—dozens of Freudian slides—then presented, over a series of days, a stream of folded garments in white, or sometimes black and occasionally grey, saying that before I even considered another piece I should always meditate on *votre look*. She gave me a piece of black leather with words stamped in serif: *Surgeon. Sensei. Colonist.* I left her bill, which was insane, on Moe's desk.

"What about Tender?" I say.

"Told him you were putting out fires with Irene."

"Did you book the call with Gulf?"

"They suggested Wednesday ten or Thursday four."

"Wednesday, I guess."

Viv cocks her head. "So you're planning on coming in on time tomorrow then?" Her glossy bangs, cut straight and heavy, give her the appearance of a precocious twelve-year-old, always mocking me from within her immaculate ensemble. *Votre look: Aristocrat. Company man. Queen of the Detention Hall.*

"Shut up," I say.

"Rough night?" Viv is also too interested in personal things, mine and the clients' both. She is excellent, for a twenty-five-year-old, but still she is twenty-five. The entire office is twenty-five, except for Moe and me, and the nineteen-year-olds.

"It was fine," I say. I was dealing with the lawyers and publicists about Irene's ex, but that's not why I slept so late.

The dream runs in tandem harness with reality, but it is separate and unique. It's hard to twist out of. In one night I can wake up a dozen times, still deep in it. Time fogs like it's long gone already. Last night in the dream I came to work, then went home and worked. I came to work, then went home and worked. You see why I have trouble telling everything apart.

"What did you tell everyone?" I ask.

"That you were out with a potential client."

"A client."

"Yeah, like, Rihanna."

"Rihanna?"

"I didn't." It disgusts her that I don't understand her jokes. "Obviously I did not. Do you want a coffee?"

I pause, blank. "Do you want one?"

"Sure," she sighs.

"Can you get food, too?" I dig a card out of the purse that woman bought me. "And whatever you're having."

Viv leaves the door open. I unfold my computer. Since closing it at three a.m. I've received another hundred emails, which puts me at twelve hundred unread. I've left so many fires to burn while dealing with Irene's ex. The email from Irene is titled *thank you* and it says, *everything feels so much better already, see you at 2*. I hope that means that she'll show up to our meeting unweeping. Although maybe it'll be just as well to give Tom, her new tour manager, a holistic picture.

"Here you go, Mad," says the mail guy. The package is white plastic ribbed in black electrical tape.

I don't look up because he is too attractive. Tattooed, narrow. I grab the package from the edge of my desk after he turns away, saw it open with my car keys. A handheld audio recorder. Some little band wanting attention. Or the lawyers? I press play.

A high whine.

They told me the glass walls fractured and crashed to the floor, but the fern beside my desk was unruffled.

In the dream, I'm skinning a kiwi on my patio. The valley below is emptied of houses, streets. The leaves on everything are primordial. I admire what the light does, gilding them. I'm unstructured in silk robe, slick hair. Irene and her ex confer in my kitchen, shrieking celery in the juicer.

Together in the same room, hands touching and re-touching in the coral-reef current between them, they make each other more beautiful. Irene's always hanging back like she's been strung from the ceiling. Grey skin, ashy hair. His name is Ryan. She has a tendency, in public, to speak inaudibly, but her laugh is huge and braying because she was raised with good brothers. Beside her, Ryan's alive: long, wall-scaling arms. He's pixie-faced, sparkle-eyed, currently wearing a moustache that would be unremarkable on a uniformed park ranger. He'd be an insolent waiter.

Irene is crying, her mascara a watercolour blackwash across her cheekbones. She says, "Leave, please. Look." Then to me: "I'm sorry. This is your house."

"Don't worry," I cross my arms over my breasts.

"I'm so embarrassed," she says. I guess they've been in my spare room all night. He would've come in through a window. There's no question the two of them were fucking like cats while I was an absurd lump, sleeping with my hand on my phone under the pillow, irradiated.

"Please just go," Irene says, and covers her face.

Ryan looks to me. I shake my head and shrug. I've never actually met him. She's my client. I've heard everything. I know in reality we've taken out a restraining order against him, but things are allowed to be different here. Some of the pain could be stripped from them, maybe.

"I'll go," I say. "Take your time. Call me if you need anything."

I pick up my car keys. My feet are bare. In the garage it's not the Audi, it's my old shitty Jeep, and my dog is waiting in it, though she won't look at me. We go to the beach and she swims into the ocean and keeps swimming. She doesn't come back.

White curtains and the tops of trees twitch outside the window. I will my body to move but it won't. A doctor comes in. My arms are swaddled like infants, the left one stopping six inches short.

"What's wrong?" I ask.

"Do you feel any pain?"

"I don't think so," I say.

"We cleaned up the forearm. We're waiting to see about the other one."

"The other one?"

"We'll see, but we're fairly sure it'll be fine."

"Where's my phone?" I ask.

"I have no idea," she says. "Did she have a phone?"

Moe is standing in the door. He's gleaming with sweat. It's droppletting the front of his beautiful white shirt. He's fat and handsome. When he hired me he promised he'd never interfere with my clients, that I'd take my twenty percent and he was just happy to have my name around. The man never shuts up or stops laughing. He doesn't come into the room. He gawks.

"Do you have my phone?" I ask.

He moans. He leaves.

The bandages are yellowed, yellowing. I can't move my arms, but then I can. One swings like a construction crane. It hits some tubing that's attached to me, and I draw it back in across my chest.

Moe comes back. He says, "Holy shit, Mad. Vivian's looking for it. But I guarantee you it melted with the rest of everything on your desk. It's probably lodged in the fucking ceiling right now."

"I'm really behind, Moe," I confess. I've been wanting to say it for months, but immediately I want to unsay it.

He doesn't acknowledge me. He comes to the bed and looks at my left bandage. "Do you remember what the package said? The police want to talk to you about that. Is she up for that?" He looks for the doctor, but she walked out ages ago.

"Everything got away from me," I say. Heat leaks from the sides of my eyes. I shouldn't admit it. But I'm so relieved to tell him. There's nothing he can do. My throat closes up. My clients are all angry. Everyone but Irene. I could lose Tender, I could lose Bishop Weyland. I wouldn't blame them.

"Mad," he says. "Madeleine."

I open my eyes. "Listen. What is going on here? Is Irene okay?"

"Irene?" Moe says. "Jesus, forget her melodrama for a second."

"Was there some kind of car accident or something?" I ask.

"What? No," Moe says. He sits down in the chair beside me. He's staring at my chest, or my arms crossed vampirically over it. He's hot and red and his face has a fixedness to it that is becoming terrifying. I don't recognize his features in this shape. "Holy shit," he says, again.

Irene refuses to bring me to her favourite bar for meetings, and she also refuses to come into the office because there have been times, yes, when we've ordered in lunch, and dinner, and another dinner. I don't always know when to stop. That was when we were first getting set up, though, and I was untangling the mess Poseidon had made. Crew, accounting, booking agents. A real tour manager. Now we meet at this bar she hates, the one with expensive artisanal cocktails that she thinks will motivate me to wrap up quickly. She orders gin, I order soda. The server is wearing a vintage tuxedo and a tiny moustache. Of course the place has no name. Moe's friend Marcus owns it and calls it Bar No Name. Irene will wither under any glint of attention. At first people just see her jawline, her poltergeist figure, the negative oxygen suck of her strikingness, but then there's the spread of recognition. This is not the kind of place where anyone will approach her, though the server is embarrassingly familiar. He brings us a plate of olives, "Viz our compliments," he says.

"He's faking that accent," Irene says. "He can't make up his mind between French and German."

"Swiss?" I say. I open my laptop. I don't know, I avoid travelling too much. All my clients know I won't tour with them. It's part of the deal. I'm supposed to be worth it. My email chimes and Irene, leaning back into the white leather, wreathed in waxy palm fronds, smiles. No one's supposed to work explicitly anymore, I know. Viv has told me repeatedly that looking at my phone is not socially okay.

"Gulf has some names for the new bio."

"Okay," she says.

"They have someone to shoot the interview. Turn the footage into teasers."

"Who do they want to write it?"

"No one I recognized. Some kid from London? Let me look." I click around, searching for the conversation.

"Have you heard from Ryan?" This is what she actually wants to talk about.

"I haven't. Has he been—" I stare into my silver light.

"No." She twists her gin, lifts it to cradle near her heart.

I click through labels and tabs. What is the woman who does international's name? Maude. Meghan. Meagan. I type *bio* in the search box and two thousand conversations come up.

"He's never actually left me alone before."

"It's a restraining order."

Finally, I'd called the police. The night he wouldn't leave her foyer, the door buzzing constantly, the magazine photographer—nineteen years old mentally if not physiologically—giggling and peering down through the front window to the stoop where he stood, Allison the publicist staring at me with increasing heat, Irene handing me her phone and retreating to the bathroom to sob, then coming back smiling weakly and shivering. I read his endless, contorting scroll: *You talentless, starfucking piece of shit. You've fucked me over do your own vapid soul for the last time. Don't you dare contact me again you fucking bitch. Your all I want. We're conjoined I'm absolutely fucked inside. Please. One more chance.* She curled like a greyhound on the couch. I looked outside: he stood in the street with his chin lifted. The police came up to take our statements. Allison hissed, smiling, into my ear: "This is so bad."

The sun on Irene is green-gold through the leaves. Her freckles look like worry scattered under deep-socketed, apologetic eyes. She could be a sickish art-gallery clerk, undiagnosable without health care; or some court sorceress tasked with sitting awake all night to keep the cats and night hags off a happier woman's baby. I love Irene. It's a side effect of looking at her.

"He's not stupid," she says. "He's batshit, but." Then weeping again. Not sobbing, just glossy-eyed. I know the overview: five years spiralling around him and she got three albums out of it, including the one that broke her. Even before she fired the predator of a manager she'd started with, there was a cold war for her talent: I only won because she wanted me. Me, because everyone knows what I've done for Tender. We've only had each other since Christmas, but she still hasn't signed my contract. I never forget I'm still on trial. My job is to spin her talent into money, but no one else ever called the cops.

"You gave him every opportunity," I say.

"I just—I don't know how to. Who else can I tell about this remix, you know?" She swirls a hand in the air. Bruce Springsteen or a coyote yips over the speakers.

I grimace. The server, for one, would happily listen to her thoughts, as would any number of the ostentatiously disinterested people in this bar. But this is the problem. Fame corrodes everything.

"I know, I don't mean to be. It's just what's in my head. You're not. Creatively, it was an important—"

"I understand, Irene."

"It's just withdrawal. He was always going to—" She inhales. She sips. Her eyes skitter across the room behind me. "I guess it's all the other women, now."

"Withdrawal," I repeat.

"If I just think of myself as an addict," she says.

"Is there—" I don't know what to say. "Does that help?"

She has calmed. She is wrapped in her black kaftan. Her gin dampens her knee. "I wish I could warn them. But I'd seem crazy, wouldn't I?"

I turn back to my emails. "Mavis," I mutter. The list of music writers appears.

"What if he's all I have to write about?" she says.

I don't answer her. I have no answer.

In the dream, when he comes through the window I'm there this time. He's not embarrassed to find me.

. "Can I help you?" I say. He locks the window after sliding it closed. A spider the size of my hand skitters across the glass and disappears.

He has a scar under one eye and premature crow's feet from years spent in weather. Stringy biceps. He's always so flushed, dry, burnt up. The light is yellow from the hall. I meet his eyes and then can't. My watch beeps. It's green velcro, a gift from my father when I was in junior high. I'm in a full sweat like back then. Hormones.

I try again. "Can I get you anything?"

His hands are still, like they want nothing, but his body is vibrating. I can tell because we're standing so close. If I could just be of some use to him. His mother died last year. Irene told me. Irene told me everything evil about him. The good was untranslatable. A separate stream. He has one hand on my sternum. There's a gorge open there that I'd welcome him into. I don't recognize this room. It's his, I guess. He has a whole wing of my house and this is the first time I've been into it. He kisses me with his eyes open so that he can watch Irene where she sits in an armchair in the corner by an armoire, holding her throat and sobbing so hard she's coughing, choking, pulling at a pendant around her neck until the cheap metal chain breaks.

I lie, mummified. I have questions. Who would the hospital have called if I hadn't been at work? If Viv and Moe and the hot mailman hadn't known my name and insurance details? I keep a card in my wallet with a few names blacked out: my ex-husband who remarried, a friend who lives in New York, for a while my trainer at the gym, who would text me in a friendly way that I strained into reading as flirtation. But I was paying my trainer, which meant we probably each had a different understanding of the situation, and I was too embarrassed to tell him his name was on that card, so eventually I blacked him out, too.

The cops come and go. Moe says I have to make a statement for the press release. I say, "I look forward to starting my new bionic life." Allison rolls her eyes but says that she can work with it. I don't ask if they know who sent the package, and no one volunteers any ideas.

The sharpie did not do a perfect job. A nurse walks me down the hall to the pay phone and dials the number I read through the ink. My ex-husband is newlywed. There's no mirror in my washroom, so I assume I now look demonic. Charred, scarred. We talk about his honeymoon in French Polynesia. We had planned to go to Tahiti on our fifteenth anniversary, but we only made it to twelve. He invited me to his wedding, but I declined on the grounds I'd never made myself very likable to his friends. "What else is new?" I say.

"Not much. Dog's good. She's doing that tongue thing again."

"Send me a picture."

"Sure."

"Oh, actually, you can't. My phone blew up."

"Like exploded?" He's amiable. He's driving home to his wife.

"I'm in the hospital," I say.

"Seriously?"

"It was on the news."

"What was on the news?"

"A mail bomb blew my hand off."

"Holy god, Mads," he laughs.

"Will you come visit?"

"You're kidding, right?" he says. I remember that he moved with the dog to Denver two years ago.

"No?" I say. "The nurse had to give me a special pillow to hold the phone."

"Wait."

"I look super cool right now."

"Wait," he squawks. "You're not kidding?"

He probably won't come.

There's less blood than I would've thought. The pain is mostly a frightening lack of pressure, a carsick lightness that wakes me up over and over again. My head jerks up, drifts down, jerks up. The nurses keep it sedated. Irene has not come.

Irene told me about how Ryan, three years into their relationship, was summoned by a dying hairdresser, who bought him a plane ticket to visit her deathbed. Just a hook-up, he'd said. Why would this dying woman want to see him? He didn't know. He spent six months evading the trip. The dying woman got angry, accused him of using the ticket for something else and not telling her. Coward. When he finally went, he booked the trip over Irene's birthday. "What's wrong with you?" he'd said. "She's *dying*, Irene."

I have options as to prosthetics. If I spend the money, I can have one that looks like Apple made it. Pellucid, streamlined. An improvement on the hand. I've always had short, ugly nails. Who needs the weakest digits, besides to apply under-eye cream. I'll be able to type and percolate coffee, do some light yoga. No inversions, obviously. Viv shows me my phone: screen cracked, cover blown off the back. She sits beside me and I dictate: tour support for Europe, the launch timeline, ad buys. I was never that into yoga, though. There is one vase of tropical flowers, and fifty-three more at the office. The intern at reception was lost in them so they had to start spreading them out, two per desk. I can't decide: either Viv is exaggerating the number to make me feel beloved, or everyone in the office is enjoying the swell of good feeling while I lie here with one bunch of daylilies and alpinia. Irene has not come. The pain medication makes it easy to weep constantly, weakly, about how everything is happening without me now.

"Has Irene called?" I ask again.

"No," says Viv, her eyes sliding away and back to the screen.

"But she knows."

"I emailed her. We spoke on the phone."

It's been four days.

"She's probably with Ryan," I say, and Viv's eyebrows twitch up, though she keeps typing. "They've probably run off to Morocco together."

"Ha," says Viv. She treats most things I say as a joke.

"Call her again."

"Sure," she says, in the way that means she'll forget until I ask again. She sighs. "I'll never understand women like that."

I raise my left bandage to my mouth. It smells starchy, unclean. Old upholstery, a gelatin factory. The pain, sometimes, is just the need to crack my knuckles.

Onstage at the Belvedere, Irene is her own high priestess. Her hair shrouds her as she fiddles with pedals and murmurs into the mic. I stand sidestage behind the guitar tech as he consults the set list by penlight and ignores me. I'm in situ so rarely that I'm often mistaken for someone's girlfriend, but after a week of production rehearsals for the North American run—I brought my laptop from the office, cleared some pizza boxes from a closet—half the crew can at least recognize me, though it's still only the tour manager, Tom, who'll speak to me. Tour managers are a favoured breed. *Votre look: Dive bartender. Super-mom. Warzone logistician.* Tom passes a rummy plastic cup and I hold onto it. Beside me, Tender, looking not long for this world, stands like a stork on one foot and sucks back his vodka.

"She is so beloved," he says, leaning into me. We can't see the audience, but they're shrieking like a bat colony. His mouth touches my ear, on purpose. I shiver. Tender's habits hope for an early death. He's painted his face paler, his bony shoulders and bare ribs exposed by the night-blue silk shirt eternally falling off him. I've managed him for twelve years and he's made three albums for every one he's let me release. He's too big to bill as support for Irene, but he'd begged—*I am begging you*—so we'd let it leak he would. Hometown kick-off to the world tour, Irene could've filled a stadium, but we gave away the tickets to this little one: eight hundred humans in a time machine with velvet curtains winging the proscenium, living simultaneously in this moment and the one three years ago when this song was playing on the radio and everyone who heard it knew they'd survive.

I turn away from the meet-and-greet after the show: nearing that line-up of sweating and trembling is too much. Tom cuts and aligns fans like a border collie or a coke dealer. I abandon my untouched rum on a console worth more than my car and retreat upstairs to the green room, where it's mostly Tender's locals: thin limbs and pretty faces I only vaguely recognize line the tiny room's couches like a panel of judges. Viv is in there with an aloof smirk. Good for her. Except she beckons me in, and Tender passes me another plastic cup and I wait for someone to say something I can speak to: streaming royalties, equipment carnets. But the conversation is all MDMA and rent.

Irene comes in, eyes glassed, hair dried to salted twine. The room and Tender wrap around her and she goes loose like he's snagged her by the nape. His talent's always been making you yearn like an exile. I almost put a hand out between them, but am too shocked by my jealousy. She pushes him away instantly: "God. I'll cry. Please, Nick." She shakes her head, smiling and apologizing, and fades back out of the room, which wilts after her. Viv raises an eyebrow at me.

I guard Irene's door for two minutes, then tap it myself. "Irene?"

"Who are they?" she says. A dozen pine-scented tea lights burn a witchy forest fire. Her eyes are blacked like a falcon's. "Like, I don't really know any of those people."

"Do you mean names?" I say. "I can ask."

"No. I don't care. I'd rather hang out with Tom and Gonzalo, but they're busy loading up my stupid shit."

"Is it—" I try to guess. "The show was unbelievable."

"Jesus. What does that mean?"

I blank my face. I wait. I say, humanely, "You just seem upset."

"Do I? Do you want to be more condescending about it?"

I surrender my palms.

She rattles the ice in a cup. "Just tell me where my friends are. Why weren't my friends in that room?"

I saw the guest list. I can't say I know what friends she's talking about. She didn't invite any. She takes a lighter from her pocket and lights more candles.

"No one's here," she mutters.

"None of your friends," I repeat, soft.

"They all left me," she says. She clicks the lighter. She hooks a thumb through a necklace; the long one with a tine of antler dangling from it. She grinds the tip of it into the heel of her hand. "They all got sick of it. It was too boring, I guess, when he was all I ever talked about."

"That's a beautiful necklace," I say.

Her eyes dart up. She lifts it. "Can you take it?"

"Um—"

"I promised myself I'd give it to the first person who complimented it."

"No, that's—"

"I know it's a little woodsy for you." She narrows her eyes at my dress, which makes me look like an aesthetician from the blizzarding steppe. "But give it away, whatever. I can't keep it. It's cursed."

The antler, copper-wound, is warm in my hand. I do not want to put the chain around my neck. Irene crying and choking in that armchair while he kissed me. It's easy to understand why she's allowed him to return so many times. Forgiveness is a grace.

"Sorry," she says. "I'm sorry."

"Irene, you know you can't offend me," I say. I would've held her, if she'd looked up. "Whatever you need."

I find Tom closing out with the merch guy. "Bring her some pizza," I tell him. "And blow out those candles."

Out on the floor under the house lights, the venue staff sweep plastic cups and confetti as the crew disassembles the rig. I drop the antler. It'll find its own in the trash.

In the dream, Ryan sweats the bed to soaking. In his wing, words are tamped down with crypt dust and incense. It's impossible to speak. I visit him there, dress, and leave, knowing myself less and less. "I didn't send a fucking bomb," he says. "That's insane." He lies, liar. He deletes truth like weather deletes history, imperfectly. He says Irene has victimized herself, twisted everything her way. She treats all her friends, family, past lovers the same. He is human and fallible. He could say things about her, but he won't. Time fogs like it's long gone already. I have both hands, all my fingers flex elegantly. I call Irene, over and over, but she doesn't answer. "She pretended she was going to kill herself," he confesses. "She wrote fake suicide letters. She manipulated me with her emotions." It's my house, so I watch another dozen women enter and exit, comforting him. They see each other but stay silent. Their shoulders brush in the foyer as they take off their shoes, wrap their scarves. Please—I'd say, if they could hear me—don't delete yourselves.

I am still in hospital when the Bataclan happens. "They flipped the soundboard up and hid behind it," Tender reads, voice strange. He holds too tightly to my good arm, even though the burns are ugly, and in the end the doctor decided to take off two of its fingers.

Ed calls from Zurich, voice high. "We want to come home now," he says. Cancelling the rest of Bishop Weyland's continental grind will cost as much as recording their next LP, but they're only twenty. They have pimples and the whites of their eyes are bright.

"I know you do," I say. "Give me a few hours."

Viv, on my other side, says, "Did you read about the merch guy? His girlfriend was all over social media trying to find out if he was okay. But there was this other woman who was at the show, giving him mouth-to-mouth. He died in her arms. And they're both going, 'He was the love of my life.' Word for word." She shakes her head. "Can you imagine finding out that way?"

"I don't think you're even aware of what you're saying," says Tender. "Or at least I hope you're not."

Viv pauses a half-second too long. Her voice is a crystal ting of apology: "Yes, you're right."

Tender shakes his head. "You know you have to actually try to care. It takes effort."

"Oh, definitely," says Viv demurely.

"Jesus. There's nothing more callous than a twenty-eight-year-old woman."

"Maybe just women in general," Viv suggests. "You would know."

"Please stop," I say. "Nick. Just go, for a little bit. Both of you."

This morning I saw my new reflection. They've been looking at me this whole time and didn't tell me. How is it possible that I missed it? Hyper-sensitive, that's what makes me good at this job. Perfectly attuned, no boundaries between their needs and mine. I'm part of them, until I'm not. I need to text Jonathan, Bishop Weyland's tour manager, and tell him to make Ed eat something, sleep a bit, before I talk to him again and convince him they're fine, they can keep going. But I can't text anyone. Ryan's bomb took a hand and a half. I have three fingers, three limbs.

Irene stands in my door. She looks like a vow of poverty. Soft-soled, tattered. Now I know what disturbs my visitors, but I don't turn my face away from her. She is weeping, but she is always weeping. What kind of person takes another's suffering as an attack? She keeps the rope she noosed to hang herself with coiled on a bookshelf in her living room. I've seen it. It could suit an aesthetic: *Sailor. Convict. Casualty.*

"Can we pretend that I came right away?" she says.

"Come here," I say, and she hugs me, smells the dead horse of me, the black dust on me. She lifts a hip and slips onto the bed with me. She is a bandage.

"They arrested him," she says into my neck, under my ear. "He sent one to the lawyers. They caught it right away."

"I know," I tell her.

"He never sent one to me." Her tiny voice.

"I'm sorry," I say. I lift my hand to touch her hair, then lower the bandaged stump soundlessly.

She is suffering because she could be in Morocco with him. Panama. He's tried to kill for her, which makes her more special to him than the others. We are conjoined, he'd tell her. Forgiveness is the temptation she's damned to. Eighty-nine people shot dead in a concert hall. Violence scales more effortlessly than art. We're all going to die one day. Her thumb rubs smooth the furrow in my brow. Her body holds emotion like smoke in a barricaded room. I hold her body. I protect it with my own.

NO. 10

TAMAS DOBOZY

THE FIRST bad Remembrance Day was 1984, the year Frank turned seventeen and his mother, Juliska, passed away. The old men came up the front steps in their berets and dress uniforms and polished medals, and Feri, Frank's father, met them at the door and told them to go away—"Get lost, murderers" is what he actually said—and then they were arguing over who'd fought for who and which government you should be grateful to and whether or not Feri should maybe just pack up if he really felt that way and go home to whatever fucking country he'd come from.

Those old men really knew how to swear. It was, in fact, the main reason Frank believed they'd fought in the war, down in the dirtiest trenches, in conditions so extreme everything—every moral lapse—was permitted. "Go home to whatever fucking country you came from" was actually one of the nicer things they said. Sooner or later, as Feri railed against them, the veterans would get to words like "jackass" and "selfish bastard" and then, eventually, "goddamn Nazi asshole," which for Feri was the worst insult of all.

"Hungary was not a Nazi country!" he shouted.

"Goddamn Nazi asshole son of a bitch," the old men said.

"The Allies spent the war shooting and bombing Hungarians and you want me to give you money for your stupid plastic flowers?" The vets glared at him. "What else do you want?" Feri said. "Maybe I should dance around and clap for you like a monkey?"

"We fought so you'd have a country like Canada to come to."

"If you hadn't fought I wouldn't have *needed* a country like Canada to come to!" The veterans had this fidgety look, like they were still obeying some old reflex, patting their hips for service revolvers no longer there, reaching for rifles that used to hang on their shoulders. The movements made no impression on Feri. "Or," he shouted, "if you'd fought a little *harder* and pushed the commies back to Moscow instead of being so friendly with Stalin you gave him half of Europe, I *also* wouldn't have needed a country like Canada to come to." At this point Feri hauled back the door as if he was inviting them inside, but really just so he could slam it that much more forcefully in their faces.

Frank watched the old men stumble out of the driveway that rainy November day. There was the lanky one he'd come to know as Lester, the barrel-chested one, Harlan, and there was of course Hank, who'd done all the swearing and finger pointing and stomping of feet. Frank took out his sketchbook and drew a cartoon of the three of them, Lester and Harlan with their arms around Hank like he was some comrade they were carrying home from battle, and the following year he went back and wrote "No. 1" beside it.

By 1985 Frank was sketching more than ever, something he did when he was nervous, watching Feri disintegrate, the house dirtier with each day since Juliska's death, their lives unraveling. He pulled out the big black hardcover and flipped to a blank page, dreaming of getting out of Mr. Simpson's art class with a portfolio good enough for university. He was so lost in it—drawing the changes to his father's face—that when the doorbell rang he jerked and chiseled a line through Feri's mouth.

Frank got up, his face already lined with the strain of getting Feri to work every morning, rolling the old man out of bed in that tiny guest room he'd taken to sleeping in after the funeral, so narrow and stuffy in there you could get loaded off the boozy fumes he exhaled. Then Frank would go to school, trying to finish grade twelve, shopping for groceries afterwards, driving to work to pick up Feri, coming home to make dinner, do lunches, laundry, then whatever homework would still fit into the day.

At night he'd get calls from Arlen Hassburger, Feri's boss, about how he'd caught him napping in the supply cupboard, or drinking on the job, or letting the other guys on the rigging crew pick up the slack, and Frank would have to talk Arlen out of firing Feri. He'd have to beg for sympathy—after all, who wouldn't fall apart after the death of his wife of nineteen years?—and then lie about how Feri was making "visible signs of progress." (Frank had learned this language from the high-school counsellor who'd helped him with his own grief.) If Arlen could only give him another month of grace things would improve.

"Your father was always my go-to guy," Arlen said. "It hurts me to see him like this. But I've got to hold up my end, too, you know?"

"He'll be your go-to guy again, I promise," said Frank.

"What about you, Frank? If things don't work out with Feri, I could use someone like you down here. There's always openings..."

"I don't know," said Frank. "My plan was to finish high school and go to university." He stopped, realizing he'd used the word "was" instead of "is," and wondered if it wasn't too late to take it back, to stop whatever the word had set into motion.

"To study what?"

"I was thinking fine arts."

"Waste of time. You'll blow four years in university and you'll be good for nothing but what you should have done in the first place. Take it from me—I wrote an honours thesis on Alexander Pope. Rhymed couplets, the 'incisiveness of satire,' all that shit! I've got friends who went to grad school and are serving meals while I'm making eighty-five grand a year as supervisor. Union wages. It's good money."

But it's not good *work*, thought Frank. Thirty-five years of it. Your whole life gone. He held the phone to his ear and said he'd get Feri to work on time tomorrow.

Now he came around the corner and saw them.

Hank was in front, just like last year, peering out from between his gin blossoms, pushing his face forward with every point he made, telling Feri about the war, his role in it, those of his friends Lester and Harlan, who stood to either side, agreeing with Hank's descriptions of how they'd suffered. And all the while he rattled the box filled with change, his lapels covered up and down, not an inch to spare, with the poppies he peeled off and gave away.

Feri looked at Hank like he was a freak. Feri was drunk. "You didn't fight for me," he finally said when Hank stopped to take a breath, "you fought *against* me."

Hank pushed his face even closer, as if he either couldn't believe what he was hearing or had already forgotten it. "Do you know what it's like to be trapped on some hill shaking with dysentery while mortars are raining all around you?"

Feri smirked. "Do you know what it's like to be ten years old, stuck in some cellar, while Allied bombers are blowing up the city over your head?"

Hank looked back at Harlan and Lester as if Feri's response was a prank, just the sort of thing old comrades would pull on their former sergeant, but they looked just as shocked and bewildered. So he turned back, head tilted the way a dog will look at humans who are doing something inexplicable. "Do you know what it's like leaving behind your family and country to go fight for someone else's freedom?"

"Do you know what it's like realizing that your country has been overrun by foreign soldiers, who are replacing the last foreign soldiers, who are replacing the foreign soldiers who came before, all of them promising freedom?"

Hank put his fists on his hips, not knowing what else to do with them. "Do you have any idea what the nights were like, working on three hours sleep, covered in mud, bitten to shit by mosquitoes, waiting for the bullet that's going to end it?"

"Do you know what it's like for a young boy to step out of the cellar to get water, and there's a Hungarian soldier lying on the sidewalk, his head crushed flat by a tank, and the boy realizes it's the soldier who helped him get water yesterday?"

Hank's face was red now, furious. "Do you know what it's like holding your friend, some guy who's covered you, saved your life more times than you can count, while he tries to tell you something, choking on his own blood, and you're not even praying that he lives, you just want God to give him a chance to say what he wants to say before he dies?" He stepped forward again, looking into Feri's face.

"Do you know what it's like when the Allied armies finally arrive and the soldiers—*Allied soldiers*—," Feri poked

Hank in the chest, "come into the place you're hiding with your mother and aunts and sister and take turns raping them in front of you?"

"You have no idea what it took for us to win that war!"

"You have no idea what suffering is!" Feri yelled back. "You shot your way through Europe then came back to Canada and didn't have to live with what was left!"

"And all of us died so you could come out here and enjoy it too!"

"What makes you think I'm enjoying it?" shouted Feri. And then he pulled back the door and slammed it in his face.

"We'll be back next year!" howled Hank.

"You can come back every year for all I care!" screamed Feri straight into the oak grain of the door, the words coming out in a movement so violent it jerked his head forward, teeth bared like he wanted to take a bite.

If the "No. 1" visit was unexpected, and "No. 2" a test to see if it had been real, then "Nos. 3–10" were by design. Over the years Frank would see every variant on the argument, every tactic, every cheating attempt at victory, until November 11 became for his father a kind of Christmas and Thanksgiving and Easter rolled into one, the day on which he flickered briefly to life again. The veterans tried everything. They tried shame, telling Feri they were going to go to every house on the whole block, the whole neighborhood, the whole town, and let everyone know what an ungrateful bastard he was; Feri said he didn't care what others thought, and looking at him, breathing hoarsely, flashing yellowed teeth, in that old sweater with its constellation of cigarette burns, the vets knew he wasn't bluffing. They tried hostility, ganging up on Feri and yelling at him at once; but Feri was like some master fencer, parrying every point, patiently explaining why they were wrong, even remembering things they'd said in passing minutes ago, returning to refute each of them in turn. (This, from a father who no longer remembered to wish his son happy birthday.) They tried empathy, telling him he was right, soldiers had died on both sides, that Remembrance Day really was for soldiers all over the world; but Feri just snickered and said, "Don't patronize me." Did they really think he believed for one second that they'd be happy pinning poppies on the lapels of former Waffen-SS?

So the vets had to become creative.

"No. 6" took place on a weirdly sunny November 11. Feri was sitting on the front steps drinking beer, lining up the full bottles on his left, the empties on the right, and the ashtray on the step below, between his feet. He scowled when he saw the vets arrive.

Frank was up a ladder around the other side of the house, out of sight, but he could hear everything. He stopped to listen in the middle of cleaning the eavestroughs, his arms caked in muck and weeds and leaves up to the elbows.

By the time he'd climbed down the ladder and come around the corner, Feri had gone into the house and come out with their old Atlas, paged forward to a map of Central Europe, and began pointing to the scenes of historic battles: Stalingrad, the Don River, and finally Voronezh, where the Soviets slaughtered 100,000 soldiers from the Hungarian 2nd Army. He pointed to each place on the map, then went through the invasion of Hungary, from county to county, city to city, ending at the siege of Budapest, listing off the numbers of the dead. "If Hitler hadn't been distracted by you bastards in the west," Feri said, his voice slurring, "we might have been able to mount some opposition to the Soviets. And then all our cities wouldn't have been destroyed. Women raped. Children slaughtered."

"That's not our fault," Harlan said. "You picked your side."

"We picked our side as much as Canada did," Feri replied. "There was no choice. The only difference between your country and mine was luck—yours good, ours bad. When Regent Horthy tried to make peace with the Allies, Hitler threatened his son, then kidnapped Horthy, then replaced him with puppets."

"Excuses, excuses," Lester said. "The Poles resisted. The Romanians managed to switch sides. The Greeks, the Serbs…"

"We had an underground, too," yelled Feri, "General Kiss and Bajczy…"

"That's not all that's been going on underground, Mr. Anti-Canada," Hank said, speaking now as if he'd meant to speak much earlier, totally out of synch with the conversation. He reached into the rucksack he'd brought along and pulled out a photo album that he opened with the pages facing Feri. "You say you're not happy with being forced to come here," Hank said, sweating into the wool of his collar, "but these pictures say otherwise." There they were: Feri and Frank sitting in a canoe in the middle of Frida Lake, mist rising off the surface, slash all around, whitecapped mountains rising on every side; Feri and Frank down by the marina getting on board the Princess Anne to go salmon fishing in Georgia Strait; Feri—alone this time—sighting his rifle on the hood of the truck, a bottle of *pálinka* open at his elbow; Feri—alone again—squatting on the edge of Stillwater Bluffs while a storm front opened over the sea, sheets of rain dimming the islands along the strait, an image cold and miserable and solitary.

"You've been following him?" It was Frank now, cutting in, stepping between Hank and Feri, who was staring at the pictures open-mouthed. "You can't just follow people around and take pictures of them."

"I was just getting proof," Hank said, while Lester and Harlan turned red, and Frank realized they hadn't agreed with what Hank had done, stalking Feri, that he'd done it alone. "Go ahead and tell the police," Hank continued. "They're on our side." But despite his confidence he'd already snapped the book shut, and was backing away.

Why wasn't Feri saying anything? Frank turned back to his father and saw that the old man was swaying on his seat, still clutching his atlas, face wet with tears. "Juliska liked going out to Stillwater," Feri said, having such difficulty forcing out the words it was like a stage whisper. But Frank knew it wasn't true. His mother had never gone out there. Once again the old man was reinventing the past to make it look as if he'd had some insight, some intimacy, with the woman he'd been unwilling to know.

"Maybe you should go inside," Frank said, but he wasn't talking about the moment anymore, what was happening with the vets, but of something more permanent, watching as Feri tried to pick up the beer bottles, which clattered and rolled down the stairs—not a single one broke—the old man stumbling through the door, gone into full retreat now, from work, from the world, from any thought of the future.

When Frank turned back only Harlan was still there, holding out a plastic poppy. "I'm sorry about Hank," he said. "I don't know what got into him. He's kind of gone crazy with your father. I think…" Harlan paused, still holding out the poppy, its fuzzy petals trembling. "You see, things happened to Hank in the war. He came back from over there… Well, he came back and he's been like this ever since." Harlan coughed. "Lester and I try to make sure he doesn't do anything too crazy, though we can't always... Look, I'm not trying to make excuses, and your father is as much to blame."

"I think you should leave," said Frank, not taking the poppy.

"It's not our idea to keep coming back here. It's Hank. We come because he tells us to." Harlan blushed, looked away, then mumbled, "Well, he's a sergeant and we're just privates." Throughout it all Harlan held the poppy extended, but he and Frank were too committed to their positions either to retract or reach out for it.

Finally, Harlan just let it fall between them.

It stayed there, on the ground, for weeks, for months, until the spring, when one of May's downpours washed it away. Passing it every morning going out, every evening coming in, Frank would wonder about the flowers that had come and gone since the start, and all the flowers yet to come, offered across the threshold, raining on the years of Feri's bereavement like some disintegrating bouquet. It would have been better if the old man had just taken the first poppy Hank had offered, dropped a quarter into the box they held out, thanked them for the sacrifices they'd made, then closed the door, tossed the poppy into the garbage and never seen them again. And if they'd come five months earlier, the night Juliska sat them down before dinner and told them what the doctor had said, how little time he'd given her, before that terrible scene between her and Feri on the last night, any time at all during those four months it took her to die, then maybe that's how it would have worked out—Feri too distracted by what was happening to him (because that's how it was, Juliska was sick, yet somehow the whole thing was happening to *him*) to do anything other than nod, neither really seeing them at the door, nor hearing what they were saying, nodding, nodding, nodding, absently dropping the coin into the box and then standing there holding the flower wondering what it was for. He often looked at people—especially his wife and son—like that during those four months, standing in the kitchen staring as if he couldn't figure out how they were put together, according to what design, what aim, and it wasn't until the vets showed up that Feri flickered back to life again, in a way he'd only ever do with them, every year on the anniversary of that first visit, summoning up that original energy, the man he'd been when he was still secure, before his wife's death, loss of job, before the cigarettes and bad food and booze took their toll—too soured on what Juliska's passing had done to him to notice that his son, Frank, was still there, looking in, attending to his father's needs, and to realize that if he *had* noticed they might have been in it together instead of alone.

For "No. 7" Frank was in the shower, early morning, and as usual Feri came into the bathroom, too lazy to use the one upstairs, dropped his pants, sat down on the toilet and lit up a cigarette. "Smells bad, doesn't it?" he said in Hungarian, always Hungarian when it was just the two of them, though his English, perfected from the gutter-speak of the rigging crew right up to the pseudo-formality of union meetings, was almost flawless, his accent only coming out once in a while and in the strangest of places—saying "shet" for "shit," "kwen" for "when," and "slot" for "slut."

Frank said nothing. It was just awful, the combination of steam, tobacco smoke, and his father's loose bowels, and the years had for some reason weakened rather than built up his resistance.

"I must say even *I* find it disgusting." The old man shook his head, completely bewildered. "And yet I am the source of the smell."

Frank wondered if this is what had killed his mother, not this specifically of course, but the slow accumulation of such incidents—the oncologist had told him that stress was a contributing factor with cancer—back when they still lived together in this house, when the place was clean, kept up, when he'd get home from school with the smells of his mother's meals wafting through the place, when Feri would return from the mill having actually worked, tired but satisfied, having accomplished what was expected of him—back, in other words, when things were relatively normal for Frank, when he could still look forward to the sorts of things sixteen-year-olds looked forward to: getting his driver's license, girls, bootlegged beers, at least a decade of odd jobs and irresponsibility before work, marriage, and kids set in—the rewards of a life kept on track.

The doorbell rang. Frank popped his head out between the curtains. "Is that the doorbell?" he asked. But instead of answering Feri wiped himself, stood up, belted his pants and pressed the toilet lever. "Watch out, I'm going to flush," he said, knowing that flushing always cut off the cold water to the shower, though he always did it anyway.

Frank pushed himself into the corner where the scalding spray couldn't reach, pressed shivering against the cold tiles until he knew the toilet had filled up again and the temperature gone back to normal.

By then, he could hear them shouting through the bathroom door Feri always forgot to close as he left, the heat and steam escaping with him, so that when Frank got out of the shower he was freezing. The veterans had brought along a woman, Frank's age or so, and he crept out at the sound of her voice, barely remembering to wrap a towel around his hips.

She was beautiful, women were all beautiful, they got more beautiful the longer Frank was trapped in this house with Feri—the women, the thought of women, the possibility of women, receding from him as if Feri was a boat carrying him off to sea, even though he could still make them out, all of them, throwing confetti and lifting champagne bottles and waving from some distant pier for him to come back.

She had black ringlets down to her shoulders, a narrow face, cheekbones so high they ricocheted the sun right into his eyes, and the pinkest lips he'd ever seen without actually having lipstick on them. She was already talking to his father while Hank, Harlan, and Lester stood behind her, arms crossed, like some geriatric bodyguard.

"...moreover, if the Canadian and American soldiers hadn't come, my grandparents would have died there, along with the six million others," she finished.

Feri looked incredulous. "Are you kidding me?" he said to the three vets.

"Really. If not for men like these," she indicated the vets, "I wouldn't be alive."

Feri pretended to gag, though it could have been a cough.

"It's not like the soldiers of your country were doing anything about the concentration camps," Hank said, nodding along with the point she was making. "Or I should say—they weren't doing anything to *empty* the camps."

Feri turned to Frank, who stood there in the towel dripping wet, then rolled his eyes at his son's lack of social graces—even as he was still wearing one of the three sets of clothes the veterans had seen him in year after year—then turned back to the visitors. "Very nice. So if I agree with this young lady, then I might as well thank you all for fighting Hitler. If I say who cares, then it proves I was a Nazi." Feri crossed his arms and tapped his temple. "Here is what I say to you—what is your name, Elena?—" she nodded and Feri continued, "the Red Army did more to free the Jews than the British and American armies put together. So maybe you should send a thank you to Russia."

"It was the great Anglo-American alliance that won the war," yelled Hank. "It was the triumph of conservative principles over socialism!"

"Ha!" yelled Feri. "You remember nothing. The Red Army did most of the fighting and most of the dying." He lifted a thumb. "Their leader was a communist. The Americans came second," he said, lifting his index finger. "Roosevelt was a very liberal president, maybe the most liberal in American history. And the British third," he said, lifting his middle finger. "They didn't do as much fighting or dying as the other two." He shrugged. "And Churchill was the only true conservative among the three." He dropped his fingers and chuckled. "One communist, one liberal. It was actually the socialists who defeated Hitler." Here Feri laughed out loud, not because he cared who'd defeated Hitler, or who was or wasn't a socialist, but because he was just so happy to destroy the veterans' argument and see the look of hatred on their faces.

It looked like Hank was going to start jumping up and down in rage.

"He has a point," Elena said, though she was looking at Frank as she said it.

"He has no goddamned point," said Hank, who then stopped for a minute to think about what the point was. "The Brits fought hard," he finally said, unable to come up with anything more concrete, but Elena cut in, saving him from the lapse.

"Yes, but Stalin and Roosevelt were both to the left, politically. Not to the same degree of course. But, I mean, if Roosevelt was running for president today, with his policies, the Republicans would call him a socialist."

"Those people don't even know what socialism is!" said Feri.

"That's not the point!" yelled Hank, responding to Elena, not Feri.

"I'll tell you the point," said Feri, getting into the old man's face. "The point is you stopped the Nazis from killing people, then you let Stalin kill twice as many." He pulled the door back shaking his head. "No plastic flower for me this year, no thanks, no thank you," he said, and slammed it in their faces. Through the crack Frank caught a last glimpse of Elena looking his way, and for a moment thought of putting his hand out to catch the door and find out if what he saw in her eyes was attraction or pity.

Frank was still drawing her picture months later, even though he'd tracked down her name, Elena Prager, and phone number, which he was building up to call. Sometimes while Frank was drawing, Feri would enter the room and come up from behind and place his hand on Frank's shoulder and just stand there like that, breathing hard, with the rattle in his throat growing louder and louder as his daily dosage of cigarettes increased. "She was a pretty girl. Maybe she'll come back next year!" The old man laughed. But when Frank didn't laugh along with him, Feri lowered his voice, "Maybe I'll be dead by next year." Frank just kept working on the picture, ignoring him. The old man coughed, not too long, not like in the morning when he couldn't stop, standing by the sink as if he was going to heave up his lungs, but just once or twice, as a reminder. Frank looked up at him, put down his pencil, and asked Feri if he'd like a beer. Or wine. Or *pálinka*. "As much as you like," Frank said, angry now, pushing out of the chair, moving into the kitchen with his father stumbling behind him, locating the old man's stash, always shifting but never so well hidden Frank couldn't find it sooner or later, pouring the booze into a shot glass, holding it out for Feri, who just stood there pretending nonchalance, as if he could say no, as if he could resist. Then Frank remembered his promise and shook his head, angrier now with the hopelessness of it all, and in the last second, just as Feri was reaching for it, he turned and dumped it into the sink.

"You'll never call her," Feri snarled. "Never, never."

By "No. 8," Feri was three-quarters rotted, breathing in rasps, too tired now for the effort of hiding his drinking or maintaining his dignity, to do anything other than sit in his chair with the crossword puzzles his brother sent every week from Hungary, back issues of old *Füles* magazine bought at flea markets, relics from the communist era printed on cheap newspaper stock, black and white, though every issue had pictures of naked women posing seductively in the middle of the darks. If Feri somehow managed to finish one, which was rare, he always made sure to rip it up and throw the scraps into the garbage in front of Frank, something he'd been doing for fifteen years, as if no time had gone by since his son was ten. It was the demonstration of superiority that mattered, not the naked ladies, because God knows there were always enough unfinished crosswords lying around the house, sometimes for years. Nonetheless, Feri would stand there, tearing them up page by page, smirking at Frank, who no longer had any idea what his father could be thinking, lost in another empty ritual, another idiosyncrasy the old man clung to—like his feud with the veterans, or his constant demands that Frank drive him out to the places he claimed Juliska had loved, or the way he always said, *"Guten morgen, mein herr"* when he entered the kitchen for the coffee and eggs Frank made; or "salt, *bitte schön*," once they'd sat to eat; or *"tostada, por favor,"* when he needed another slice of toast—always the same, every morning, year after year.

There were other idiosyncrasies, of course, and far more malevolent. All of Frank's girlfriends had commented on how Feri would sit around talking about how he was too old and tired to help with cooking or cleaning up, but the minute the food was on the table he was there instantly, fast as teleportation—it didn't matter if he'd been in the next room, on the toilet, in the garden—and then complaining loudly for everyone else to hurry up so he could eat. He was too old and sick to get up from the couch for the TV remote control, five feet away, yelling to Frank to get it for him, but when it came to driving to the liquor store for another week of booze he was good to go, keys in hand, shoes on, no help necessary. But what really bothered them was the way he stood and stared, never making clear what the stare implied—Monica described it as a leer, Judy as a glare, Vera as a form of psychological blindness—except that there was a kind of violence to it, as if Feri knew exactly who and what they were.

"Don't leave," Frank always said when the girls suddenly sat up, checked their watches, and said they needed to go, though he always said it low, under his breath, not wanting to beg. He was tempted to add that Feri wasn't going to live much longer, if they could just be patient, but he decided this might jinx it, his father's death, and the old man would somehow recover, his lungs turning pink and elastic, and he'd live to be a hundred.

The girls always smiled. "You're a great guy, Frank, but I can't sit around like this." They made it sound like they were waiting for something else—to move in together, get married, have kids—but Frank knew exactly what it really was: that even if Feri died tomorrow it would have taken too long. They'd seen Frank come home from a dead-end day with the riggers, driving Feri to visit doctors the old man never listened to, refusing to quit drinking or smoking or eating sandwiches slathered with chicken drippings, and all of them knew that every week Frank would peel the sheets off his father's bed, stained yellow with the nicotine the old man excreted in his sleep. Worst of all, they'd witnessed the pride that kept Feri from admitting how much he owed Frank, which would have meant admitting how hard Frank worked for him, which would have meant admitting his absolute lack of gratitude, all of which was impossible since Feri was never wrong in anything he thought or did. He deserved it all, automatically.

No, it was easier to belittle Frank, Feri sitting with his crossword, asking his son's advice: "What is a four-letter word for the Greek goddess of victory?"

"Nike," Frank would say.

"Nike? That must be another of those goddamn Anglicisms." Feri stared at the page. "Nikusz! That's what it must be." He turned back to the crossword. "Wait a minute, that's six letters—too many."

"N-I-K-E. Four letters," said Frank.

Feri smirked. "It's a Hungarian crossword puzzle. I wonder what it is in the original Greek. Must be closer."

"Maybe it's Nike in Hungarian, too," said Frank, but Feri just snorted. "What?" continued Frank, coming from the kitchen carrying the long knife he'd been using to cut up a chicken, "you think just because it's English it can't be right?"

"Hungarian and Greek are European languages. They're closer."

"English is a European language."

"No it's not. Ask the English if they consider themselves part of Europe. Go ahead—see what answer you get."

"It's Nike," said Frank. "Why can't you just admit it?"

Feri looked at him in total silence, which was the closest Frank ever got to winning an argument—the old man saying nothing, not having a comeback but refusing to concede. And in the background, some girl or other, there only for the two weeks Frank ever managed to have any girlfriend, would sit in quiet witness, sometimes shaking her head, unable to understand why Frank stayed.

"I promised I would," he would say later, after Feri had been put to bed.

"Your mother couldn't have expected you to put up with this," she'd answer.

She hadn't, Frank thought. She'd lain in that bed, a shawl over her bald head, and listened to Feri weep and go on about how he'd look after Frank when she was gone, how he'd make sure their son went to school, studied hard, avoided the pitfall of getting an easy job in town rather than a university degree. Then she'd leaned up on her elbow and motioned to Frank.

"Promise me you'll leave," she'd hissed, whispering into Frank's ear with the last of her strength. "He has no idea how far he'll sink. Run away. Promise me!"

And of course Frank had promised, knowing it would never keep, that there would always be that *other* father—now disappeared completely into the wreck Feri had become, killed off in fact by the suicidal indulgences the old man permitted himself—the one who'd taken Frank fly fishing as a kid; and hunting and skiing and swimming at night, laughing as they jumped into the water off a log boom at Mowat Bay; who'd gone over to Harold Bosco's house when he complained that Frank had been trespassing on his property, running through his strawberry patch on the way to school, and set him straight in no uncertain terms; and who most importantly had seen to it that when he took sixteen-year-old Frank back to Hungary the kid had the freedom and license to get laid, something Juliska would never have permitted. None of these things had ever been presented to Frank as a debt to be repaid, and he himself didn't see it that way, only that looking after this terrible old prick was his last chance at communing with the dead, with that long-departed father who would have loved Frank looking after him.

Besides, he thought, holding his mother's dying hand, it was easy for her to ask for this promise now, passing off the responsibility for something she should have done years ago, if the security of being with Feri hadn't been less scary for her than the thought of going it alone.

When November 11 came around again Feri was at the door before Frank could react. The old man responded to the doorbell like he'd been waiting for it, shuffling along the carpet with the kind of speed he only ever used for dinner, or if too much time had gone by between shots of brandy. Frank buried his head in his hands, expecting another battle, voices yelling, drowning each other out, but it was quiet, so quiet that after a minute he lifted his head and saw that the scene had changed.

It was the veterans, as usual, but Lester was missing, and in his place were two young men, cadets, carrying clipboards and maps and handling the money and poppies.

"Where's my friend, Lester?" Feri asked, looking around as if he was truly bewildered by the vet's absence, as if they really had been friends.

"Lenny?" Hank rubbed the back of his head and looked at Harlan and the cadets.

"Lester's dead," Harlan said.

In that moment of silence, Frank thought of Juliska, and what she might have said to all this, standing at the door telling Feri to stop teasing the old men, get back inside, mow the lawn, put up a shelf, re-roof the garage, all the chores Feri had hated but which ultimately kept him functioning, off to work, away from the bottle, alive. "You'll all be dead one day," Juliska would have said, "and replaced by other old men keeping to their wars." She'd have glided over to run a hand down the fuzzy faces of the cadets, all the while looking at Frank, "And enlisting boys like these to do your dirty work."

Feri looked at Frank, and then in the direction his son was gazing, his own face draining of color as if he could see Juliska too. Then he turned to Hank: "See what you've done to my son! Do you see? It's the same thing you people did to me! It broke Juliska's heart, having to come out to Canada, to this place. I've never told you about that, have I? Back in Hungary she taught literature. Do you realize what coming to a country like this—where you can't do the one thing you were born for—does to a person?"

Frank rolled his eyes. Feri had been delighted to tell Juliska there was no point in looking for work, that he was making more than enough to keep her at home doing laundry, washing dishes, cleaning toilets, in what Juliska would, at the end, refer to in broken English as her "pushed-underwater life." But she'd done it, drowning her days, and the only time she complained was at the end, trying to keep Frank from doing the same.

"You did it to yourselves," yelled Hank, "you and your Nazi government."

"We weren't Nazis!"

Frank turned and walked away from the door. By the time he'd reached the kitchen, the argument was in full swing.

Feri lived another two years. By then he was attached to an oxygen canister, wheeling it along behind himself, covered in stickers that said "danger" and even one showing a huge skull and crossbones. Frank thought of it as his father's pirate flag cruising the high seas of the Uptown Mall, Hendricks Liquor, the Hollinger Hill Tobacconist Shop, and, of course, that last November 11 the old man would ever see, "No. 10" on the list, when he hobbled in sight of old Hank, who was more befuddled than ever, standing outside the liquor store in full military regalia, mechanically jingling a set of bells while three or four cadets stood around in camouflage and black berets handing out poppies. "I guess I'll see you at home later," said Feri, shuffling over, aggressive as always. Hank stopped jingling for a second as if he wanted to say something in return, but then a wave of blankness passed over his face and his hand resumed the side-to-side motion with the bells.

Feri looked at Frank, but it wasn't with the usual mix of rage and arrogance—that sort of listen-and-learn widening of the eyes Frank remembered from every November 11— but a kind of withdrawal, even fear, as if Feri was asking for help. "I'm Feri Kovacs," he said, turning back to Hank. "Your enemy."

The cadets stopped what they were doing and closed in, not yet alarmed but wanting to know what was going on. Hank's arm continued jingling the bells as if it were detached from him, some cartoon arm he could unscrew and leave hanging in space still doing its job while the rest of him turned to the cadets, uncertain, waiting for instructions.

"My brother stayed in Hungary," Feri said, verging on desperate. Some of the people coming out of the liquor store stopped, a small crowd forming. "I told you about him," Feri continued. "It was what the communists did to family who remained behind after someone got out. They made them suffer. Bad jobs. No promotions. Terrible places to live. The guilt was supposed to discourage people from trying to escape. My brother used to write me letters about how bad his life was, blaming me."

Feri stood waiting, wondering why Hank wasn't fighting back. It was as if his words were nothing but sound for the old vet, rising and falling, glimmering for a moment like some firework at the top of its arc, then fading as if it had never been there.

Hank stopped jingling the bell again. "Feri Kovacs," he said, speaking as if there was a hair on his tongue. "Fuckin' bastard…" His voice trailed off.

"That's right," said Feri, smiling with relief. "Fuckin' bastard. That's right."

Hank jingled the bell a few more times, then his eyes brightened, a phrase occurred to him and he spoke it: "Canada is your home."

"Canada is my prison!" said Feri, his tone light, relaxed, slipping into the old argument like a pair of slippers. "Canada is the place you forced me to live in. The place filled with my dead wife. The place I keep coming back to whenever I visit Hungary and realize I don't belong there anymore, the country went on without me, when you people forced me out you forced me out forever!" The phrases were so easy, streaming out of Feri, and Hank seemed pleased by them too, smiling so wide his eyes crinkled at the edges, and he jingled the bell in time with Feri's syllables so perfectly Frank thought the crowd was going to start clapping along. But one of the cadets stepped in.

"Better leave him alone," he said, straight and simple.

"Who are you?" asked Feri, and Frank knew that if this had happened twelve years ago, when Feri was still in his prime, the answer wouldn't have mattered.

"That's irrelevant," the cadet said.

"Dysentery means you shit yourself," interrupted Hank, sounding a flurry of jingles on the word "shit," and smiling like he'd pulled off a complicated riff.

Everyone stopped, looked at Hank, and for a moment Frank thought Feri was going to walk over and put his arms around the old vet, fold him into an embrace, but instead Feri just looked down, saying nothing. And so it was up to Frank once again, whispering to his father that maybe it was time to go, Hank watching them walk back to the car like he had no idea what country he'd just wandered into, the nature of the enemy he faced, standing there like some fresh-faced recruit at the moment of the landing in Normandy. Feri, gazing back at him, looked much the same.

When they got home, Feri moved silently into his chair and picked one of his unfinished crosswords off the pile. But he didn't read it, just sat there staring over top of the page mumbling about the time that had come and gone, his days wasting away, what little remained. The old man's voice rose and he began speaking in fits, between the fitting and removal of the oxygen mask. It was all nonsense, stories that hadn't happened, a past invented on the spot, romantic excursions with Juliska she'd never for one second entertained, not even in the most wistful of daydreams, and Frank would never know—speaking to the ambulance driver hours later—whether this fake history was just lack of oxygen in Feri's brain, or something the old man had come to believe.

"We—your mother and me—had a picnic once on Stillwater Bluffs," the old man said, the words exiting him like a breeze pushed through a pinhole. "You wouldn't believe the color of the ocean that day... like hammered gold." He coughed and whispered, "She loved me so much." He looked at Frank. "You, too."

Frank nodded, holding back his response. It was like swallowing a cactus.

"Night after night I sat with you and worked on the math, remember? When Juliska left the room I always had chocolate for us. I made it fun, didn't I?"

"Chocolate..." Frank said, his voice trailing off. "Math." But he couldn't quite bring himself to say, "I remember that."

"That time we all went out..." Feri said.

"We went out cutting wood," Frank broke in. He couldn't take it anymore. "Do you remember?" Feri's eyes softened. Here was something real. "It was winter. We still had the truck." Feri nodded. They'd been out cutting down snags, sawing the wood into rounds, splitting those into quarters, stacking them back in the truck. They were on the edge of Cranberry Lake, in the brush off a side road on A-branch, keeping the cold away with the heat of work, the two of them so quiet they could hear the snowflakes touching down, in a hush that seemed, that one time, like an arrival, an understanding.

"I brought along some of your favorite beer that day," said Feri. "Do you remember? That beef jerky you loved. And afterwards we stopped by the Beach Gardens and ate steak... Wow, what a day that was!"

Frank closed his eyes, shaking, wanting to strangle the old man.

When he opened them again Feri was looking at him sadly, some word playing about his lips—what was it? "I'm sorry?" "Thank you?" "Goodbye?"—trying to become sound, but Feri couldn't quite make it, and after a while he put down the crossword, got up, rattling the canister behind him as he went into the bathroom for one last cigarette and a shot of *pálinka*. Frank sat for a moment, then picked up the crossword his father had dropped on the floor, finished years ago but for that four-letter word still blank after the rest had been filled in, as if the name for victory was also the name for defeat.

CALM

CYNTHIA FLOOD

S TRONG FEET stepped into the boy's dream, came nearer down the hall, and he sat up, but the sounds went past, outside.

Quick, to the window.

Down the dark quiet street came four horses, two by two, with police on top. Streetlights shone on the animals' rumps, the riders' yellow vests. Clop clop. Harnesses glinted, tails waved, manes lifted and subsided. The horses too wore reflective yellow, in bands round their ankles. No heavy traffic here, though, not like the last time he'd seen them, at rush hour, walking calmly, single file, between a moving bus and a line of parked cars.

Hesitation. *Bad.* His bruises still hurt.

I have to know where you are, she'd said, you can't just wander alone. You don't know this big city. And stay out of the Park! Who knows what's hiding there?

Also, they'd taken his keys.

Clothes—he found them.

As he felt in the "secret" pocket of her rain jacket, from the other bedroom came sounds he disliked. Good, they'd sleep soon.

He left the building via the rusty fire escape off the third-floor hall. At the bottom he must swallow then jump down to damp earth—better than taking the dim stairs to the basement door.

He hurried then. Clop clop, and the horses headed west past shabby low-rises like his, past the corner store with posters stuck on its outer wall. One said *Resist!* What? Then past the school, the one he went to, with a map of all Canada on the classroom wall. Vancouver, a dot. The town where he'd lived before, not even that. On the bewildering drive to the city, she'd kept saying *Look at the map, see where you're going!* He didn't. Hadn't ever asked to make this move. Back there, the cops only had motorcycles.

The boy kept half a block between himself and clop-clop, scuttling from hedge to street-tree to shrub. Where did they live? He'd seen them often, on busy West End streets or near the big beach. Sometimes the police halted them, so people could ask questions or even pat those enormous heads. He saw the cops' holsters close up, and the animals' big nostrils, and their strange eyes, bluish-brown. Such big teeth. Soon the horses moved on. Their steady gait—lots of videos showed that, how the animals just kept on coming, calm amidst furious crowds. Did riots happen here?

As the quartet neared the big street he stayed further back, waiting while the traffic light changed and changed again. On the restaurant at the corner, someone had half-scraped off a *Resist!* poster. Near this intersection, he did know his way. Homeless men slept in store entrances, their hidden faces probably familiar to him from the network of local alleys, of bins behind cafes and groceries. Once, he'd taken home a cold burger, untouched in its box. They'd found it. *Bad.*

When green shone a third time he sauntered across, then hastened after the lifting hooves. Along these blocks, richer landscaping fronted tall condos. To hide and move and hide: easy. Ahead waited greater darkness, though moonlight came and went as the clouds moved.

By day he'd wandered this terrain south of Lost Lagoon, grasping at its geography. Some lampposts in the Park and at its edges displayed a map for tourists, so he'd learned some of the main routes. In the middle of the map's big green stood a tiny, surprising coyote. He hadn't known they could live in cities. Mum said *You never see what's right under your nose*. Not true. On his own he'd spotted a real raccoon snoozing in a tree, and a dead bird with a beak like a sword, and sleeping bags inside bushes, along with piled bottles and cans.

Once he'd even circled the Lagoon, peering up at the forest north of it, but had never entered the Park after sunset. In the small town, he and other kids spent hours nightly in the local park, only vacating when the teenagers took over, but no map was needed. You could see right across.

Now he followed the horses into the dark. Near-silence, but for the stepping animals. One lifted its tail. Plop plop, and that warm smell mixed with the night's leafy earthiness.

Would they turn at the tennis courts, head for the bay? No. A right turn. Where to? At first following the horses, the boy dared to move sideways into the damp understory of salal, laurel, giant rhodo—and then ahead, to crouch and peek as the nodding heads approached. Even when a rare midnight car drove past, the animals didn't change pace. The videos showed that too— horses proceeding while police trainers waved flags and noisemakers in their faces, fired blanks, came unseen from behind to beat garbage-can lids. Calm.

Next they went west. On one side of that road, he knew, lay open lawn, on the other just patchy shrubs, low. All the way, streetlights. Now what? Could he scrabble downhill, unseen, unheard, to the underpass, and so move roughly west too? His insides heaved. No, not that tunnel in the dark—nor by day. It curved, so the exit wasn't visible from the entrance. *I'm not a little boy any more. I'm not!* They'd laughed till they cried, though later Mum said *Sorry,* and then they smoked. Also, the meadow beyond the underpass gave no cover.

He slowed, guessing, and turned from the horses, south and then west in a long watchful arc through both open and wooded areas. Breathed leaves, a trace of skunk, of cigarette. Uphill then, on to the high bank overlooking the ocean. Here he squatted under a shore-pine distorted by wind and weather, smelled algae, watched the incoming tide's long frills of white collapse on the sand. Soaked runners, cold sockless feet—he didn't care, looked north. *I was right.* Only a hundred metres away the quartet walked towards a ramp that sloped to the beach. Touching the concrete, the lead animals snorted, and the riders spoke gently, stroking them.

When hooves met beach the four horses trotted south almost as far as the point, almost gone from view—then back again, under the boy's high perch, to and fro, to and fro. The animals' muscles created light patterns on their coats while the waves gleamed under the moon, fell into silver-marbled froth and made their *hssshing* sound.

When the riders headed straight at the water, the boy gasped. He couldn't swim. Nodding, the horses waded in. They stepped freely, splashed, came back to shore, reversed and went forward again into the waves, whinnying. *They're happy!* The riders turned them tightly, splashing through the shallows as if in an enclosure rather than the Pacific. Turn, turn—and out of the water they came, dripping, tossing their manes, to shoulder sideways, back and forth, steady pairs dancing while the sand bounced up by their hooves.

They stopped. One cop said something, and within a minute the horses walked two by two up the ramp and trotted eastward into treed darkness. Where?

Clop clop, clop clop, fading. At last the boy felt cold.

Once he slipped on wet leaves, falling.

Without the horses ahead, he got muddled in the darkness.

Emerging from the Park, he found the street wasn't his but took it anyway, for traffic lights winked ahead. *Resist!* was stapled to four street trees.

At the corner he checked a tourist map. *I'm just two blocks over.* By day he'd go again, figure out the lay of the land. As the signal changed, he noted at the map's edge a legend matching images to numbers dotted on the Park's green expanse. Seven: tiny horse. *Police Stables.*

Somehow the key's noise woke them at home. *Bad.* His wet, dirty clothes enraged his mother. The man never needed a reason, but used that one too.

In bed at last, he thought a bit about how one day he'd shove them off, shove as if they were an enormous ball, six feet in diameter, rolling about a training ring to impede his progress. As horses do when skilled in crowd control, he'd shoulder them. Lean against them, step sideways, step and step and another patient step till, like him now, they'd have no choice. Steady he'd be, calm.

Mostly he imagined stables. He'd stand close, look up. Touch? Feed? Once he'd seen a girl hold out an apple. Big teeth showed as the hairy lips lifted back, and the horse crunched the fruit.

The boy raised his hand, held his palm flat.

SUTURE

DAVID HUEBERT

I MAGINE IT'S you facing the loss of the still-ripening cherries between your legs. Imagine you're the black-and-white splotched Jack Russel mix with a knuckle in your tail from getting run over by a mountain bike. Imagine you have no idea that a vet might soon be opening your scrotal sac and scraping out your testes and your vas deferens like a chef spooning seeds from a cantaloupe. Imagine you have to wear a cone on your head to keep you from licking your own stitched and scabby genital region. A cone to stop you from sniffing and tonguing the sore and pungent spots you desperately want to tongue and sniff. Because tonguing is how you treat your wounds, sniffing how you sculpt your world. Picture these humans you desperately adore, the male with the scars and the female with different coloured eyes. Conjure these companions who walk city streets stooping to collect your steaming excretions in winter chill, handling the warmth of your digested kibble through the coarse and rustling plastic of a poo bag. These people who nuzzle and spoon you, who snoog you softly in their beds at night. Who named you Ezra but mostly call you Chèvre and Bedrock and Nebuchadnezzra. Who cook chicken necks to mix with your food, placing those gizzards in a special Tupperware marked "dog chicken." Microwaving that rangy poultry for fifteen seconds to take off the chill before mixing it with your grain-free kibble. These people who refuse to eat meat themselves but who care enough about your health and pleasure to bring chicken necks into their kitchen. Now imagine that these same people decide to remove your genitals. Because your dispatched testes mean an easier life for them. Mean not having to show face at the dog park and say "intact." Because this way all your erotic drives can be channelled into puppy playdates and doggy daycares and vigorous Kong-tossing sessions. Imagine that these people who call themselves animal lovers want to reroute your sexuality, to sluice your eros—to make every light in you beam for them and them alone.

This is the quiet perversity looping through Gavin's mind as he watches Rubix drop a drool-slathered frisbee at his feet. This is the societal hypocrisy that has caused the first real disagreement between Gavin and Zara.

Zara. The vegan with optic heterochromia who works the counter at the neighbourhood microbrew and volunteers at the Ecology Network. Zara who was born in Mumbai and has never been back but has vowed to take Gavin there one day to watch cricket and swim with sea turtles and sip tea under whispering fronds. Zara who did not turn Gavin's life around but pushed it into a delirious cartwheel of pleasure and something larger. Zara who said yes he should go to cooking school at NSCC and no he was not too old to start a new career. Zara who read his chapbook of poems about teeth decomposing in Coke cans and said she liked their gothic ecstasies, said they read like the music of blood-drunk mosquitoes and what better compliment could she have given? Zara with one blue eye and one green and Gavin never able to say which was more ravishing against the opiate dusk of her skin. Zara the woman who is adamant about the benefits of neutering their dog.

Gavin stoops to grab that drool-slick disc as Hermione the red-coated duck toller takes a vigorous interest in Ezra's crotch. He tosses the frisbee and watches Rubix blast across the pitch while Hermione continues to sniff Ezra's privates, tail thwacking Gavin's shins. Gavin knows Hermione was spayed last April but still he follows protocol—tugs Ezra away and tells Hermione's person that Ezra hasn't been neutered yet, prompting a grimace from that toqued barista. Kijiji trees a squirrel and Ezra charges over to howl up at the quivering tuft of russet. Gavin watches Ezra leap at the tree, watches that gangly puppy coil and spring and wonders how it happened—when did such joy become available through a body other than his own?

Zara is home brewing peppermint tea and as they say hello he wills the glow of this woman standing over the stove they share to seep through him. She pecks his cheek and he says he missed her and they embrace like nothing is wrong. She pours him tea and puts peanut butter in a Kong for Ezra. Much as he wants everything to be resolved between them Gavin finds himself saying about Hermione's person. Saying who does she think she is and all this bourgeois nuclear dog family bullshit. Zara scoffs and they glitch into the argument that has come to define them. Gavin says about the banality, says it is just so perverse to have this nation of so-called pet lovers scraping out their companion animals like Halloween pumpkins.

Zara mentions the safety, the docility, the trainability.

They throw cancers back and forth.

Gavin adds weight gain, surgery complications, the cone.

"Would you feel the same if it was a female?"

"Of course," Gavin lies. He has weighed this question many times and remains deeply, shamefully unsure.

"How much of your life are you willing to spend on these same words, this same conversation?"

"A lot, I hope." He tries to be cute but sounds petulant. Meaning Zara heads to the bathroom to take a triumphant shower. Gavin picks up his collected Baudelaire and stares at a poem for a long time, not turning the page. Zara sings a Springsteen tune into the shower head and the notes come to Gavin thick and muddled through the bathroom wall.

They were sixteen and they'd set out swimming in the harbour—Theo and Gavin and Drew. Sixteen and swimming in that sewage-slick elbow of the Atlantic and they knew it wasn't safe but the mushrooms did not care for prohibitions, did not fear bacteria, did not respect sanitation. Swimming among the tiny jellyfish and the tampon applicators, among the unrecorded suicides and the debris of 1917. They'd set out together but soon they were alone, each boy on his own journey through water and body and mind. Drew and Theo disappeared and Gavin was not concerned with them. The water moved over him and each slither was an undreamt dermal rhapsody. He swam through the black, swam beneath the surface and found to his pleasure that he had no need for air. Through the darkness he saw a hulking shadow, gnarled and round.

Gavin and Zara met on a rideshare to Montreal. He'd borrowed his mother's car to go to there for the launch of his poetry chapbook, *Agricola Dentata*, and he didn't want to do the twelve-hour drive alone. His ad got a few responses and of course he chose the woman's name and when she climbed in the car wearing a romper that showed the floral tattoos stitched up her thighs he felt sleazy and fearful and awed. There was traffic on Robie Street and Gavin brought up the city's need for light rail but Zara said that was what she loved about the place, that they were stuck on this peninsula within a peninsula so the city couldn't possibly get any bigger. He said she was right, said the only way to build was up but the people wouldn't abide that because they didn't want to ruin the view from Citadel Hill.

"Fucking perfect!" she laughed. "This place is so brilliantly backward."

Zara was from Halifax and had gone to St. Pats while Gavin went to QE. She was only a year younger but they somehow knew none of the same people— she'd been in French immersion and the high school musical while he was drinking Colt Forty-Five and skateboarding poorly and secretly writing blank verse sonnets about fingernail clippings.

Dropping her in Mile End he wanted to ask for her number but only managed to blurt about the poetry launch. She said "that could be cool" and slid out of the car and he assumed he'd never see her again until he was two poems deep in the dark room full of hostile strangers. She strode in with her shoulder bandaged from a fresh tattoo and laughed with the bartender in the middle of his poem. Laughed and flicked back her hair and became a streak of neon in a sepia photo. After his set he bought her a cider and as they chatted their mouths and knees drew closer and closer. When he went to the bathroom she crept up behind him at the sink and hissed "whatever you want" into his neck but another poet walked in and they stumbled out giggling.

They met Zara's friends at a dangerously packed bar on the Plateau. Zara found a storeroom and thieved two six packs of Stella, stashing the beer in the corner where the two of them kissed and rubbed thighs and drank free until close. They stumbled home with five or six of Zara's Blundstone-wearing girlfriends, all of whom were vocally unimpressed by Gavin's skate shoes and straight-leg jeans. Gavin peed in an alley and got a ticket from a police officer in camo shorts and when he looked up Zara and her friends were gone.

He drove home the next day hungover and cursing himself for not getting her number. Lying in his bed in Halifax he told himself not to but finally got up at three in the morning and emailed her. She wrote back a single, unpunctuated line—"what's your address?" Three days later she showed up with a growler of IPA and a toothbrush and she hadn't left since.

Gavin goes for post-work drinks with Theo and Drew, who won't stop swiping his phone. Drew is bragging that he never swipes left and using words like "Tinderella" and Gavin is wondering how this culture can believe it is the dogs of the world who need their sexuality adjusted. Gavin starts a conversation about turning thirty, how people suddenly stop looking at you as if you were always about to throw a stink bomb. Drew says girls love thirty-year-old guys and points to the grey streak in his lumberjack beard and Gavin can't tell how serious he is. Theo snorts but he is not there, he has drifted. He's been euphoric since Corrine got a job at Halifax Grammar and they moved back to town but tonight he seems punctured. He says something about how we're all nothing but deteriorating bodies and the comment looms in the acrid bar air.

They order tequilas and Gavin asks the waiter for a lemon. Drew scoffs "training wheels" and Gavin thinks as he often has about how dogs are like practise children. All the thirtyish couples he knows who didn't want or couldn't afford or couldn't commit to human children got dogs instead, their nurturing instincts channelled into doggy daycares and doggy spas and doggy treats. Gavin thinks that a dog might be better than a kid anyway because it never grows up, never turns teenage and gets caught shoplifting. Never totals the car. A dog never winds up staggering across streets heedless of lights and horns and intersections, face scaled with meth sores.

But dogs come with their own set of problems. Such as the one facing him now as these three old friends sit together ignoring each other at a table. Three faces lit by the ionic cosmos of Drew's phone. Gavin is considering how silence is alright between old friends, how silence between long-time pals is even kind of pleasant, when Theo blurts the news about his mother. No warning whatever and then the words "early onset" and Drew and Gavin sitting there in the dark, gulping. Drew asks how could this have happened and Theo shrugs and downs his beer and Gavin finds himself saying it's okay. Saying it's okay and not believing it and thinking of Nancy, cosmic Nancy, her tanned calves in platform sandals just two summers ago at Theo's wedding. How could a body that sleek and sure ever break down? He is thinking of Nancy in all her ageless splendour and putting a hand on Theo's shoulder and saying it will be fine, these things take time, it will be slow, very slow.

Theo says no. It's fast. Last week she got lost on Barrington and parked in front of the house on Morris where she hasn't lived for fifteen years. She sat there for five hours and missed two work meetings before she called anyone. Gavin cups his friend's hands and Theo gives in to a long silent sob and they are three thirty-year-old men sitting in a dark bar with eyes wet and throats burning, helpless against the gnaw of decay.

Gavin and Zara and Ezra are sitting in bed watching a documentary about Margaret Howe, a British researcher who lived in a place called "The Dolphin House" in the 1960s. Ezra lies on Zara's belly, legs splayed like a frog's, grinding his nose into whatever hand he can reach until the head-scratch continues. The Dolphin House was run by a hippy scientist named John Lilly who performed experiments such as injecting dolphins with LSD. Howe's job was teaching English to a bottlenose named Peter. The research ended with Peter moving to a tiny, dark, half-septic pool in Miami and choosing to simply stop breathing, to descend to the bottom of that toxic, lightless pool as the air seeped out of him. But before that there were the dolphin hand jobs. A vet mentions that dolphins often prefer humans to their own kind and implies that Peter was in love with Howe. Howe herself is strangely forthcoming about the fact that, when his desire got in the way of her research, she satisfied Peter manually.

After the film, Zara tells Gavin about the time she swam with dolphins. Her family went to a resort in Mexico and she spent the days sunbathing and playing ping pong with a boy from Rhode Island whose mouth was a snare of braces. She and her sister begged until her mother took them on the overpriced excursion and when they got there it deadened something in her. A small pool and a smell like sewage and cheap old fish. Dolphins chirping in that tiny stinking pool and she knew it was ridiculous but nonetheless felt they were asking her personally for help. She'd once seen a *National Geographic* video with dolphins swimming wild off the coast of Florida. Racing fast through the wide and blameless blue and leaping out of the water before darting back in and she didn't know much about dolphins but as she watched them in that pool chattering for food she knew it was wrong. The whole thing was wrong.

Though Gavin wants to, he doesn't say who are we to be the arbiters of animal life.

They lie together in silence for too long and then Zara says, "We're okay, right?" Her eyes pulse like minute oceans, one blue and one green. Gavin says of course and believes it. Believes that they are okay, fundamentally. Believes that this crisis will make them closer, the way collagen thickens a broken bone.

Gavin ushers Ezra out of the room and the dog watches plaintive as the door swings closed. As he pulls Zara in, Gavin finds himself thinking of that lonely dog curled on the far side of the door, listening to the squelch and creak of their union. He wonders whether Zara, too, is thinking of Ezra. But he doesn't ask.

Gavin's task is pulling the meat out of the lobsters, putting the big chunks in the fish tray marked "lob fet" and the small stuff in the one marked "lob rolls." Gavin, who has dreams of starting a vegetarian bistro with Zara and growing their own rosemary and oregano and cucumbers on the patio, is the person the red-faced chef chooses to boil then vivisect these crustaceans. Gavin who is studying cooking at NSCC and works here at minimum wage because of an agreement between the restaurant and the college. Gavin who plans to get his red seal, who has plans to stage in Chicago and Brooklyn. Gavin who has recently mastered garlic-scape pesto, who dreams of tapping his own maples and baptising pistachios in their syrup, who has designed a seven-course meal including onion confit and cayenne mushroom bisque and ending with salted caramel-apple profiteroles. This is the person they elect to drop live animals into boiling water before manually dissecting them, the person who will go home and wash his hands again and again and still be unable to rid his flesh of the chalky aftermath of the bodies he has torn and plucked and mangled.

With each exoskeleton he slices open and snaps off, with each intact tail he eases out of its sheath, with each pea-green sludge of tomalley he spatulas into the fish tray, Gavin thinks about Ezra. Ezra lying inert under general anaesthetic as a faceless surgeon slices open his scrotum, seeking the small slick planets she is paid to extract.

Gavin makes an incision and turns a lobster over to tear the tail off, finds the underside coated with a slick beard of eggs. The green-black beads clinging to that pale red tail and Gavin thinking of the lives these creatures might have had. He remembers reading about a lobster that traveled 273 miles between Maine and Nantucket, knows they often walk vast distances to lay their eggs. But these ones would have lived differently, conceived in hatcheries and grown in a suburb of tanks and filtration systems, of regular testing and men with thick gloves. Gavin thinks of all these dark, alien animals growing strong and fat and reproducing and none of them marching freely through the ocean, none of them hunting by night or hiding their eggs in the swaying deep, none of them birthed amid the dark and flowing greens of rock weed, alaria, or kelp.

Gavin comes to live in thrall of the procedure. His mind a gothic slideshow of veterinarians and gleaming surgical steel. After weeks squinting through screen-blue darkness after Zara goes to bed, he knows the operation so well he thinks he could perform it. He becomes enamoured with the epididymis and the term *vas deferens* derived from the Latin for "vessel" and "carrying-forth." This glandular circuit an escape route for sperm, most of which will be released into hostile terrain and die. The term reminds him of the great, churning tides of the Bay of Fundy. The tide and the sperm, the mind and the moon, all of it always carrying forth and this scientist species wanting to mute that motion, to dam the waterways of life. He writes a suite of poems based on this metaphor but it brings him no closer to a decision.

And the dog ages steadily, the surgery more traumatic by the day.

Two mixed terrier puppies entered their world and Gavin had no precedent for the way they would bend his life, the way his mind would buckle and zing. They called the smaller one Ezra and the bigger one Pound and when Gavin lay down to read both of them would crawl onto his chest and stare at him, the breath gradually slowing in their tiny puppy lungs. They eventually gave Pound to a friend of Zara's and it was just the two of them and Ezra, their one-bedroom flat with the screeching bathroom fan and the warped back door with the glitchy lock transformed into a palace of canine glee.

Gavin had never had dogs as a child and the bond was baffling to him. The trill in his heart when he let Ezra off leash and watched him take off across the grass, front legs barely visible as they scooped and dug into a pinball blur of forward, forward, forward. Gavin was baffled by the joy he took in Ezra's habit of carrying a stick that was far, far too large for him, bouncing it off the calves of anyone who walked near. And he was astounded by his despair, his bottomless torment the day he watched that pup scamper too close to a fat-wheeled Norco, heard the crunch of busted tailbone and the dog's awful pinse of betrayal. A sound Ezra had never made before and how could Gavin not hear it as his own failure, stooping to comfort his puppy and wishing that he himself could have licked that frail bone back together.

And now Gavin has to choose. He has to decide whether or not to wilfully hurt this creature he has done everything possible to protect. He must decide whether or not to extract something vital from this beloved companion's insides, something that could bring him pleasure and excitement and riveting carnal bliss. Gavin must decide whether to permanently maim this cherished friend, whether to flatten Ezra's world.

The shadow was dark and round and when he looked closer he saw it was a mine. A massive underwater mine, the curved and rusted iron slick with a mucous of algae, a gnarled barnacle braille. He thought of Mr. Healy in Social Studies class, talking about the 3,000 unexploded bombs left in the harbour by German U-boats. A chore to remove those explosives and most of them dead by now so the traffic passed through in the hopes that nothing shifted or changed its mind.

Gavin was drifting towards the rust-gnawed mine when Nancy appeared, beckoning him. Nancy flickering in the watery dark and it was only the two of them there in the liquid emptiness where no pollution or creatures or bombs could harm them. He saw her beckon and without a movement of leg or arm, felt himself drifting closer.

Gavin gets up early to walk Ezra around the block and then he makes Zara a burrito fried in handfuls of the garlic he plucked last week from the backyard. She roams naked and fat-eyed into the kitchen, cups him from behind as he whips the guacamole. "Smells gorgeous," she says and he is surprised, as always, that all it takes is the fragrance of bulbs frying in oil to blend this discord of rooms into a home. He says she smells gorgeous and she laughs, filling a mug with the coffee he's just pressed. She sits down at the table, steam rising from her cup, and Ezra nuzzles into her calf. Gavin wonders, briefly, if the dog is stirred by the sight of this naked woman. He wonders this but does not say anything, does not say anything of the sort as he serves breakfast and sits down to eat. They talk about Gavin's work, about his fall courses, about the cherry tomatoes finally ripening in the one patch of full sun. Zara asks about Corinne and Theo, suggests that they have them over for dinner. Gavin says they're doing well and Theo has a gig teaching environmental philosophy at SMU in the fall. He's reached the middle of a spiel about the student-as-customer model before he realizes that he's not telling Zara about Nancy. He's not telling her and he's not going to and what does this mean? Ezra is rising onto his hind legs to sniff at the table scraps and Gavin knows sharply, darkly, that he will not tell Zara about Nancy or Blue Velvet or the early onset. Instead, he sneaks Ezra a peanut and scratches the dog's eager ears and thinks about swelling ventricles, a shrinking hippocampus. He smells Ezra's fetid breath as the dog's tongue licks the sweat from his neck and thinks of the plaque and tangles in Nancy's head, the disease boring her brain like sugar mining a tooth.

There's a bald man Gavin has never seen before at the dog park. He has a little black pug mix and a T-shirt that reads *#alldogsmatter*. When someone asks him what breed his dog is Gavin hears him answer, loudly, "He's a rescue." Gavin stays to the outskirts, talking to Chimichanga's owner and trying not to hear the man lecturing about microchips and puppy mills and shock collars. But the rescue takes an interest in Ezra as he raises his leg to mark the fence and when the smaller dog approaches Ezra yaps at him. The owner scuttles over as the dogs bark and growl. Ezra lunges, teeth bared. Gavin races towards Ezra but he's not quite there when the owner bends to scoop his dog up into his arms, the worst thing he could do.

Ezra goes manic and leaps for the pug mix, who squirms out of his owner's arms and lands on the grass in a rage of growls and bent necks, a fury of teeth and bulging eyes. Turf and fur spin in the air as the dogs tussle and snap and bite, both owners trying to wrangle their snarling pets. Gavin finally grasps Ezra's collar and the bald man yanks his dog back up into his arms and Gavin tries to say sorry but the man is shouting at him.

Gavin hears curses and gibberish and finally makes out "Jesus man, get a hold of your dog!" The adrenaline swells through his neck and chest, his biceps coiling. He knows whatever he says will be brash so he stays silent as the man asks with a quavering voice, "Is your dog even neutered?" It is not a question but an assault. Gavin gets Ezra on leash and as they walk away he hears the man shouting, "How dare you!"

At home he is trembling as he tells Zara the story then announces that he won't be going to that dog park anymore. He can no longer abide the PETA brigade, these people with all the answers. He will take Ezra to Point Pleasant or the Commons and he will simply walk, walk where he and his dog are not cornered in this bastion of norms.

Zara shrugs and says, "Do what you've got to do," turning back to her laptop. He feels it like a foot to the gut. Wishes that just for once she would simply take his side.

Gavin sits down at his desk and starts a poem about doggie pills and doggie condoms. At the end Bob Barker appears on the stage of *The Price is Right*, wagging his liver-spotted fingers at a nation of suburban dream-home gamblers, commanding: "Thy dog shalt not fuck."

Pro: less prone to aggression.

Con: may not reliably reduce aggression.

Pro: dog will be calmer around unspayed females.

Con: almost no unspayed female dogs left in urban dog culture.

Pro: more focused on companion human.

Con: dog will spend two weeks healing with head in cone.

Pro: reduces leg-lifting.

Con: triples risk of obesity.

Pro: reduced likelihood of testicular cancer.

Con: dog will be unable to reproduce.

Pro: dog will be unable to reproduce.

Con: coat may become patchy and haggard.

Con: may lead to hip dysplasia.

Con: ligament rupture.

Con: hypothyroidism.

Con: osteosarcoma.

Con: geriatric cognitive impairment.

Con: risk of death from anaesthetic complications.

Con: risk of death or injury from surgical complications.

Con: wilfully mutilating another living creature.

Con: wilfully mutilating another living creature.

Con: wilfully mutilating another living creature.

Cindy, who'd clearly had a couple of pinots before they got there, has already put her hand on Zara's thigh and winked at Gavin while hissing "this one's a keeper" and now she's talking about cats. They had ordered Thai food because

Cindy claims not to know how to cook vegan and now the table around them is a Styrofoam jungle. Gavin tries to ask his mother about her new boyfriend the Via Rail conductor and then tries to ask about her job at Canada Post HQ but she glares over her glasses and keeps on about the feral cats. There are swarms of them in the neighbourhood, she says, fucking and fighting and eating all the songbirds, spreading diseases among the housecats. Cindy looks right at Zara as she rants, one eye drooping and the other fierce with an intimacy not natural between two women who've only met six or seven times. Cindy says one night a feral cat got trapped in her basement and it was spraying and crazed and she had to try to beat it out with a hockey stick but it would not move. So here she was, Cindy, alone in her own house with this cat locked in a room and the window was open but the beast would not vacate. They stayed up all night like that. Cindy tried to sleep but she could feel the cat there, poised and fearful, and in the morning she found it precisely where she'd left it in the corner of the room. She had breakfast and watched it some more and finally realized it must've been desperately hungry so she put some cold chicken by the back door with a saucer of milk and she left the house. Went around the corner to get a coffee. Waited as long as she could. When she came back the cat was gone, the dishes licked spotless.

Cindy smiles smugly and pours herself more wine. Gavin exchanges a look with Zara and asks what the story has to do with feral cats and Cindy says sterilization. We need to sterilize them, of course. A silence thickens in the room and Gavin lets it linger.

Gavin is readying himself to leave when Cindy invites Zara downstairs to see the collection. Zara looks surprised and says of course and so they head down to the basement where Gavin's mother keeps her hoard of children's body parts. They stand among the dust and the suitcases, looking at Gavin's umbilical cord—grey and curled and stiff in its dusty Ziplock womb. The teeth come next. Why would his mother have kept every baby tooth and wisdom tooth and molar Gavin's growing body ever shucked? After the teeth there are jars of hair: Gavin's grade two rat tail, his grade ten Mohawk, his grade twelve surfer curls. As Gavin stands embarrassed in the midst of his personal mausoleum he wonders what would become of Ezra's testes if they were removed. Zara recently told him about rendering and deadstock, about how "livestock management" companies cruise farms collecting horse and goat and cow carcasses, pulping those bodies into the stearic acids and slip agents that become bike tires, shampoo, plastic bags. Now he finds himself wondering if Ezra's gonads will be cycled into kibble, fed back to other dogs in a canine parody of *Soylent Green*.

This is what Gavin is thinking as Cindy unveils her masterpiece—a hand-made cedar box containing Gavin's hospital bracelet alongside newspaper clippings from the electrocution and curled polaroid photos of the burns that permanently marbled his torso and sent purple tentacles flaring up his arms and calves. The burns he's had to have cut and grafted twice since the accident because the scars stay still as his body grows and ages. Seeing those polaroids Gavin feels the burns brighten under his shirt, feels his gut turn tidal as he recalls the inane and drunken choice to climb that tower. Recalls the strange teenage logic that made him believe he could somehow reach Nancy up there. Gavin burns shameful but Zara is calm and sweet as she looks at each photo and newspaper clipping, nodding at Cindy's comments then leaning into

Gavin and whispering, "All of this is what you are, and I love all of what you are."

When Gavin was ten he went with Theo and Nancy to their family cottage in Hubbards. Nancy had just broken up with Theo's father and it was just her and the two boys. They spent three mosquito-droning days at a two-bedroom cabin thick with the smell of pine. There were dunes with prickly grasses and a beach strewn with sun-bleached driftwood and ancient, sagging lobster traps. Each night they had bonfires and watched the stars and Gavin learned to love the taste of burnt marshmallows. On the last day Theo got an ear infection and had to stay in bed so Gavin and Nancy went down to the beach without him. Gavin found a dried-out lobster claw and pretended it was his hand as he put his arm around Nancy's shoulder. When she saw that gnarled pincer at her clavicle she laughed and laughed and he felt himself large and noticed. When they went out into the water she watched him swimming and said "no no not like that" and then taught him how to do a proper breaststroke, taught him it was all about timing—the smooth arc of the arms pulling you forward, the legs coiling together as the arms reset. The frog kick and the forward dart of the hands and that moment of skimming effortless across the surface. She explained it, then showed him. He watched her gliding seal-sleek in a black one-piece and then he got it, felt the astonishing ease of it as he shot through the brisk Atlantic on that still and sunny day.

The cabin had an ancient, rusted outdoor shower with a rotting plywood door. Gavin was eager to wash off the salt and sand and so he rushed into that shower thinking Nancy was still down at the beach and found her naked and stooping to pull the sand from her toes. Her breasts dangling freely, dappled by the patches of sun leaking through the slats. They stood there looking at each other like cats crossing paths in an alley. Gavin took no more than a glance at those breasts—curiously pale, nipples like sand dollars.

She did not say a word to Gavin on the drive home, even though Theo was in the back seat still suffering from earache and he was sitting up front. They drove in silence and Gavin stared out the windshield at the road slithering beneath the bright open blue, saw Nancy's breasts in every cloud.

On the walk home Zara says she likes Gavin's mother. Gavin scoffs and asks why and she says how else would Gavin have developed such a dazzling corkscrew mind. He stops her and they hold each other in the middle of the street, a warm wind cloaking them in a swirl of grass and ocean. They make a pact not to talk about Ezra or sterilization so Zara talks about the tidal turbine in the Bay of Fundy. Highest tides in the world so of course they want to squeeze that churning power into dollars. And of course this green energy might not be so green and the lobster fishermen are concerned about the impact to the ecosystem, about the noise pollution diluting the whale song not to mention the plankton being sucked into the 1000-tonne rotors churning the waters of the ancient cove. The cove that bears the world's only fossilized trace of the moment life managed to scuttle out of the ocean and stagger onto land.

He'd been alone in the dark ocean among the lurking mines until Nancy appeared like a beacon. A younger Nancy, a less complicated Nancy, and as he watched her swim astride him he saw her legs melt and flick into a tail. A tail scaled with glimmering greens and blues, a glowing blur streaking the dark water. The water a volatile blackness and he knew it was cold but he also knew he could not feel that cold, felt nothing but Nancy's pulsing proximity. She swam closer still and he was nothing but the thrill of her. He felt himself dancing in her nimbus and he wanted her. A vague want, a desire that did not involve genitals or fluids or climaxes. He felt himself drained of the precision of drives, acquiescing to a novel, blunt euphoria.

They arrive at their apartment and find the back door swinging open. The dog is gone and Gavin is thinking of course. Thinking of fucking course and he and Zara are grabbing the leash and some treats and blasting outside wailing the dog's name into the clammy summer sky. It's almost midnight but some neighbours are out on the porch and they join in and soon the neighbourhood is a clamour of *Ezz-ra, Ezz-ra* and they are rounding two corners and coming out onto Gottingen. Gavin thinks they should split up but he doesn't say this because he doesn't want to be alone he just wants this to be not happening. He wants this not ever to happen but it also seems inevitable that their dog, their puppy, is gone. Inevitable that this tender love would swell and swell and burst.

And likewise inevitable that Gavin should round the corner and turn out onto Gottingen and see a dark furry hump in the middle of the road. See the still-wet blood slanting across the yellow line and say Zara's name in a tone that makes her stop and follow his gaze and sprint into the middle of the road through hornbleat and headlights.

Gavin waits for the traffic to pass and walks slowly behind her, knowing already all he needs to know. He hears Zara sobbing as he gets closer but then her sobs become crazed laughter and he sees that the furry hump in the road is a raccoon, still wheezing. Its tiny mouth quivering, paws scrubbing together.

Gavin looks stupidly around for a shovel but then he is back on the sidewalk, calling Ezra's name again, and Zara is with him. They walk down Gottingen and through the square and then turn back, tracing and retracing the grid between Gottingen and Agricola, fattening the night on the name of their dog. Finally they agree to split up and Gavin says he'll go home to notify the SPCA which is no doubt ridiculous but he does not know what else to do. When he gets home he finds the back door still slung open and Ezra cringing in the kitchen, sitting obedient and fearful. Gavin bends down and hugs him, feeling a brilliant and boundless love. More love than he'd known there could be in the world.

Nancy is wordlessly calling him closer as she sways her green and gleaming tail but he can't get near enough to touch her. Something keeps him an arm's length from her face and shoulders and when he reaches up he finds that there is a large cone over his head. A cone that he cannot remove. He looks down to see whether there is a scar between his legs but he cannot see past the cone. She is calling to him, begging him closer, but the cone is between them. Has always been and will always be between them. Eventually she turns away from him and starts to pump her tail. She swims slowly, looking over her shoulder, her hair luffing like seaweed in a current. She is leaving and he is sinking down into the accumulating darkness, watching her shrink into the distance as he drifts into the bottomless below.

Gavin awakes in the gut of night to find the bed empty. He listens to the quiet, locates a ripple through that silence and hears it swirl into murmur. Zara's voice. He thinks of calling her name then thinks no. Instead he rises quietly and leans into the hall, watches her stoop over Ezra, rubbing the sweet spot above his haunch. Gavin hears her cooing and talking a formless gibberish that sometimes settles into "oh yes" or "Ezzy" or "good boy."

And then he sees it, a slick tulip blooming between Ezra's legs. A tube of lipstick winding upwards from a bulb of fur. He knows Zara cannot see that wet and urgent flower as she leans over and rubs his back, and he knows that this canine erection might have nothing to do with her. But he also knows, as he watches this scene of intimacy, that there is something in that small sprout of flesh that he detests. Something that makes him uneasy. And he knows, knows and hates himself for knowing, that for all his talk about hypocrisy and repression and consent, he would be happy if that organ were to disappear.

Zara turns and sees him standing there in the door frame. She does not appear surprised. "I've decided," she announces, still stroking Ezra's neck. "It's up to you." Gavin has to ask her to repeat herself and she says again that it should be up to him, that he cares more than she does and so if he feels like he needs to leave Ezra's genitals intact that's fine with her.

Gavin puts a hand on the door frame. His heart is a fish flapping on a beach. No way out of the choice and no way to make it. "It's on you," she says and the onus slithers down his throat, fattens there. He thinks for the first time in their eleven months living together how easy it would be to leave her. How possible. To leave Zara, leave the lobsters, take Ezra to a cabin in Bridgewater and write poetry, live on beans. The thought is ugly and rank and he tries to dismiss it but it lingers like an eel in his sternum.

Give the animal a mild sedative and inject with general anaesthetic. Place the gas mask on the muzzle or slip a tube down the animal's trachea to administer the isoflurane. The anaesthetic gas will ensure the dog remains unconscious throughout the procedure. Once the animal is fully unconscious, make an incision at the tip of its scrotal sac, taking care not to sever the urethra. Pull one testicle out through the seam in the animal's skin. Trim away the fatty tunica vaginalis, exposing the testicle. Clamp the testicular blood vessels and the vas deferens to ensure blood does not flow upon laceration. Slice the spermatic cord above the clamp, severing the testicle. Discard. Repeat. Suture.

Gavin is walking Ezra on the main path overlooking the Northwest Arm as sunlight flickers down through the spruce. Squirrels scamper after bird feed. A seal chirps in the distance and Ezra bounds through the forest, staying close to Gavin and mostly ignoring the dogs on the main path. This is what Gavin likes: just walking. No standing in parks talking about groomers and breeders and crate training. What he likes is walking with his companion, the dog off-leash and racing through the forest as Gavin treads the gravel tongue running through it. Ezra returning now and then for a check-in, tongue curling out of his delirious grin. What Gavin likes is watching Ezra tear after squirrels, reaching full speed on the straightaway and then bounding impossibly over stumps and rocks. Watching Ezra stand ankle-deep in the glint of the surf and tilt his head to make eye contact, to share the measureless wealth of his glee.

Gavin is basking in this primal rhythm, the yoked locomotion of human and dog, when they run into her. He doesn't realize it's Nancy until she bends down to pet Ezra.

He is thirteen and stealing her personal sex toy and parading it around the neighbourhood. He is thirteen and unable to forgive himself and climbing an electrical tower and shooting deathbound across the night. He is thirteen and seeking Nancy in each rung, finding her in the brilliant wattage that sends him soaring through the cloudless black. Finding her in the tree that catches him, its leaves lush and soft as velvet. He is recovering in the hospital from six broken bones and third-degree burns across his torso and limbs and feeling all of his pain, all the lifelong scars on his back and thighs as penance. A penance he craves.

Nancy finishes petting Ezra and looks up, looks straight into Gavin's face. He can tell she recognizes him, but distantly. For a moment he inhabits her and sees himself as blur, as echo.

He wants to say hello, wants to tell her it's him, Gavin. Gavin whom she's known for twenty years. Gavin who accosted her and professed his rabid, lifelong desire two years ago at her son's wedding. Gavin who charmed her with a lobster claw and saw her pale breasts swaying in the patchy Hubbards light.

She is gone, loping casually down the path, before he can say any of this.

How could he know, then, that after taking Ezra to a beach strewn with six-pack rings and cigarette butts he would walk down to the parking lot and see Nancy drifting ghastly from car to car, her white hair streaked with a memory of black. That she would turn shrunken and ancient, old as the Sibyl of Cumae. That she would hold a set of car keys in her hands and glide about, pressing the button over and over but hearing no welcoming beep. That when she saw him approaching she would turn to

Gavin and, still unable to conjure his name, ask if he had seen her car, a red Toyota, and he would see the exhausted frenzy in her eyes and almost hear the frantic pant of her thoughts. *The car is Red. No. Yellow. The car is red no yellow or was that the last one the car is definitely yellow or red no yellow and where has it gone someone must have taken it, stolen it. The car is a Toyota. A little yellow Toyota Yaris and I bought it yellow for precisely this reason and now I cannot find it in this parking lot. This horrible parking lot and I've been here before been lost here before and why can't somebody help? Of course they can't help because the help I need is not someone asking what kind of car and are you alright but someone crawling into my brain, burrowing through the cavities of my aged and rotting psyche and whispering gentle music, lathering my mind with tea leaves and eucalyptus and mint. The car is red no yellow maybe blue and how I wish I could howl, how I long to wail into the ocean wind and all I want is my car who has taken it someone must have stolen my car. The vehicles like liquid, like gelatine oozing through the lot and none of them mine. A slur of greys and blacks, Nissans and Fords spinning crookedly together in this cackling concrete funhouse and now this boy, this strange familiar awful boy and has he stolen the red no yellow Toyota?*

Gavin makes all this from a twitch of her eye and he says let me help you, maybe you're in the upper lot, let me call your son. Her eyes flit about and she shakes her head in vigorous refusal but when her mouth finally open she is saying yes, saying okay, sure, thank you.

How could Gavin have known that a full third of his lifespan would seem to burn and wither, that his entire life thus far would seem to melt as he phoned his friend Theo, found out that the car was a blue Kia, took Nancy's hand with its colony of liver spots. How could he have known that as she drove out of the parking lot he would glimpse her face through the driver's side window and wonder once more how someone so lovely could possibly decay. He would realize, then, that he would one day have to tell Zara the whole story. But how could he possibly explain this cosmic beacon, this wounded siren, this disintegrating god?

Gavin would always carry two parallel versions of the experience. He knew what happened and what didn't happen. What didn't happen was he didn't float endlessly underwater, not needing to breathe. What didn't happen was he didn't meet Nancy and watch her sprout a mermaid's tail and beckon him towards a rhapsodic unknown.

What did happen was three kids on a freakishly hot day in early June doing mushrooms and traipsing through Point Pleasant, thinking it was a fun idea to go swimming in the harbour. What did happen was a poor choice. What did happen was Gavin lost Drew and Theo and wound up crawling ashore in Dartmouth and the night got a little colder than expected and he walked alone and soaked in just boxers across the McDonald Bridge. What did happen was he did not shower that night and when he woke up he knew instantly. Even before he looked down and saw the red sores and the slugs of plasma he knew it was bad. Cindy made him eat some cereal and take a shower and she didn't say anything because she didn't need to. She drove with all the windows down to mute the reek of his flesh. The doctor was a kind old grandmother until he said about the harbour. At which point she made him repeat that he'd swam in the harbour and asked what had he been on and as he admitted about the mushrooms he felt as if all the water had fled his body. What did happen, as the matronly doctor explained in arduous detail, was that every miniscule laceration on Gavin's body—every paper cut and bug bite and shin nick from his walk through Point Pleasant—had become infected. What did happen was the doctor took a semi-permanent marker and drew circles around every one of those infected wounds and said if the red reaches this line then come back for antibiotics. What did happen was Gavin spending two plus weeks at school wearing long sleeves every day to try to hide the strange new nipples blooming all over his body and the doctor-drawn circles framing them. What did happen was shame and agony and even less interest than usual from girls and constant ridicule from Drew and Theo.

But what did happen remained much less important to Gavin than what did not happen. What did not happen—Nancy, the mine, the mermaid's tail—was a companion that would always travel with him, a beloved phantasm that would shape and sustain him more than the bland and barren real.

Gavin and Ezra walk home along the waterfront and there are men fishing in the harbour and somehow this has never signified as it does now. Ten or twelve men standing along the wharf and two of them pulling up small wriggling mackerel or cod and the harbour does not reek as it used to. Men out with their sons and daughters fishing and possibly even eating what they fish, which means there is life blooming in the water Gavin knew as an embarrassment of sepsis. There are fish living and thriving and the colour of the water has changed. The water is blue-grey and swaying with seaweed where Gavin remembers a childhood of looking down to see nothing but the spectral orb of a jellyfish, a tampon applicator drifting like an orphaned pinkie.

Gavin walks into their apartment and loves it—loves the clusters of cobwebs and the peeling paint, loves that warped and finicky back door, loves this place that has become a cradle for him and Zara and Ezra. He drops the dog's leash on the floor and holds Zara. Holds her as if his squeezing could weld them into permanence. Ezra scurries about their feet and Gavin delights in this dog and this woman and the things that he now clearly knows. He knows that he has never resented Zara. Knows he has never begrudged this strange-eyed person blending cashew butter in the apartment they share. He squeezes her and tells her he has confused freedom with desire. He has invested far, far too much in a satchel of fluid and hormone. He has seen Nancy lost and confused in a parking lot and she has whispered in her oracle way that what he wants is to take care of others, these others. That she, Zara, is a lovely confusing slash of colours and scents and all he wants is to keep discovering her, to brew her French-pressed coarse-grind coffee, to make her mango salad and coconut curry and vegan chocolate torte, to trace letters on the back of her hands as she lilts into sleep, to watch the streaks of white bloom like sun-bleached seaweed in her black, black hair. He tells her that he has agonized over this decision but now he knows it is not a decision, it's a feeling. That there are different ways to care and he can only do it the way that feels honest and real.

He says all this to Zara and she does not need to ask about Ezra because she has always known his decision. She says they will be alright, that things will change and things will stay the same but life is astonishing. She tells him life will churn on and there's no way to know what will happen, let alone control it. She tells him there were palm trees on Antarctica once, tells him this peninsula is just the blunt crown of a weary mountain, a drawling collision of Gondwana, Avolonia, Laurentia. She tells him things will flourish and things will melt. That nothing will be the same but she will protect him. She will hold him against the tidal drone and the vanishing whales and the waters rising to subsume them. Guard him from the acid ocean gnawing the soft sandstone of this peninsula. She vows to keep him safe from the glaciers, melting awake from their long sleep. Safe to listen to the lullaby—chirps and bellows of humpbacks pealing through the oceanic vast. Safe while the restless currents of mind and memory carry forth into the wavering beyond.

THE LAST TRUMPET

K.D. MILLER

L EN SPARKS has started to look forward to the advice column in the *Sackville Tribune-Post*. Reading about the situations people get themselves into charges him up in the morning. "Idiot!" he will all but snort over his cereal. "How and *why?*" Crackling the paper, shaking his head, while Sister watches him with her worried beagle eyes. "How and *why?*"

This morning, what he reads makes him go so still and quiet that Sister comes close, needing his palm on her head to forestall a whine. A woman has written in about her impending death. Specifically, her burial. She wants to be placed in her late husband's coffin, turned on her side to face him, so that when the last trumpet sounds and they wake to the Resurrection, they will embrace each other with joy and rise together.

Len has to read the letter a second time to be sure the writer is serious. She must be very old, he thinks, then reminds himself that he's eighty-six. But still. Are there people today who actually believe that kind of thing? Take it literally?

The advice columnist's name is Fran, and she gets it right most of the time. With this poor soul she is gentle.

Tactful. She suggests that the woman talk to her pastor, then perhaps discuss the matter with an undertaker. Len feels a stab of pity, imagining each man wondering whether to laugh or cry.

Sister is resting her chin on his knee. He starts in on a good scratch, neck to tail, that makes her close her eyes and sigh deep in her throat. "That's enough now," he says after a minute. "Go lie down. Go." Sister obeys, padding to her wicker bed lined with the cushion whose plaid is dim under a layer of shed hair. Len supposes he should have the thing cleaned. Did Joan ever send it out to be cleaned? He can't remember.

He stirs the coffee he poured before he sat down so it would be cool enough to drink when he got to it after his cereal and canned peaches. He can't stop thinking about that letter. What would it be like to have a rock-solid belief in something like the resurrection of the body? To be able to put aside all logic, quiet all questions and doubts, simply not see images of putrefaction and protruding bone?

He sips his coffee. Puts more milk in from the small pitcher, his shaking hand making it slop a little into the saucer. It used to drive Joan nuts, the way he drank his coffee almost cold. "I can pour it the night before and leave it in the fridge for you if you like," she said more than once.

He'll visit her this afternoon. It's the first of the month. October. Might not be able to do it again till spring. For years after she died, he kept his monthly appointment at her grave regardless of the weather. But the last few winters have been fierce—deep snow and ice storms. Last year he actually got one of those pronged attachments for the tip of his cane. He'll have to look it out soon. He hates it, the way it resembles the claws of some strange beast.

"I've become a strange beast, Sister," he says aloud. The dog hears her name and raises her head, looking at him hopefully. "No, not yet. Just settle down. We'll go for a you-know-what in a little while." Even now, in her twelfth year, she goes all puppyish if she hears *walk*.

He wonders if she still misses Brother, or even remembers him. Brother was always the more rambunctious of the two, and one day when he was barely a year old he ran into the street and was hit. Len insisted on letting Sister see and sniff the body so that she would understand that Brother was dead. But it didn't seem to work. She took on a puzzled air, poking into every corner of the house, searching the face of each visitor as if to say, "Do *you* know where Brother went?" Or at least, that's how it seemed to Len. Joan was more prosaic. "She's not all that bright. Just give it time. She'll forget he ever existed." She never said so, but Len knew that of the two Joan would have preferred to lose Sister. Brother was definitely her dog. Their personalities matched—curious, adventurous, demanding.

The dogs got their names by default. It was how the woman at the kennel referred to them as puppies—Sister and Brother. "Whatever you do," she said, "don't get two males from the same litter. They'll be like Tom and Jerry— egging each other on and wrecking the house. Two females are better, even though they can get a little territorial sometimes. But a sister and a brother? Bingo."

They couldn't decide on names. Fred and Ginger? George and Gracie? Beatrice and Benedict? One day they realized the dogs had decided for themselves, the female turning her head if she heard *Sister*, the male thumping his tail to the sound of *Brother*.

Len folds the last section of the paper. Places it on top of the other sections and squares the pile. Then he stacks his breakfast dishes—plate, saucer, cereal bowl, fruit bowl, coffee cup. Readies himself to get up. He still refuses to bring his cane to the table. The cane is for outside. Its place is in the brass umbrella stand by the front door. The day he'd allow himself to hobble around with it in the kitchen—

He pushes his chair back and gets carefully to his feet, thinking through the distance from table to sink. So far, so good. None of that sickening light-headedness he's had of late, forcing him to sit right back down. Now. Dishes to the counter. Then. Papers to the recycle bin under the sink. Two trips.

Is the stack of dishes rattling more than it did yesterday? Would a tray help? He could maybe assemble his breakfast things the night before on a tray. It's the turning around that's a bugger. Well, he could set his place at the other end of the table. Facing the sink. Six steps. There. Set the pile on the counter with a minimum of clatter and slide. Now do the whole thing over again to get the newspapers into the box. Jesus.

A tray. Does he even have a tray? Joan used to bring drinks out to guests. He tries to picture her. Would she have used a tray for that? She'd never let him help, that was for sure. His job was to entertain, be all chuckly and urbane in the living room. If there was ever a crash and a whispered "Shit!" from the kitchen, he would rise and go, saying, "My lady wife hath need of me." Then, when she hissed at him to just keep out of her way, he would re-emerge, give the company a seraphic smile and say, "Every day a honeymoon."

Company. Joan did love a party, for all her fussing. Probably loved the fussing too. Mostly couples they'd have over, back in the day. Neighbours. His colleagues from the school. Hers from all her volunteer jobs. A few singles. Men, usually. Joan was a man's woman. No doubt about that.

Len pauses in the middle of gathering up the papers. There was that one guy. Tall. Balding. On the arts festival committee with Joan. Was he the one with the silver Honda? Would he have come to the house? Taken a drink? Shaken Len's hand?

No way to know. And no point dwelling on it now. It's in the past. He's made it to the sink for the second time. The papers are in the box. He'll wash the dishes, sit for a bit, then take Sister for her walk.

It's cold for early October. He should have worn his heavier coat. His November coat, as he thinks of it. The windbreaker that got him through September is just light enough this morning to leave him chilled. He could have used gloves, too.

How do animals manage the temperature extremes, he wonders, watching Sister meander and sniff, seeking the perfect place to squat. All this one has is the same short pelt all year round. True, he does tie her coat on her in the winter, and puts booties on her feet for the salt. But still. He doesn't know much about beagles, where they originated, why they were bred to be the way they are. Something to do this afternoon. Google beagles.

Sister has finished, and watches apologetically as Len plants his cane, bracing himself with it to go down on one knee and pick up the mess with the hand already inside the plastic bag. It's all about preparation, he thinks, hoisting himself back up onto his feet.

He stashes the plastic bag in the first waste container he finds, then heads down Bridge to Main. He and Sister always enter the waterfowl park near St. Paul's, where Joan was rector's warden the two years before she was killed. Her funeral was huge. Crowd spilling out the door. People he barely knew coming close to take his hand or squeeze his shoulder and murmur something. None of them the face he kept looking for, in spite of himself. Surely the guy wouldn't have the gall. Or would he? Slip in the back at the last minute. Slip out again just before the end. Take off in his silver Honda.

They pass St. Paul's, then take the path to the boardwalk. They're a bit late this morning, so the mist has mostly lifted off the water. Still, there is that point on the near horizon where everything dissolves into grey—no distinction between water and sky. The sight always cheers Len, for some reason.

Cattails knocking against the handrails on either side are already crisping, and most of the songbirds have left. But there's still plenty of chatter and chirp to distract Sister from her sniffing. She woofs at a squawking raven overhead, then gets so fixated on some gum underfoot that Len has to pull her away.

When they come to their usual first resting spot, one of the little look-outs built off to the side and ringed with benches, they find it occupied. A young couple. Both smoking. Both wearing dark glasses on this cold grey morning. As Len passes by, pulling Sister back to his side and already trying to sight the next lookout, he hears the young woman say, "There are other. Issues. Besides. That."

One of *those* conversations, from the sound of it. Remember them? Joan pelting him with words. Him just waiting for it to be over. Do all women do that? Stir things up just when they've gotten settled and calm? Insist there is some *other issue* whose existence was always news to him, yet for which he was somehow always to blame?

He never repaid her in kind. Could have. Could have pointed a finger. Said a few words of his own. Would it have changed anything, if he had? Or would she have found some way to turn it around and as usual blame him?

Sister whines softly at his side and he realizes he's been tightening up on the leash. "Sorry, old girl. Let's have a bit of a rest." They've come to the next lookout which is vacant, thank God. Len sits stiffly down on the bench, feeling pain transfer from his feet to his knees. It never leaves now, just moves around.

The fog has lifted. He can see where the boardwalk zigzags out into the marsh, then back around to solid ground. The surface of the water is pocked with single raindrops. A muskrat noses open a seam, then submerges again.

This is usually when the simplicity of the place, its birds and animals living so completely in the present, settles him down and cheers him up. But he's morbid this morning. Brooding on things best left buried. Must be the effect of that letter to the advice columnist. Damn fool woman wanting to wake from the dead in her husband's arms. Beats opening your eyes alone inside your own coffin, he supposes. Having to heave against the lid, lift all that weight of dirt, claw your way to the surface in answer to the last trumpet sounding. Except he doubts she sees it that way. Probably imagines things being all lovely and easy and miraculous. Likely hasn't occurred to her that when her husband opens his own eyes and sees his wife again—this time for all eternity—his reaction might be something less than unmitigated joy.

Len hasn't a clue what happens after death, and is not sure he cares. He stayed away from the church for a year after Joan's funeral. Kept telling himself he'd never go back. But in time, he did. And now he's there most Sunday mornings. It's an outing. A chance to see people.

When Joan was alive he only went because she was so involved with the place. She ran it the way she ran the arts festival committee and the library board. Hustled him into his tie and out the door every Sunday morning so as to have time to perch on the kneeler in front of their pew to pray—eyes shut, slightly smiling lips moving. Len himself just sat. He had been raised a Presbyterian, and his parents had looked little and lost at the Anglican mass Joan had insisted on for their wedding.

Joan knew how to insist. It was her gift. How she got things done. They never talked about her habit of praying prior to a Sunday service—what she prayed for, what she believed in. Besides herself, that is. Yes, Joan Sparks definitely believed in Joan Sparks.

A pair of mallards glide past. Perfectly in sync, they upend to feed. Do they mate for life, Len wonders. Something else to look up. Imagine how serene that would be. *This is your mate. There will be no other. So just paddle your feet and don't even think about it.*

But what if one of them dies? When the police came to the door with the news that Joan had been hit by a van while jaywalking across Main, Len's first thought was, *Just like Brother.* His second was, *I never told her. She'll never know that I knew.*

It had been close at times, over the years. Oddly enough, the day he found out, it was easy. Maybe he was in shock. He got through dinner with the usual small talk about work. Had no problem leaving out the part about getting a headache after lunch, asking another teacher to supervise his spare, knocking off early. Walking home as usual, wondering if Joan would be there, or off doing one of her projects. Then, from half a block away, seeing a silver Honda just pulling out of their driveway. Joan on the porch watching it. Suddenly running down the steps. The car pausing. The driver leaning out. Joan bending to kiss him.

Len seemed to know exactly what to do—step quickly back behind a tall hedge and watch as the Honda passed him by, the driver invisible through the sunlit windshield. He felt as if he was in a play, performing a role he had been rehearsing all his life. Next the script directed him to turn and walk to that little cafe around the corner. Sit over one cooling cup of coffee until his usual coming-home time.

That night he lay in the dark beside Joan, aware of the inches between them. Feeling words crowding the back of his throat. *Why? How long –? What does he –?* It had been weeks since she'd wanted him to touch her. But she had always been temperamental that way. And he'd always just ridden it out, relieved and grateful to have her back when she came back.

So that was what he did. And when, in time, she did come back, did slide those few inches to press up against him, all he felt was the usual gratitude and relief. And though he never stopped looking for it, he never saw the silver Honda again.

Although beagle-type dogs have existed for 2500 years, the modern breed was developed in Great Britain around the 1830s from several breeds ...

Len resisted getting a computer at first. Held out as long as he could against Joan, who started agitating for one in the early nineties.

Beagles are scent hounds, developed primarily for tracking hare, rabbit, deer and other small game. They have a great sense of smell and tracking instinct that sees them employed as detection dogs for prohibited agricultural imports and foodstuffs in quarantine ...

He gave in, of course, thinking that would be the end of it and discovering it was only the beginning. Updates all the time and always the latest gizmo Joan just had to have. Then the desktop/laptop debate, which Len conceded almost before it began. Then, within months of acquiring the machine he is using now and will likely take to the grave, Joan went her own way with an iPad and iPhone, claiming she needed to be free of anything plugged in at home. *Does she mean me?* Len remembers musing at the time.

Joan's phone became a third presence, their electronic child, never asleep, forever interrupting. She claimed it consolidated and streamlined things for her, but it seemed to Len that it complicated her life, harassing and obsessing her. She was in the middle of texting someone when she stepped off the curb and was hit.

Beagles are intelligent but single-minded, and popular pets because of their size, even temper, and lack of inherited health problems.

What if human beings were bred for specific tasks, the way domesticated animals are? Not for the first time, Len fantasizes some extraterrestrial race, whose intelligence compares to that of homo sapiens the way his does to Sister's, arriving one day on Earth and taking over. In just a few generations, humans would be sorted into functional breeds—some to do menial work, some to invent or create, others to organize and keep records. Len is aware that he finds something attractive in the notion. Knowing one's role, one's nature, and being unwilling, even unable, to deviate from it.

But what if it had actually happened in his lifetime? Where would he have fit, in the scheme of things? He was fifteen when the Second World War ended. His father had fought in the Great War, and never stopped talking about it. Unlike other boys his age, Len did not chafe at being just too young to join up. He felt secretly relieved, as if he'd gotten off scot-free.

He took a general bachelor's degree and became a high school teacher in Sackville, New Brunswick. He was good enough in the classroom to keep order and impart his subject, which was geography. An inoffensive discipline, neither soft art nor hard science, offering a smorgasbord of topics from tariffs on trade goods to tectonic forces shifting the ground beneath his students' feet.

Somewhat to his surprise, he married a strikingly beautiful woman who got more so with age, her white hair contrasting dramatically with her dark brows. A woman, however, who was not unlike one of those tectonic forces— never resting, never satisfied, incapable of engaging with an individual or a group without pushing them around.

Joan was scornful of Sackville, for all she practically ran its cultural and spiritual life. She was furious with Len for refusing a vice-principalship in Moncton—*A real city, at least! This place is a village!* But Len for once put his foot down and refused to move. He had found his place. Sackville *was* a city, albeit a cozy one, with its historic university and fall fair. It was small enough that he could walk back and forth to work each day. Walk to church each Sunday morning. Afford a big old house with a wraparound porch that never failed to move him when he turned the corner at the end of the day and sighted it. He was used to his life. Even the discomforts of his marriage were accustomed discomforts. He never cheated on Joan. Not for lack of opportunity. A high school teacher in a small place like Sackville gets a certain number of eyes turning his way. But it stopped with the eyes. Sometimes Joan would even have to tell him— *Didn't you see Trish Bromley just throwing herself at you?*—after some gathering or other. All he would remember would be the woman's upturned face, her expression interested. Well, all right. Maybe a bit more than just interested. But such occurrences always left him mystified. He knew he was not unattractive. He just felt so thoroughly married. He had been made to be married. To Joan. He felt safe in his life. Out of harm's way. And there was nothing wrong with that.

He may have spent all his political capital as breadwinner when he refused to move for that promotion. And it's possible Joan was paying him back when she had that affair—if that's what it was—with the guy in the silver Honda. He doesn't know. He never will. It's in the past, he reminds himself, shutting down the computer.

The cemetery gates always strike him as a bit pretentious—two big gothic wings wafting him in. But here he is, as usual. First of the month. A little later in the day than he would have liked. The dark comes down early, and they shut the place up at five.

He almost didn't make it out the door. That damned light-headedness again when he tried to get up out of his desk chair. It dropped him right back down with a *whump*. All he could do was sit and wait for the room to stop spinning. He thought about just staying home, leaving the visit till tomorrow or the next day. But no. That would be the start of something. Something he does not want to start.

Sister was so sound asleep that he decided not to wake her for a second walk. She's sleeping more and more these days. He supposes the time is coming. But not just yet. She can still get around. Still likes her food. And she's a presence in the house. Sometimes he'll lower his paper or look away from the TV and see her eyes upon him. He'll wonder how long she has been quietly studying him, and why. Maybe she knows he's all she's got. Maybe she senses that he will one day decide she has lived long enough. *Oh for God's sake, Len,* he can just hear Joan, *she's a dog. They don't think beyond their next bowl of kibble.*

Joan's grave is not far in, but it is up a bit of a rise. Len has to stop half way and catch his breath. When she died, there was actually a sale on cemetery plots and he got a two-for-one deal. He paid a little extra even so, because there was a bench facing where their headstones would be. At the time, he didn't care all that much, but now he's glad of a place to sit during these monthly visits.

He leans on his cane and looks around at the acres of graves. Generations upon generations. Taking up land. Would the day ever come when the needs of the living shredded the last notion of what is sacred? He imagines graveyards being excavated for condominium foundations. Earth movers lifting jaws dripping with dry and not so dry bones. Shards of mahogany. Crisping bouquets. All of it loaded onto trucks trundling up out of the deepening pit and taking it—

"Hey, you got a light?"

Where did he come from? A boy. Maybe fifteen. Wearing jeans and one of those hoodie things or whatever they're called.

"I'm sorry?"

"I *said*. Do. You. Got. A light."

Rude young—"No. I haven't."

"You sure?"

"Yes, I'm sure," Len says, stumping past. "I don't smoke. And neither should you." Honestly.

The bench is just a few steps around a bend in the cemetery path. When he reaches it he grabs onto the armrest, braces with his cane and sits gingerly. Even through his heavier coat, the seat is hard and cold.

Joan's headstone is a plain white marble tablet. Name and dates. No *Beloved Wife Of* or any other sentiment. He did want to make the right decision. Searched his memory for any hint she might have given about preferring to be cremated. Except Joan didn't hint, and she didn't prefer. If she wanted something, she opened her mouth and—

"You just out takin' a walk or somethin'?"

Damn. He didn't hear the kid following him. Len tightens up on the handle of his cane. Draws a calming breath. "I'm visiting my late wife." He nods toward Joan's grave.

"Oh yeah?" The boy sits down beside him. "How long she been dead?" His face is a pale oval, the eyes dark-lashed, the lips fleshy, curled in a smirk. There is a pink constellation of pimples on his chin.

Len moves his left hand into his lap. He's wearing his good watch—the one he got at retirement. And his wallet— cash and credit card—is in his lapel pocket. But he has his cane. One good crack across the bridge of the nose—

Oh, calm down. The boy hasn't done anything wrong. As a teacher, Len learned to focus on the question asked and filter out any attitude. It usually worked. "As you can see from the date on the stone, my wife passed away eight years ago," he says firmly, then faces front.

"What she die of?"

Is he being baited? The way the young sometimes bait the old? He wants to say, *You'll be like me some day. I know you don't believe it, but it's true. Unless you die young in some damned fool way. Racing a car. Putting some garbage into your veins or up your nose or whatever your type does.* Keeping his voice steady, he says, "It was an accident. She was hit crossing the street. Now if you don't mind, I would like to be quiet."

"Sure. No problem. Quiet as you want."

Len tries to ignore the boy after that, but he must have a slight cold because his breath snuffles. He wants to focus the way he usually does, calling up memories of Joan. Just fifteen minutes or so of acknowledgement. It's what he does. Once a month. He was her husband. She was his wife. All the difficulties and disappointments notwithstanding.

Len sucks up all the integrity in the room. Did Joan ever actually say that? Or can he just imagine her saying it?

No matter. Focus. Try. But his mind throws up a picture of how she—her body—must be now. Why didn't he just go ahead and have her cremated? Scatter the ashes wherever? Except he wouldn't have scattered her, would he? No, he'd have kept her in a box or an urn somewhere in the living room. Ridiculous. Superstitious. Still, he did want her to be in a specific place. That was another odd thought he had right after she died. *At least now I'll know where she is. What she's—*

"You come here a lot?"

Len sighs. "I come here once per month. For just a few minutes. Of quiet reflection."

"You and her married for long?"

"Forty-eight years."

"Wow. All that time. Just you two. What's that like?"

"I'm sorry?"

"Like, didn't you get sick of each other?"

Len says nothing, just looks steadily ahead at Joan's grave, thinking he might as well leave but unwilling to let the boy force him out.

"Like, didn't you fight or nothin'? My folks, they fight all the time."

Maybe, Len thinks resignedly, this could be a teaching moment. "There are always tensions in a marriage," he says. "Especially a long one. But you adjust to each other. And if there is a foundation of respect—"

163

"You ever give her a little tap?"

"What?"

"You know. Just a swat now and then. Keep her in line."

What kind of home does this boy come from? "Absolutely not." Then, quoting his father, "When a man raises his hand to a woman, he ceases to be a man."

"She pretty good, then?"

"Excuse me?"

"You know." .

"I'm sure I don't."

"You get what you want? When you wanted it?"

"Look, I don't know what you're—"

"Or did you have to beg for it?" The boy's adenoidal breath is almost in his ear. "Did you have to say, *Pleease, Honey! Pleease! Pleease?*"

Len plants his cane. Pulls himself to his feet. Feels the blood drain sickeningly from his head. Lands back down. "Oooff!" One slat of the bench bruises his tailbone. His cane clatters to the ground beside him.

"Hey! Geez. You all right?" The boy is crouched in front of him, peering into his face. Grinning. "You know what? You should put your head down. Between your knees. Yeah. That's what you're supposed to do."

And that is what Len does, because the boy puts his hands on his shoulders and pushes him down hard until he is bent double. "I can't breathe!" he squeaks, and the pressure eases a bit.

"Now, you just stay that way," the boy says tenderly. "You hear me?" When Len does not respond, he presses down hard again.

"Yes!" Len even nods—wags his head between his knees. He can see the end of his cane, where it fell. Could he reach it if—

"Good. That's good." A pale hand picks the cane up. Pulls it out of his line of vision. He hears a whoosh of air. Another. Is the boy swinging his cane around? Revving up? Len braces for the impact. He'll be found beaten to death in front of his wife's grave. Because he always visits his wife, doesn't he? Every bloody month. His wife with her prayers and her good works. His wife who cheated on him. Opened her legs. Took him for a bloody—

Whump!

He winces at the sound. Dares to look up. The boy raises the cane. Brings it down again. On Joan's grave.

Whump!

"Bitch!"

Whump!

"Cunt!"

Whump!

Len jerks with every blow. *Right. Wear yourself out. Take it out on her. Give it to her. Give it to her.*

The boy stops and stands, breathing heavily. Len quickly looks down again. Hears the sound of a zipper. A splashing. "Drink it, bitch!"

Drink it, bitch.

A clatter. Running footsteps. Getting fainter.

After a long moment, Len looks up. There, a few feet in front of him on the path, is his cane. No sign of the boy. He listens. Hard. Nothing.

Carefully, he half-rolls off the bench onto his knees. Feels cold gravel through the fabric of his pants. Crawls to his cane. Braces with it. Pulls himself to his feet. Hobbles to Joan's grave and leans on the stone. "I'm sorry," he wheezes. "I'm sorry." He is tired to death. He could lie down right here and now with Joan and fall asleep. But if he does that, Sister will die slowly inside the house of hunger and thirst.

She won't howl or bark at a window the way Brother would have. And even if she does, who will hear? No one comes to the door. There's no mail delivery any more, just that bloody community box he has to walk to. He should have asked a neighbor to look in on him every other day or so. But that's how it starts. The exchanged looks. The being talked about. *Poor old Len...*

He's getting his breath back. Patting the headstone now, saying, "All right then? All right." He checks his watch. It's not yet five. If he starts back now, he'll make it to the gates before they lock them.

Once he's home, should he call the authorities? Report the boy? He did get a good look at him. But his mind veers from the thought of a young officer, perhaps even a woman, sitting in his living room and listening to his tale of what happened. What was done to him. And to Joan. Then asking questions. Forcing him to reveal more and more detail. It would be like having to describe a humiliating but deserved punishment.

So the boy will get off scot free. Maybe Len will even encounter him one day when he's out walking Sister.

Sister. She'll be waking up. Wondering where he is. Making that worried little whine in her throat. He starts toward the gates. Is he actually hungry? What does he have in the house?

He should start getting his groceries delivered. He hasn't been eating well, because he can only carry one bag home at a time from the store and he doesn't want to be seen trundling one of those old-lady bundle buggies. So yes. Delivery. He'll set that up. Tomorrow. Nothing wrong with it, either. Not as if he's getting meals on bloody wheels.

And what was he thinking about this morning? Setting his breakfast things out on a tray the night before. At the other end of the table, facing the sink. He must have a tray somewhere. He'll take a look tonight. Pick one up tomorrow from the hardware in town, if necessary.

It's all about preparation, he reminds himself, stumping down the hill. Catching sight of the gates.

THE SHOE EMPORIUM

LISA MOORE

D O YOU feel that? Steve asks. The customer, a leggy junior high school teacher, has just taken up running.

Steve rubs small circles on the inside of his own knee.

Right there, he says. He doesn't break eye contact. The customer has large grey eyes and a habit of hyper-rapid blinking that suggests permanent incredulity. But her weak, caving chin gives Steve hope.

The customer reaches down to touch the inside of her knee, unconsciously mirroring him. Rubbing little circles. She blinks.

I guess so, she says.

Then she says, Yes.

Steve nods. Slow, small nods, like a translator with an invisible ear bud hearing foreign things of life-altering importance and simultaneously transforming them into colloquial, sales-savvy koans about bones and joints and mortality.

His nodding effects a reluctant intimacy, as if many a customer could not get this kind of attention out of Steve, the kind she's getting right now, nobody could, under normal circumstances, but look, lady, you are golden, I can see right inside you, the things you want, you are some kind of charismatic junior highschool teacher and the eyes on you, and I get it, you want to run and it hurts. You are hurting.

She is nodding right back.

Yes, she says. I feel it.

When you're running, Steve says. A pain, right here, this muscle?

Now he's stroking the inside of his thigh.

Yes, that's absolutely where it hurts, she says. He doesn't break eye contact because that's how good he is at selling shoes, but he intuits that, behind him, another customer he's also agreed to help, is on tiptoes stretching for a buttery suede hiking boot with fringes, reaching for it, reaching. And he feels the eyes of his manager, Cathy, riveted on him.

You're right, Aiden, yes, the junior high school teacher says to Steve, and she blinks. His nametag says Aiden. She's caressing her own thigh.

See this right here, he asks. He's holding the foot measurer.

The new heat-sensing foot measurer came with the spring shipment and Steve was the first to embrace the technology.

The old metal foot measurer has sliding parts that cup the ball of the foot and the top of the toes. The measurements are in the grooves that run down the side, like the foot measurers of yore. The new device introduces the first innovation to the original design since 1927, when it was first invented;the metal has been fitted with a magic, footprint-shaped inlay.

Can I get you to take off your boot, Steve asks. He is careful with tone. He speaks atonally. Okay, yes. He has a husky hue, a tamped-down friskiness this side of overtly sexual that is spontaneous, comes over him unbidden with the promise of a naked foot.

I'm not wearing any socks, she says. Does she blush? Steve drops to one knee in front of her, a signature move the other two salespeople, including Cathy, the manager, occasionally adopt, following his lead.

Steve pulls a scrunched little ball of nylon out of his back pocket and, without another word, tugs the zipper on junior high school teacher's black suede ankle boot, gripping the heel and toe and, gently rocking, breaking the sweat-suction seal of smelly leather: black glitter nail polish, toes like unearthed baby potatoes, a bitsy little corn on the side of the big toe, yellowed, hardened but porous, full of character.

He slips the sockette over the toes, slithering it up to the heel, letting it snap into place.

What do you teach? he asks.

Ukulele, she says. Blinking hard.

He places the foot measurer in front of her on the floor.

Do you want me to, she says. The Shoe Emporium is packed right now and there's a lot of noise and distraction but Steve is built. He has a worked physique: balls of tough flesh bulge all down his arms as he moves, ropes of muscles ripple over his back, the curving waist. His face is clefts and crags, a boxy, unbeautiful lean-to of a forehead, shovel chin. He has eyes that came to Newfoundland four hundred years ago, straight from Waterford, Ireland.

Those eyes are a particular blue: Jell-Ovodka shooters at bachelorette parties in 1992 were that shade of blue. Mr. Freezes. Blowtorch blue. Iceland's blue lagoon.

I'll just ask you to scootchie your foot back against that heel holder, he says. She steps onto it. He adjusts the sliding metal cup so it snugs the ball of her foot and then slides the other movable metal part so it touches her toes.

Does that feel good? he asks.

Tickles, she says.

Does it, he says. But he's doctorish, scientific. His pinkie nevertheless brushes her instep. Her foot curls in on itself, but she does not haul it away.

Okay, step off, he says. He hoists the foot measurer so one end of it rests on his hip. The plastic foot-shaped inlay holds a skim of surging liquid as alive as the primordial plasma from which life first sprang.

It captures the imprint of heat from the sole. Cathy had once pressed it against her heart and showed the print to the other salesperson on the floor, Marty, whose nametag actually says Marty. There had been a beautiful flare in the plasma, a boiling cherry with a penumbra of aqua surging out all over the place and a black star with a chartreuse aureole off to the left that may or may not have been an imprint of her nipple through the rough nylon lace of her bra and the polyester blouse. The image seemed to Cathy an exact and nuanced impression of her emotional state because of Marty, her other co-worker, besides Steve, both of whom answered to her and basically had to do what she said, both of whom nevertheless made fifty cents an hour more than her, even though they all got hired at the same time and they didn't have to vacuum after closing, or do the scheduling, and both of whom had seen the impression of her nipple, but only one of whom (Marty) had thrown her so far off course from anything she had previously known about love, or lust, or that heady combo, last weekend in the too-small storage room full of boxes of shoes and boots, floor to ceiling, behind the cash.

The chartreuse flare of her nipple in the heat-sensing footprint had bruised up black pretty quick and disappeared.

Steve had seen it, though, and the impression of Cathy's nipple in the foot-measuring, heat-sensing pad, made in a moment of collegial goofing around(very rare because she's usually so angry, working two jobs and going to school, not making as much as them, and also hell-bent on winning the trip to Toronto and the tickets to the Broadway musical Kinky Boots, the reward for the highest commission sales this fiscal year throughout all the Shoe Emporium franchises across Canada), was sexy as fuck. It made Steve's mouth water. He got hot, flushed. He got hard.

He might be in love.

But after what happened in the storage room last weekend, he is somehow both addled and deliberate.

Steve points out, with the tip of a pen he's drawn out of his breast pocket, an indigo flare at the instep of the junior high school ukulele instructor's foot.

That's what I'm talking about, he says. He taps the pen against the plastic inlay.

Oh my god, she says.

Pronation, he says. You've got a problem. Can you see that?

I definitely see something, Aiden, she says.

Right there, Steve/Aiden says. That's causing a misalignment that is travelling from your knee all the way up your thigh, all the way up, basically, to your core.

And as he says this, he steps backwards two, three steps, and reaches behind him, still holding the eyes of the ukulele teacher, who is abashed by the imprint of her own foot which is aflame with furtive bitterness, bush fires and comets. He sweeps down the buttery suede hiking boot for the other customer, tossing it to her.

Marty has an elbow stretched over the top of the Saucony display unit, a hand holding up his head, fingers spread through his gold buzz-cut and he's taking in Steve's charisma.

Marty's eyes are russet brown, that feral, ferric sun-struck rust of turning leaves just before frost, his eyelashes orange, his mouth tender. So many freckles they join together in golden tan patches on his neck, his left wrist. A single opal earring in a gold setting surrounded by diamonds in his right ear.

Cathy had kissed Marty's closed eyelids in the storage room last week. His eyelids were the only parts of Marty that didn't have freckles, as far as Cathy could tell.

One, then the other, the eyeballs jittering under her lips like the eyeballs of someone in the midst of a flying dream, someone taking in swathes of city, warp speed, black roofs, green roofs, a few pools, little toy ATVs ringed around garage doors, then the prickled carpet of treetops at the outskirts, wrinkled mountains on the left, tinfoil lakes on the right. Eyeballs flicking back and forth so fast under her lips.

Because what was that?

That was the storage closet of the Shoe Emporium at the Avalon Mall at four o'clock on Saturday afternoon, a week ago to the hour, basically, where there was not really enough room for two people, at the beginning of the Buy-One-Get-the-Second-Pair-Half-Price Blow-Out Sale that was still in progress and during which Cathy fell in love with a gay guy, Marty, who is totally gay, who says on the spectrum, if there is a spectrum, he's way over here: and he cups one elbow and holds his hand up straight like a blade and then lets it swing down flat against the Saucony display unit to show he is at the very end of the spectrum that basically isn't interested in women at all.

Cathy, you're going to have to take my word for it, he says. Marty, who does, though, admit to a preference for straight men, and has lots of secret love affairs with straight guys with girlfriends and can't explain to himself or anyone else, including Cathy, what happened in the storage closet, the why of it, if he's so gay, like he says, totally gay, nor has he given it much thought, because it just happened is all, and besides he's suffering because his grandmother died three weeks before, on the same day, a Saturday, and the same hour, maybe, that the thing happened in the storage closet last weekend.

His grandmother used to press his shirts for him and return them in a neat stack with a sheaf of white tissue paper folded around each shirt. She made lemon roll dusted with icing sugar every Sunday and the smell of it, when he walked in, all through the house. She was professor emerita of marine biology at Memorial University specializing in the reproductive cycles of sea cucumbers.

She had died in a sauna tent that Marty ordered for her over the web, at her request, because she'd heard it would be good for her arthritis.

He'd been over when the sauna tent was delivered and they'd unpacked it together and rolled it out on the Persian carpet. He'd consulted the instruction pamphlet and poured several litres of water in through the nozzle and twisted the cap, untied the twist-ties that bundled all the extension cords, plugged that sucker in, and watched the folded, rubberized tent unpook and lift and sigh until it was bloated with steam while they had tea and ate lemon roll dusted with icing sugar. There was a little stool in the tent, and you just got in it was what you were supposed to do, the zipper tab inside and you zipped it to the neck so your head stuck out, just your head, your arms and everything else inside. You sat on the plastic stool that came with it. Marty had assembled it, screwing the four short, fat legs into the seat and the plastic backrest before he went to work. Because he'd had to go to work.

She'd agreed to wait until he got back in the evening before trying out the sauna tent but she had also given him the pair of opal earrings, like she knew. She put them in his hand and closed his fingers around them, and she patted his loose fist and then grabbed it tight with both her hands, rocked his fist up and down three times before letting go and he didn't want them. He told her that. But she got very serious and said, If anything happens to me.

Nothing will happen to you, he'd said.

If anything happens to me will you take care of the cockapoos? And he said it was all nonsense, but she made him promise. She had basically raised him.

Marty has been watching Steve, who has passive-aggressively forgotten his own nametag. This morning Cathy was all, Where's your nametag. You're on the floor; you wear the nametag.

And: This is something you can consult in the memo I sent out last week.

She'd dug around under the counter where there were a bunch of defunct nametags in a Tupperware container and she drew her hand back out fast because a name-tag pin drove deep into the tip of her index finger. Cathy flick-flicked her hand, really hard, back and forth over her shoulder and the tag, bright red with embossed white letters, flew across the counter and hit Steve in the face, the corner of it, just below his left eye.

Cathy stuck her finger in her mouth and was sucking it and then the look on her, seeing this thing hitting Steve just below the eye. She hates Steve's guts but she would certainly never maim the guy on purpose or try to take out his eye.

Oh my god, Steve, I'm sorry, she says. At first Steve just stands still with his eyes shut and his lips pressed tight, his cheeks getting red. Then he bends down and picks up the tag and fixes it to his shirt pocket.

You get the feeling Cathy is really going to be sorry when Steve gets a chance to make her sorry, which, you get the feeling, he is well equipped to do.

For the time being, though, Steve obviously plans to sell the shit out of shoes all day long, drawing the highest commission ever out of the Shoe Emporium in order to win the two tickets to Toronto to see the Broadway musical Kinky Boots, and right now Cathy and Steve are both streaks ahead of the rest of the staff, in all the franchises across the country, in terms of winning that prize.

Steve has no desire to go to Toronto or to see a musical about shoes, if that's what it is, but he solemnly believes that if you find yourself, ever, in the middle of the ocean in a dory with a helicopter hovering over you, and if you're dressed as Santa Claus in the middle of July, and the dory is loaded with cod, two days after the food fishery has shut down, and if you have a bottle of rum in one hand and you're yelling Fuck you at the top of your lungs and waving the rum bottle over your head and if the RCMP are waiting for you on the wharf and half the community is cheering because you staged a one-man protest is basically what it was but you get arrested anyway, cuffed even, and then if you find that Solcor have come out and said they must manage expectations around chartered flights from now on, so if you wanted, say, to continue working six weeks on, two weeks off, as you've been doing for the last twenty-two years in Fort Mac, if that's what you wanted to do, then you'd have to start booking commercial flights, which would mean landing in St. John's in the dark and driving three fucking hours back to Marystown and eventually hitting a moose, only a fender-bender, popped the dent with a toilet plunger, but the bawling of the animal, pitched so low and baleful, the anguish of it nearly startling the fuck out of him, and so Steve solemnly believes that, if that's what's happening to you, if you find yourself in that situation, you might as well sell the shit out of some shoes.

Steve is serving two women at the same time, and tilts his chin up at a third woman. With the tilt of his shovel chin, Steve is saying: I'm coming for you, girlfriend, hang tight, love of God.

Cathy is stuck with a mother and three sugar-blitzed youngsters, the youngest of whom is headed for a full-on implosion because she wants shoes with blinking lights in the heels, which are not one of the brands of shoes where you buy one get the second pair half price and because she (the little girl) has a lollipop, slimy with saliva, the size of her face and because some children are born with a willpower so fully formed and flinty they are ungovernable after the first gasp of oxygen and ever on.

But what can you do for me? In terms of price? This is the mother—nervy, a knee jiggling, arms crossed tight over her chest, a nicotine patch on her neck.

Cathy does not care to explore the possibilities of a reduced price on the shoes that flash with each step. All she cares about at the moment is Marty and possibly getting back into the storage closet with him because of what happened last weekend, even though Marty is gay and grief-stricken.

Marty, in the meantime, is still dreamily looking on as Steve comes out of the storage closet with five boxes of shoes held in place with his shovel chin, handing them out to four women now. And Marty is not doing anything else except holding up the Saucony display unit, practically draped all over it, because his grandmother has died and because he's been doing MDMA for three nights in a row and last night, at a house party, he'd taken a handful of prescription pills from a big glass salad bowl next to the front door that everybody at the party had contributed to, and he hasn't really slept very well since he found her.

It's actually making him physically weak, this grief, and he got home from the gay dance bar that everybody went to after the house party and put on his work clothes without ever going to bed and then stepped outside into the below-zero frost and fat tumbling snowflakes and slanting light, dropped his skateboard with a clatter onto the asphalt and stepped on it, and rumbled downhill in the middle of Thorburn Road, cars swerving around him all the way to the Avalon Mall.

So he's draped that way, over the display unit, unable to do anything at all, because she raised him, his grandmother, and he understands with a one-time, ultra-sensitive, drug-enhanced clairvoyance that nobody will ever love him like that again, not with that depth and intelligence and appreciation for who he is in the very marrow of his bones no matter how much he fucks up or triumphs, loves him the same amount, with the same intensity no matter what because she knows him. Knew him.

Cathy is on her knees before the youngest child, who is probably seven, pasty and shrill with desire for the shoes with red lights in the soles, shoes that are unforgivably expensive and built to fall apart in less than a month. Cathy has altered her tone, a child-friendly falsetto, airy and uncertain. She closes her eyes tight and turns her shiny red fake fingernails toward her own face and rakes down the air between the tips of her fingernails and her face, several times, the nails floating down over her face without actually touching it, showing the child how one can calm oneself down if one needs to: Come on, try this with me.

And here she flings her fingers to the side, the way you might flick water off your hands after doing the dishes—and with her eyes still closed, she tells the little girl: The whole mall is alive with negative ions, but we've just basically brushed them away.

Steve is full of admiration. She's theatrical; she brings a theatrical touch to selling shoes. If all three kids get new shoes, she'll be ahead in sales and they're fifteen minutes to shift change.

All the grief Marty feels for his grandmother, he realizes, has been turned into a hard opal of love/lust for Steve/Aiden. And he's draped over the Saucony display unit not willing to sell anything but his heart.

Because: Shoes? Is this what he's doing? Selling shoes? Under this kind of lighting, which washes him out, basically, coming to a mall, three times a week?

He'd let himself in with his key and called out to her and stood listening and he could hear an inhale-exhale that was reptilian, like rubbery scales, sliding and unsliding and even as he approached the living room with its white corduroy curving sectional couches with the round glass table between, and the bevelled glass in the windows throwing rainbows and the crystals too, throwing little rainbows everywhere, and the gold-trimmed china plates, lined up on the white marble fireplace with the big hearth and the cold lemon roll on the side table on a silver tray with a white paper doily under it and the silver pie server with the pearlized handle, as he approached the door, he both knew and didn't know what the hellish hissing could be.

And at first he thought: Just asleep. Her head drooping forward and a line of drool still attached to the lower lip, the sauna bag inflating, deflating, like it was breathing for her.

The zipper on the sauna bag was pulled up on the inside, and it had gotten stuck in a fold of the rubberized fabric that had bunched in the head of the zipper.

The heat: she had been as good as poached alive. Of course he picked up the pearlized pie server with a serrated edge and hacked through the plastic and tried CPR and called 911 on his cell, but she had been dead, the doctor estimated, two hours or more before his arrival.

The moose on its side, Steve/Aiden thought, foreleg bent in the wrong direction and the bone sticking out, trying to lift its head, the sloppy, swinging eye, humanly begging, wielding its dying like a cudgel, begging limply for mercy.

Begging you to pick up a Jesus boulder off the side of the road and bash its skull, but you get back in the car and reverse away from the rising sun and swerve around the animal with its panting ribs and terrible eye. You find yourself at forty-two years old, poster boy for what happens if you don't finish high school, and go instead after the big bucks in Alberta all swagger and Look at me. House taking up every square inch of a building lot and the ATVs and flat screens and barbeque big as a Cadillac, all in hock to the bank.

The legs on you like the bloody water, standing on the side of the highway with that dying animal, and then driving into the inky dark. The fine from the Santa Claus fishing, and the commercial flights, and then it's fuck Solcor, the move into St. John's, the one-room apartment, the job at the Shoe Emporium at the age of forty-fucking-two with the manager who is twenty-four, hot as a barbeque coal, the lip gloss and the languid flick/curl, flick/curl of a strand of her long, shiny hair around a finger and then holding it out, the split ends, lost in that inspection for a solid thirty seconds, and the lava boil of chartreuse and turquoise and molten copper that is her nipple in the heat-sensing pad, while the mall breathes and coils around all three of them.

You're standing there with somebody else's nametag, and, yes, you'll bloody well win the fucking trip to Toronto just to see she doesn't get it and then give it to her, just to spite her. To see if she'll take it.

Go on girl, have it. Have the trip. I insist.

You don't get the right shoe, Steve/Aiden says, you could be misaligned for a long time and the joints grind together, become dust inside there. Dust to dust. You may have to quit running.

I just started, says the junior high school ukulele teacher. Incredulous blinking. The woman with the suede hiking boot waving it in the air, saying she needs a six-and- a-half.

I don't ever say quit to a customer, says Steve. His ancient blue eyes and how easy for Marty to imagine him in the dory waving the bottle over his head, the white cotton-batting beard, the red velveteen hat with fur trim, water all aglint and the black rubber boots sunk to the knees in writhing silver bodies and fish stink, raging in the chuffling air, whipped up by the helicopter that dips and zooms, and drunk, yes, loaded, yes, but lamenting the loss of something big.

Anybody tells you to quit running that's a different story than I'm going to tell, Steve/Aiden tells the customer. In the end, you make the decision. But I have something for you.

He's speaking with his back to her. He has put the foot measurer down on the bench beside her. The colours fading, the gelled pad a cold, murky blue, opaque and mute.

Steve/Aiden whirls around to face her. He's holding a Saucony runner by the toe and heel, balancing it on the tips of his fingers. It's the most expensive runner they have, and pushes him well over Cathy's commission balance.

I want you to try this, he says.

But I can't afford that.

I'm not saying buy it, Steve says. He sounds affronted.

That's more than double my budget, she says.

I just want you to put it on. I want you to feel what that's like on your foot.

And here's what Cathy thinks: The last fifteen minutes of a shift, there is a lulling of everything. A lulling of all that you are because you don't have time to notice anything but the roar of whatever it is in the ceiling, mall air-conditioning, maybe? Or the noise of the glass elevator near the food court, rising, descending, the torpid stomping of a beast full of sinew and cables, huffing the sugary, charred food-court breath of fat and fries. And this amorphous monster, coming, always coming for them, to drag them under, is maybe the mall itself, the exoskeleton of a serpent, swishing its weltering tail of withdrawal and spend, the thrashing of swipe, insert, tap, charging through the ether, all bling and brand, pleather, sequins, sex, and here at the Shoe Emporium, a lot of garish neon, spiked heels, leopard print, and Can I help you.

This is the sort of situation that arises: You can fall in love with your co-worker without deciding to, even though he's so not straight. All of what you believe to be your "self" does an about-face and stands at attention, salutes all of what you believe your co-worker's "self" to be.

The mother says, No, not today, sweetie. And the child opens her mouth as wide as it will go, clutching a single shoe so the heel lights up her chin, bright red, the hollow cave of her open mouth, glowing red, and her eye sockets sunken and red, her very irises, red, on/off, on/off, while the mother tries to wrestle the shoe from her.

And your co-worker with his sunrise hair, beefy buttocks and biceps, the winding rose-bush tattoo tucking under the sleeve of his employee-issue The Shoe Emporium T-shirt, still high from whatever all-nighter and foxy-eyed and whose grandmother was the leading expert in cold-water sea cucumbers, no joke, at the Marine Institute and who (Marty) is not even bi but straight-up gay for gosh sakes, like definitely that end of the spectrum, according to him. Sea cucumbers.

I mean, this is involuntary, but what gets unleashed is a pressure hose of, Whoa, love. You turn evangelical, the lingo/babble of gel sole versus extra-foam sole and soles with lights and now the first blasting howl welters out of the child's open mouth.

The wham-splat, a hose in your chest, is spraying this pillar of, My god, love all over your unsuspecting gay not-even-slightly-interested-in-girls co-worker. And who is more surprised than you?

So there she was last week, Cathy, in the storage closet where she had wedged a heel against the second-lowest shelf, her back jammed against the shoeboxes stacked from floor to ceiling, these shoeboxes wedged in one against the other, like the stones in an archway, one shoebox (inside which happened to besling back, kitten-heeled patent-leather shoes with velvet bows and clasps of rhinestones) kept jutting out, like jut, jut-jut, once Marty had penetrated her, first tearing a hole in the leg of her nude nylons because, let's face it, this is happening, this is really happening, and how wet she is, how slippery, how yes, yes, but silent, because she's the manager, and after all some sense of the professionalism, Please.

The hole in her nylons that Marty has torn has a creep, it creeps, widening in an oval big as the palm of her hand, peeling back or unravelling, a gazillion filaments, small and laddering down the leg, invisibly giving, breaking, no, not breaking exactly, more evaporating, and it is her desire, a spreading, licking, a hole in the nylons because even though she comes to work put together because what are these stockings but a petroleum product made as thin as a lick of light, tickling, so that her skin pudges through, like dough rising or anything that rises, and then the keystone shoebox is knocked maybe half an inch with each—let's take a moment to acknowledge the paradox—very gentle, controlled but forceful, holy thrust/bang, tinged with maybe a little love for her, however ephemeral, so that the tightly jammed shoebox, maybe twelve shoeboxes above her head, juts itself out of the tightly packed wall of shoeboxes that rises from floor to ceiling all the way down the very narrow storage closet, and keeps jutting farther and farther with each lovemaking rock of Marty's hips and buttock contraction and the tilt of his head, bent as if in prayer, but also, pouf, blowing a mouthful of her hair away from his lips because, he stops just for a sec, because a hair, one of her hairs, seems to have gotten into his mouth and they're both caught up in the micro-work of What is it? A hair? Phwah-phwah, he's trying to get it off his tongue, and there he has it, Have you got it? Pinched between finger and thumb and saliva shine, he rubs it away, and the engorged freckled dong deep inside, now, slow at first but deliberately slow, sea-cucumber slow, in the deep cold is what they have down there, holes in the bottom of the ocean where everything is eyeless, groping but sentient, and phosphorescent, and just as if they were not in the mall, as if the blow-out sale were not in progress, as if you couldn't buy one, get the second pair half price, as if Steve would not be in here any second to get a load of shoes, slowly and at the same time, warp speed, she is kissing his white eyelids.

Marty, like some kind of expert, knowing exactly what to grind against, attentive to the tenderness of dumb lips, inner cling and grab and slippery ripple, and the shelving unit digging into her spine but never mind, let Steve barge in, and the shoebox with the patent-leather slingbacks shoots out another whole inch here, two inches, another half inch, and the tempo picks up because she's coming, which doesn't always happen, let me tell you, the shoebox above their heads topples free and a seam opens then, a seam in the wall of tightly packed boxes opens up, a gaping, jiggling crevasse, unzippering, so that they begin to topple, each box losing its lid as it falls, spitting puffs of white tissue paper—pwah—and a New Balance running shoe, a stiletto, and a hiking boot toppling down while Cathy digs her nails into Marty, who she knows, or intuits, well, how could you miss it, is gay, really, and they are, yes, having sex in the storage closet, and she is having, yes, a second orgasm, and because she has it, seems to be falling in love with him, which can happen in the hepped-up exhaustion of working two jobs and going to school full-time especially with the added but uncompensated responsibility of the title manager, which will look good on a resume, but Fuck them, whoever they are, fuck them.

And the truth is, it is Cathy's experience that orgasms are hard to come by, multiple, come on, who has that, really, a myth, right? And two and one so fast on top of the other that the pleasure-ripples of the first one bash right into the pleasure-ripples of the second and what's this, My god, a third fucking orgasm, pounding home the second that's still riding on the back of the first, so who cares if he's gay. What is gay? What is anything?

In the midst of which: Steve. Just as Marty slumps against her, Steve steps into the storage closet, boxes tumbling, shoes birthed from tissue cocoons, a corner of a cardboard lid hitting the top of her head, hurting, actually, a surprising amount, before wafting to the floor, and Steve blocking the door of the storage closet, standing there, unable to understand what he's seeing, and therefore not moving out of the way.

What was this?

And it's completely different from sea cucumbers, which are, if you put your hand in the aquarium that is fed by the actual sea and pick one up, leathery with the mouth at one end surrounded by tentacles, but clammy and cold.

He'd paid with his grandmother's credit card and it arrived and though he said don't try it until I'm there, after he left she got in and put the thing on bust though he'd asked her to wait for him to visit and whatever happened, some kind of stroke they said, and when he went over, because he went over every day to walk the cockapoos, Minke and Killer, she was in that bloated bag with steam hissing like a goddamn dragon and her head tilted and the eyeglasses askew and Nanny, Nanny, because he loved her more than anything and wanted to please her and everything he did was for her, and he hacked through the bag and Holy shit it was hot and the zipper, crying and pulling at the vinyl around the neck and CPR and the dogs licking her face, but you know he just had to accept, leaning back on his heels, wringing his hands.

And here he is at work, trembling against the Saucony display unit because what was he supposed to do, not go to work? He had nowhere to go, and he just followed her into the storage room, he did, and turned her around and leaned her against the shoeboxes and he had kissed the very full lips of his twenty-four-year-old co-worker/manager whom he out-and-out told he wasn't into women kissing him and stuff. And then full-on fucking, like nobody's business.

And Steve standing there had a religious visitation: the inlay, heat-sensing impression of her nipple and the Kinky Boots tickets, roaring at the helicopter overhead, waving the sun struck amber bottle and the fish, boxes tumbling.

There she is on her knees getting the crying child to run her own fingers over the thick, living pelt of negative ions that coats them all and to shoo it away. Shoo. Shoe.

Fuck it, Steve/Aiden says to the junior-high ukulele teacher he is about to ring in and thereby secure the record of highest commission in the Shoe Emporium for the 2016–2017 fiscal year.

Don't buy those running shoes, he says.

Excuse me? she says. And he leaves her at the counter and approaches the mother of the prostrate seven-year-old who wants the shoes with the red lights in the sole, who is still screaming and now down on her stomach hammering her fists and kicking out, and whose mother is grabbing her by one elbow to try to lift/drag her out of the mall.

I'll buy her the goddamn shoes, Steve/Aiden says.

What?

Fucking right I will, he says. Right out of my paycheque.

But you realize I win then, Cathy says. The trip to Toronto and the tickets to the musical.

The child, still trembling, has gone still. She stands, straightening what she can of her snowsuit, and retrieves the giant lollipop abandoned on the vinyl bench in the centre of the store. It's dyed red and white, and the colours spiral toward the centre of the saucer-sized candy like op art.

It looks like a storm or an evil eye and it's gleaming with saliva and has been licked all over.

Cathy: You'd do that?

I'd do that. You're the goddamn manager, says Steve. You deserve it.

Cathy is still on her knees and the little girl approaches. She touches the lollipop down then, against Cathy's hair, like a sceptre, anointing her.

SHIMMER

ALEX PUGSLEY

I t's the biggest Deedee party ever. Walking up to the house, Sheri and Celeste can't believe how many people they don't know. Some people they recognize, like the stoner kids who hang around the school parking lot, and those jocky guys, and the girls doing cartwheels in the snow Celeste remembers from gymnastics. But those guys by the cars—aren't those the guys from *shop*? And is that like a basketball team from a whole other high school? And these punk-rock guys with green hair staring at them—whose friends are they? Look at them, unloading guitars and stuff from a van, what school are they from? How does Deedee even *know* them?

I can't breathe, says Celeste, shivering. There's too many people.

Can you believe this? Sheri says. There's like two hundred people here already. I hope Deedee's parents really went to Florida.

Fuck. My mom wants me home by eleven tonight.

Like that'll happen.

Maybe I won't go home tonight, says Celeste. Maybe I'll just kill myself first.

I hate that joke.

I'm serious.

Yeah well who isn't, Celeste?

I'll probably commit suicide around midnight. In case you can't find me.

Then can I keep your black sweater?

No, I want it back.

Too bad. You'll be dead.

You have to give it back to my mother and make sure you wash it so it doesn't smell like cigarettes.

As if your mom doesn't know you smoke, says Sheri. Fuck. Some people actually *do* commit suicide, Celeste, you freak.

Inside, it's more crowded. In the basement, Sheri and Celeste walk by some people doing hot knives with a blowtorch. There's kids smoking dope in the furnace room. Upstairs in the kitchen there's twenty cases of beer. Everyone's drinking beer. Want a beer? Celeste takes a beer from a guy she knows, Donny, he has a car, how old's he? Like nineteen. She pushes her thumb against the curve of the bottle but she doesn't feel like drinking. Who are all those people in the backyard? Through the kitchen window, Celeste sees thirty more people she doesn't know. The backyard goes right into the woods and it seems like people fade away into trees like they're at a bonfire. This is so crazy. Fuck, though. What should she do? It's the biggest party of the year and already she's feeling anti-social and not that drunk anymore. She sips the beer. It tastes weird. She doesn't really feel like drinking. Oh great she's going to be the only person to have a shitty time at the biggest party of the year.

You all right? Sheri asks, unzipping her parka.

Yeah it's just freaking me out how many people I don't know.

What a weird night, says Sheri. It was cold and now it's muggy.

Sheri! Celeste grabs her.

What?

I told you not to say that word.

What word—muggy? Why?

It's like when people say nuggets. My mother says it all the time. It's disgusting. It makes me feel like I'm throwing up in my head.

Muggy nuggets, says Sheri. Muggy nuggets.

I'm serious, says Celeste, swatting at Sheri's beer. Fuck off. I won't be your friend anymore. You'll never borrow my clothes again.

What're you doing? Sheri slaps at Celeste's hand. That's my beer! Steal my grave that fast?

The front door opens and two people in ski jackets come in.

My God, says Sheri. It's Owen and Rowan.

The student *council's* here?

Owen and Rowan, says Sheri. Rowan and Owen. Everybody's favourite fucking couple. I'm so sick of hearing about Owen and Rowan. Who cares anyway? Why should we cow-tail to them?

Celeste lights a cigarette and gazes at them. How long they been going out?

Five years, says Sheri. Since grade six. Think they'll get married?

Celeste blows a smoke ring. I hope their baby's retarded.

She's so fake, says Sheri, frowning. I can't think of a prissier, faker, more stuck-up person. I'm glad she's short.

You should see her mother, says Celeste. She's like four-foot-nothing. She's a total midget. She's a shrimp.

Who's she talking to?

Celeste recognizes the other girl. She was one of the girls doing cartwheels outside in the snow. That's that bitch Angela Silver.

Who is she? Why does she have blue hair?

She's that stupid little jerk that got me kicked out of gymnastics.

How old is she?

Grade nine.

Didn't you used to hang around her all the time?

When I was in elementary.

How'd she get you kicked out of gymnastics?

I missed three practices and said I was sick and she told them I was lying. But Celeste looks down, remembering something else, something someone said Angela said—that when Celeste got tits she became some big slut and stopped being everyone's friend.

Yeah meanwhile Angela Silver's probably a virgin with all her teeny-bopper friends still playing dress-up and tea-party in the attic and they're how old? Fourteen, fifteen? And now she's dressing like a punk rocker? Give me a break Angela Silver's a punk rocker. Excuse me while I barf she's a punk rocker. That's pathetic.

She's looking a little skanky tonight, Sheri says, noticing the girl's blue hair, black nail polish, the safety pins in her jeans. Whatever. I'm going to go find Deedee.

Sheri starts up the stairs then comes back to grab her beer. And try not to be too much of a klepto, okay, Celeste? You big freak.

Celeste locks herself in an empty bathroom and looks at herself in the mirror. She doesn't look that drunk. She takes a breath, pulls at her bangs, checks her eye shadow, then turns to see what her ass looks like in these jeans. She undoes a blouse button. The best tits in grade eleven, that's what Robby Delano said. And those other guys said she and Alison Andrews were the hottest girls in school. So with all these people here, there must be *some* cute guy she can flirt with. She should just turn on her fake personality and mingle and see how many guys she can get to like her. That used to be fun. Just the moment before, wondering if she can get them to make out with her, she loved that. That used to be everything.

Someone's knocking on the door.

Just a minute. Fuck! Celeste opens the mirror and looks in the medicine cabinet. Little bottles of Valium and aspirin, Handi-Wipes, a yellow hair elastic, Q-tips, a vacation photograph. Celeste snatches it. It's a photo of Deedee in front of the Grand Canyon. She remembers when Deedee came back from there. The most unbelievable place you ever saw, Deedee said. She couldn't even describe it. No one could explain it till they were there in person. All this nature. Looking at the photograph, Celeste wonders if she'll ever see it before she dies.

Someone knocks again.

Okay, okay, says Celeste. She grabs the Valiums and the aspirins from the medicine cabinet and stuffs them in the front pocket of her jeans. Opening the door, she sees one of the punk-rock guys, the guy with green hair. Is he ever tall—who is this guy? He kind of blushes and goes by so she smiles but it's too late, he's gone.

In the hall Sheri's talking with a bunch of people. There's some grade nine kid, somebody's lurpy little brother— that's Darren Myer's little brother—and some girl hanging off Sheri, barely standing up, she doesn't even know where she is. Fuck, it's Angela Silver.

Celeste walks over. What's going on? What are you doing with her?

Sheri shoves Darren Myer's little brother. Get the fuck away from her, you horndog asshole! Can't you see she's intoxicated? Can't you see she's practically passed out?

What'd she drink? Celeste looks at Angela Silver.

That guy made her drink it.

What was it?

I don't know. Sheri grabs a bottle off the carpet and reads the label. Bacardi. She chugged it. She chugged a pint of Bacardi.

Sheri and Celeste help Angela Silver downstairs to a bedroom and lay her on a bed. Celeste is taking off the girl's sneakers when Angela Silver lurches forward and throws up.

Fuck! Celeste jerks back. She puked on me!

Sheri finds two towels and a facecloth in the laundry room. She puts the towels over the puke then sits on the bed and wipes Angela Silver's mouth with the facecloth.

How you doing, Puke Face? You all right? Sheri looks up at Celeste. She should probably eat some bread or something.

Why? Standing beside the bed, Celeste checks her shirt for puke stains.

And someone should probably call her mother.

And what, Sheri—get the party shut down?

She might have to get her stomach pumped, all right? She could die from alcohol poisoning, you know, Celeste. And we'd be responsible.

Like I'm going to go to jail over a fourteen-year-old.

Remember Crystal-Anne Hobday? asks Sheri. She almost died in a snow bank. Think about it. She passed out in a snow bank after she had sexual intercourse with her own father! You think everything's a joke Celeste, but it's not funny.

Sheri gets up, leaving the facecloth hanging from Angela Silver's nose. I'm going to find Deedee, she says, running up the stairs.

Celeste watches Angela Silver cough a few times. Hey Puke Face, how you doing? You going to puke again?

But Angela Silver is hardly conscious. She lies on her side, her eyes slow, her skin pale. There's puke on her shirt, one sneaker off, one sneaker lost. Celeste sits beside her on the bed. She smooths Angela Silver's blue hair away from her face and studies Angela Silver's jeans. The seams have been torn out and pulled skin-tight with safety pins. Written on the faded denim in red ballpoint pen are names of bands Celeste doesn't know. She finds a Keds sneaker with black-and-white checkers drawn on it with black marker. Inside is a wrinkled pink sock. Celeste squints at it. Seeing the pink sock makes her remember something she doesn't want to remember. It makes her feel sick in her head like when Sheri said muggy. She's thinking about that when Angela Silver starts patting Celeste's knee with her fingers. What the fuck? Celeste stands up, disgusted. Jesus. She spits a mouthful of beer on Angela Silver. Go fuck your mother, punker, she says, leaving Angela Silver alone in the bed, burping, murmuring, not knowing where she is.

In the backyard the sky's clear all the clouds are gone it's cold again what a weird night—it keeps changing—and Celeste finds Veeper staring at the stars.

Quite the bed-head there, Veeper, she says. What're you looking at?

Meteor shower, says Veeper. Always at the end of February. Because the earth passes through an asteroid belt. Probably one of the asteroids will crash down here just like the one in Siberia that wiped out all the dinosaurs.

God is he stoned. She's never seen him this stoned. Hey, says Celeste, pulling on Veeper's sleeve. Where's Wendell?

Fuck knows. But don't quote me on that.

It's me—Celeste—over here.

Veeper doesn't say anything for a second. Hey Celeste over there, he says, looking at her now. His hair's kind of greasy so he's not as cute as he is normally but his eyes are smiling. Celeste loves Veeper. She doesn't really know what he thinks about—his mind is so everywhere and embarrassed—that's why he's shy with girls. She remembers back in elementary when he had really long hair like a girl she used to follow him around when she was so bored she'd do anything she'd love to blow his mind one day and fuck his brains out.

How many T-shirts you wearing tonight, Veep?

Three.

Only three? What's wrong? Aren't you the guy that wears four shirts to school?

He pulls at a shirt. That was the old Veeper, he says. I'm the new Veeper now. But don't quote me on that. He looks again at the sky. In physics we learned the light from those stars left when the Cro-Magnons were inventing ketchup.

I'm so behind in physics it's not funny, Celeste says. I don't have a clue.

But he's hardly listening to her. She can never say the right thing around him. Maybe he doesn't like her. Everybody's smart now. Oh well.

Yeah, Veeper you're definitely on your own wavelength tonight, dude. What're you on?

This hash from Eddie Fong. I'm so fucking wasted. Veeper starts giggling and looks at his boots. Here we go, he says, taking a step. Walking in the snow. Walking in the snow. He closes his eyes. I'm so fucking wasted.

There you are, Sheri says. What're you doing out here?

Hiding, says Celeste. Talking about dinosaurs.

What'd you say to Veeper?

Secret boy talk. Later we're going to a mystery land of pink forests and purple rocks and green water.

Celeste! You're being weird again. I need you to be normal.

Why? Nothing ever happens, and if it does it's going to happen to somebody else anyway so who cares?

Your boyfriend's here.

Fuck off—he is not! Celeste looks inside the windows of the house. She doesn't want to see her boyfriend. She doesn't want to deal with him and already she feels herself hating him. He's just so urgently gross, she says. I'm sorry but I'm going to fucking vomit if I ever see him again. She leans over and spits in the snow.

Sheri is staring at Celeste as if she's crazy. Are you all right?

Yeah.

Then stop being such a freak, okay? You've been in a weird mood ever since we left my house.

Okay, Mom. Okay.

You want this beer? says Sheri. I can't finish it.

Celeste takes the beer and drinks from it.

You want me to go talk to him? Sheri says.

Why didn't he call me to say he's coming out tonight?

I don't know, says Sheri. He's *your* boyfriend.

Celeste sighs, frustrated. God he's boring. He's the most boringest guy. Okay go talk to him. Tell him I want to break up.

Sheri is staring at her. Again? But you've only been back together a week!

Far in the woods, Celeste runs away from the party. It's steep uphill past the backyard maybe rocks sticking up she has to be careful oh fuck so what if she cuts her jeans or a branch scratches her eye out or she falls and smashes her head on a stone. She runs faster, and in her hand she has a forty-ouncer of Bombay Sapphire gin she stole from the freezer in the basement. Celeste watches her breath rise up in the cold air and into outer space and all the meteors. Finally she can breathe again just finally she can breathe, and she takes the top off the gin and brings the bottle to her mouth. God she loves the smell of gin in winter like perfume in air she just loves the Jesus smell of it. Gin smells so beautiful because it smells like there's always more of it. And finally when she drinks she knows she doesn't have to be in the world anymore because she can just be in some weird cartoon land where everything goes and nothing's boring. She puts the bottle to her lips and swigs it to the sky. Air bubbles up. Remember the first time she got drunk? At the parish dance, she split a jar of moose piss with Cathy Charles except Cathy didn't show up and Celeste drank all of it. Inside the gym she got so hot she had to go outside and barf. When the paddy wagon caught her she was directing traffic in the middle of the street. Is this your daughter? the police officer asked when he got her home. You little ten-dollar slut, her mother said. Thanks, Mom. Takes one to know one. Her own mother said that and now she remembers what she didn't want to remember before and wouldn't let herself remember before but it gets remembered anyway, like a car flashing down the street the wrong way. She remembers when she was a little kid and her mother stayed out all night the first time. Remember that? Her mother coming home at seven in the morning. Celeste watching Saturday morning cartoons and playing with her Polly Pocket when she finds her mom's panties in a shoe in the front porch, wrinkly pink panties with white elastic. Why would her Mom leave her panties in her shoe? Where was she that she was taking off her fucking panties? Celeste chugs from the gin bottle. It's quiet. The smell of skunk somewhere. She lets fresh darkness seep into the trees and feels for the pills in her jeans pocket. She could really do it this time. So what who cares whatever fuck off. Her body found the next day frozen in a snowbank like Crystal-Anne Hobday. Why is she always thinking this stuff? But it's so easy. How could you *not* think it? Why wouldn't you want it all over and done? She takes out the pills and empties them into her hand. When it's like this, when the feeling gets inside her head like this, it's like keeping her finger over a candle or slicing her thumb with a pocket knife, the slit of her skin like a mouth with no eyes. Fuck, why is she *thinking* this? She doesn't even know if she's thinking it. How can she tell if she's thinking it? It's dominizing her thoughts. Dominizing? Is that a word? Celeste laughs, loud, drunk again, thank God, and knows she has to pee. She stuffs the pills in her pocket, pulls down her jeans and underwear, and squats down, her pee whizzing and steaming in the cold pine needles, into the ground, like when she peed in the middle of the street at some slumber party. Celeste remembers watching her own pee stream down the pavement and gather in a puddle at the bottom of the street. Someone dared her to do it. Angela Silver or somebody. When was that? Summer of grade six. Playing hide-and-seek with Angela Silver and her friends. God, that was fun, all those rich kids in that nice neighborhood, hiding under the train bridge, making up songs, eating that gum, what was that peppermint gum, the gum with the liquid center? You can't get that anymore, Freshen-up gum, she remembers when a snowball explodes against a tree.

Who's that? Celeste stands and pulls up her clothes, her underwear twisting in her jeans. Who the fuck is that?

She hears a kid running in the woods.

Fuck off you little maggot, she says, striding away, untwisting her underwear and fastening her jeans. She doesn't notice when the pills, the pills she stole from the bathroom, spill from her pocket and disappear in the grey of a snowdrift.

Celeste sits drunk outside with the stoners, cross-legged by the woodpile, burning a hole through a leaf with a cigarette. But it's so cold her fingers are numb and she can't make the hole perfect. Three of the stoners throw matches at each other and they fizz and bounce on the frozen snow beside her. A match flames by her head, pffts, goes out.

Fuck off you little pyros, Celeste says. You could have blinded me! Do that again and I'll smack you, douchebag.

Go douche yourself, a kid says.

And I find out who the little dinkweed was that threw the snowball at me, you're dead. I mean if you're going to throw something at me, at least do it to my face.

Inside the house someone starts playing an electric guitar. Everyone looks up. Celeste watches the punk rockers jump up and down in the living room. That tall guy with green hair is screaming into a microphone, green bangs caught in his eyelashes. It makes Celeste want to go in there and flip them out of his eyes. Another guy gets pushed into a drum kit. So why is everyone into punk rock now? Like skater kids and flumpy girls in drama, okay, but normal people like Angela Silver? And don't punks hate everything? Why are they so mad? They're mad at stuff they do anyway, like posing and being pretentious. It doesn't make sense. Why do they get to be so mad?

Sheri stumbles by with somebody—she's got her arm around somebody—it's that lurpy little guy, Darren Myer's little brother. Oh my God Sheri's getting together with a grade nine?

Celeste grabs Sheri's foot. Hey, Sheri, you freak. How you doing? You all right?

Fuck you scared me! Where were you?

Doesn't matter.

What were you doing?

Something else that doesn't matter.

Sheri turns to Darren Myer's little brother. This is my friend, Muggy.

Hi, Muggy.

Hey.

So Celeste, what time's it? What time you staying till?

I'm going soon. It's like one-thirty.

You're going? You need to stay at my house?

Celeste looks at Darren Myer's little brother and smiles at Sheri. Don't worry about it, she says. I'll just act normal and go home. It's okay. I'm probably not that drunk. Did you talk to my dumb boyfriend? What'd he say?

Sheri wipes some hair off her face. He thinks you hate him. He thinks you hate him so he's being like "Oh she hates me so I don't like her first" type thing. I said Celeste doesn't hate you.

It's such a fucking diddly-bop thing. Did you tell him I want to break up?

No. Because I know you don't mean it. But Celeste he's going to try and get everyone against you, I can tell.

I don't care. Let him go play his fucked-up little games. He's got mental problems. Trying to make it so complicated. It's not complicated. It's obvious. *He's* obvious. Fuck. Celeste stands up. I'm going.

Wait for us, says Sheri. I'm just going to say goodbye to Deedee.

For a second, Celeste watches Sheri walk off with Darren Myer's little brother. Behind her in the woodpile there's a bug, a silver fish, frozen in a crack.

From the backyard, Celeste walks between the houses toward the street. This is obviously the worst night of anyone's life so she'll just walk home like a loser. Who cares at this point? Maybe she'll break up with her boyfriend for real this time. She can get another boyfriend and tell the old one to fuck off but it won't matter. Nothing really ever happens. She makes herself take a big breath because she feels like she's about to cry. She feels like she's about to cry for no reason so she looks up at the sky, watching for the glow of the meteor shower, wondering if Veeper's still here. Veeper at least listens to people. What did he say? Here we go, walking in the snow. God that was cute. Just the way he said it. Like a little kid. Celeste clears a tear from her eyelid and between the houses a bird swoops past, a sparrow or swallow and then she remembers the word starling. She's remembering the word starling when she hears someone in the snow crunching behind her and turns to see that guy, the guy with green hair, the punk rock guy, looking at her, so she says, You got a staring problem?

Sorry.

Oh, she says. I thought you were somebody else.

Are you Celeste Tate?

Are you a police officer?

Huh? No.

Then yes I am. She smiles and he sort of blushes again. He's nice. This guy is actually nice. You can tell.

I was pretty sure it was you, he says. Because I saw you at a dance once with your friends. You were in a black sweater. I know it sounds stupid, but I always knew I'd see you again.

Doesn't sound stupid. What's your name?

Josh.

So you just decided to come out and say hi? Are you in that band? You don't exactly look like a punk rocker. Except your hair.

No. Those guys just borrowed my amp. I just sang one song. I'm in another thing. Look, I didn't mean to bother you. If you're meeting your friends or something.

You didn't bother me, says Celeste, walking up to him. Hey look. She points at the window on the side of the house. My reflection in the window's talking to you.

He turns to see her reflection in the window.

Now she's smiling. Now she's laughing. Now she's gone. What's your name again?

It's still Josh.

You hear about the meteor shower?

Yeah. He looks into the sky. I haven't seen it yet.

Yeah. I should probably stay up and watch it. But I only got four hours sleep last night. I went to sleep at five and got up at nine. She yawns and lets her hair fall across her eyelashes, looking at him, one of her eyes moist, her lips open.

I know you're probably going, he says, glancing at her. But I just wanted to say I think you're really great.

Celeste doesn't say anything. She puts her hand on the back of his neck and pulls him close to kiss him. He kisses her back, his teeth bumping hers so she makes her mouth soft, matching her lips to his mouth. One of her hands moves to his waist. But what's he doing? She moves her head to one side.

What're you doing? Are you holding your breath?

I don't know where to breathe, he says.

You can breathe in your nose, she says, putting a hand on his cheek. Or breathe me. She kisses him again. Yeah. Just breathe me, she says. Breathe me.

CURRENTS

BEVERLEY SHAW

THE STAFF at the hotel had noticed the three travellers. The deck where the woman ate breakfast every morning looked out over the sea. She arrived before the men and sat with her back to the view, sunhat shading her face and a glossy magazine or paperback by her coffee cup. Fred, the head waiter, said she had a Catherine Deneuve-like elegance, but the younger staff didn't get the reference. Fred often cut dead the straight male staff who tripped over each other to serve her. She always had a croissant and coffee and walked down to the beach afterwards.

There was speculation about who the woman was with. She seemed slightly old for the younger man and too young and attractive for the older one—the beefy, hairy, fifty-something guy who appeared to be footing the bill. The younger dining-room staff thought he was her father, but others said they had seen stranger pairings. Maybe it was a threesome, otherwise why one suite instead of two or three separate rooms?

If the men made it down to breakfast at all, they did the full buffet deal—bacon, eggs, sausages, fruit—and lingered to read separate parts of the paper, argue about baseball and movies, and lean against the railing to smoke. Once, Fred heard a snippet of conversation that piqued his curiosity: "Let me talk to her about the separation," the older man said, while the younger guy flicked ash over the side of the railing.

The older guy was the one who registered, and had put his address down as New York City. Most of the guests this time of year tended to be either German or American. They were booked in for two weeks, which was rare, even at the height of summer. No matter how scenic the view or how friendly the weather, this little resort was usually a stop on the way to somewhere else. The three travellers went out in the afternoons and came back to the hotel late most nights, but not *too* late—usually before midnight. The woman never held either of the men's hands or took their arms, but they all three walked with intimate ease, bending their heads towards each other in murmured conversation. One day, while returning to their suite, she dropped her scarf, and Fred moved in quickly to retrieve it for her. As she turned to take it from him, smiling, she said to her companions behind her back: "Think I'll take a walk before turning in. See you in fifteen minutes or so." Her eyes were fixed on Fred as she spoke, but he admitted reluctantly to himself that she didn't seem to be really looking at him.

"Watch yourself Sophie, wouldn't want to get lost in those dangerous Nova Scotia streets," said the younger of the two men.

"No, wouldn't want to do that." She headed back towards the door. The younger man shrugged, and followed the older guy towards the elevator. Fred filed the name "Sophie" away in his memory.

Fred lived in the nearby city, in a tiny but neat bachelor apartment. His car, too, was impeccably clean inside, with a tiny wooden cross hanging from the rear-view mirror, and a spray bottle of orange oil sitting under the dash.

As Fred drove, he inhaled and exhaled deeply, savouring the feel of the sea air moving through his nostrils and over his throat. Every time he returned to his quiet apartment, tips and/or pay cheque in hand, he appreciated the simplicity of his life: no more joint business ventures sucking his world dry of everything but work and financial anxiety, no more café and art gallery, just the clean exchange of a job well done for rent and food money, his car payment, and the occasional indulgence in an evening out or a bottle of wine. To avoid harassing phone calls from his ex, Fred had gotten rid of his cell phone and had an unlisted landline. Jamie's outbursts of rage followed by threats of suicide would make you think it had been Fred, not Jamie, who'd screwed around all those years.

If Fred couldn't sleep when he got home after work, he'd pour himself a glass of wine and watch the movie channel or Netflix late into the night. Fred liked to search out foreign TV shows and independent films. When he liked a film he would look up the director and writer on IMDB, search out their other works, and get to know their history and the history of the actors they worked with.

When Fred first saw Sophie's profile flash by in a movie trailer, he thought it was just someone who looked like her, but when she turned her face to the camera there could be no doubt. Her nose and mouth were distinctive; they gave her a slightly quirky look in contrast to the classic beauty of her cheekbones, blue eyes, and blond hair. He checked the credits, saw the name Sophie Langstrof, and, under the title of producer, Nathan Ackerman, the name the older guy had put in the register. He looked up the writer/director, Bill something or other, and was convinced this must be the identity of the pale, muted, thirtyish guy who smoked on the balcony while the other man talked.

Right then and there, Fred decided to say nothing to the rest of the staff —the horny little waiters and the gossipy chambermaids. He decided he would hold this secret close and savour its power to set him apart. It would give him a special relationship with the three travellers, even though he knew he wouldn't mention it to them either. Their time together here was probably a creative endeavor that transcended sex, despite the staff's constant speculation. Having extracted himself from his relationship with Jamie, Fred liked the idea of transcending sex.

He scrolled back to the beginning and watched the whole movie. It wasn't bad; a romantic comedy with some references to art and a token gay couple thrown into the mix. The gay couple were only incidental to the plot, but at least they were fairly normal people; neither flamboyant party animals nor spiritual sages. Sophie was the main character—cute, confused, coming out of a relationship that had stifled her for some reason or other. The film had been released two years ago, and was too quiet to attract much notice, which was probably why he hadn't heard of it. After turning off the TV, Fred drifted off on the couch, moving to bed when the sun started to feel its way through a crack in the grey curtains.

These days, Fred prided himself on his ability to sleep well and soundly, much better than in the old days. But occasionally he had disturbing, anxiety-filled dreams about animals, which changed from dream to dream: a snake one day, a bear the next, a cat the next. Tonight Fred dreamed that he was somewhere like a museum or a zoo, and that there were all kinds of birds behind glass. It was as though they were stuffed, but Fred knew otherwise, and slid the glass open, feeling a surge of satisfaction as they burst out in a beating of wings up into the sky. But then, to his horror, they started to fall apart, like rusty airplanes. A blue jay's tail lay spread like a peacock's fan in the grass, a grosbeak's wing nearby. Worst of all, a small sparrow, who seemed to catch a current of wind for a few feeble yards, fell to the ground as if dead, but then began moving in a spasmodic, maimed way. When Fred came closer, he saw a prickly, pine needle growth slowly covering it, obliterating feather, beak, and eye. He awoke from the dream sweaty and sick to his stomach, with a weight of anxiety that pulled him back to his time with Jamie. For some reason, his dream, or the feelings it evoked, brought back memories of holding Jamie's head over a toilet, flushing multiple substances down the drain, listening in silence to his tears and threats, his occasional apologies. Strange. He couldn't remember feeling anxious about that time in his life; he couldn't remember feeling anything at all.

The next morning, Fred was working a later shift than usual. For the past few days, he'd seen Sophie go for a walk punctually at nine and return an hour later, like clockwork, but when he arrived this time Sophie and the other two travellers were nowhere in sight and the dining room was already being cleared of breakfast dishes. A German couple argued quietly over a map and coffee, and a family from Maine were at the desk getting directions to the nearby theme park.

When Fred was setting the tables on the balcony for lunch, Nathan and Bill (he called them that in his head now) came out into the sun, Bill squinting slightly. Nathan asked Fred if he had seen "our friend, Sophie".

"No sir," Fred said in his best headwaiter voice. "I'm afraid I only just arrived. Perhaps the staff at the front desk?"

"Yeah, we asked them," said Bill. "She went out for her walk about two hours ago."

Fred kept his face blank and expressionless.

"She may have lost track of time. I'll let her know you're looking for her if I see her."

He secretly rejoiced that he'd be able to say something more than the usual "Good morning," or "Would you like coffee with that?" to her when she got back; found himself indulging in a brief and strangely adolescent fantasy about entering into a conversation with her about art or film, watching her face register surprise at his intelligence and good taste.

Fred had no idea why he was so fascinated with Sophie. The one thing he knew about himself was his absolute lack of sexual interest in women. He had tried it once with a girl when he was in college, just to be open-minded, to see where he might land on the bisexual scale. It had been a surreal and alienating experience, like trying to learn a technically complex dance to ambient music with no backbeat. It wasn't Sophie's beauty that attracted him, although he appreciated it. And it wasn't just what he had recently learned about her, or that he was drawn to the world the three travellers belonged to, a world he had only read about—screenplays, treatments, pitches, directors, producers. He'd been interested in Sophie from the time of her arrival, before he'd known she was an actor. It was the way she came to the table alone every morning, the way her manicured fingers handled her coffee cup and smoothed the pages of her magazine with care, the way she always walked slowly down the balcony steps to the beach and turned her face to the sun before walking towards the cliffs in the distance.

When, around lunchtime, he realized Sophie still hadn't turned up, Fred felt the first queasy beginnings of alarm. At the same time, he couldn't repress a voyeuristic surge of excitement. Was it possible there had been some kind of dispute? Had he detected a note of hostility on Bill's face when he had asked if Fred had seen her? Had she taken off just to teach the two men a lesson of some kind? As he stood looking out at the whitecaps, he debated asking the two men if she'd taken her bathing suit. Right away the excitement died. The sweaty, claustrophobic feeling from his nightmare that morning returned.

If he alerted the rest of the dining room staff to his fear, they would listen patiently, avoid rolling their eyes out of deference to his age and seniority. Sylvia, the desk manager, would take the reins, call 911, get together a search party. Locals would comb the beach, shout her name, the name he alone had discovered. She might turn up hours later after a peaceful walk or nap, and he would look a fool.

Sophie's companions didn't return to the dining room. Fred spent the lunch hour feeling a schism develop between his outer world—calm place settings, offers of wine and coffee—and inner world, which included catastrophic images of a sodden body washed up on the beach. The absent-mindedness with which he did his job was not pleasant. He hoped it didn't show. The smooth rhythm of his day was lost. He felt a growing anger towards the three travellers, and towards himself for becoming so interested in them. He felt a strange, unreasonable humiliation over his concern for Sophie. He felt a turning in his head, a rotation of pictures, thoughts, and potential words:

"Excuse me, I don't want to alarm anyone, but did your friend take her bathing suit on her walk?"

"Sylvia, do you think we should be concerned about this woman who seems to have gone AWOL on the beach?"

"Hello? Yes: I'm calling because I'm concerned about a guest who's been missing for a few hours."

It all sounded ridiculous, so much so that he resolved not to try any of it, but instead to take a walk on the beach during his break to clear his head. Chances were, he'd meet up with her on her way back, and exchange a word or two before she continued on her way. He told himself that this was what he was hoping, that this was what he wanted.

When Fred saw the neat pile of clothes and sandals on the shore, he experienced a moment of infinite stillness, while his heart beat in his ears. He had felt this once before, during a suicide scare with Jamie—the blood audibly pumping in his head, like the soundtrack of a movie. His first impulse was to turn and run back to the hotel. He needed other humans, a procedure, a plan. He needed to escape from this breathless, paralyzing solitude. Then he saw someone moving towards him from further down the shoreline.

At first, he couldn't be sure the woman who was walking towards him was Sophie. She was a long way off; a stick figure in the distance. When she got close enough for him to make out her features, relief exploded in his chest. He felt like crying. He felt like embracing her as a long-lost sister, lover, soul mate. Then he realized something was wrong. She was moving erratically, stumbling slightly, as though drunk.

He hurried forward, feeling his service-industry persona take over:

"Are you alright?" he asked.

"I think so," she said. "I did something really foolish. I went swimming alone and got pulled out by the undertow. I was tossed around by the waves for a while before I was able to swim free. I think I might have hurt myself, broken a rib maybe."

"You're not far from the hotel, Miss Langstrof," he said. "Can you walk the rest of the way?"

"Do we know each other?" she asked.

For one moment, he imagined telling her how he'd seen her movie and read about her on IMDB, and how much of a film buff he was. Then he realized she didn't recognize him from the hotel. She didn't know him at all. She just thought he was a stranger who happened to know her name.

"I'm on the staff at the hotel," he said gently. "My name is Fred. I usually serve you coffee in the morning."

"Right, of course. Sorry, I'm not thinking very clearly right now."

"That's not surprising," he said as he gathered her clothes and towel in one hand and put his other under her elbow. It seemed like the right thing to do in the circumstance.

"I actually thought I was going to drown," she said. "But then I remembered something I'd read in a safety manual somewhere—maybe when I was taking swimming lessons as a kid. Something about swimming parallel to the shore until you break free of the current. I guess you never know when these things will come in handy."

In her bedraggled and shaken state, the patina of glamour and sophistication had left her. She had a kind of awkward, brainy quality to her speech. She reminded him of one of his best friends in high school, a girl who was never at home in any social situation, but who played the piano like a professional. She might have gone on to do a music degree, he wasn't sure. He had lost touch with her, with a lot of people, after he had gotten together with Jamie.

"Your friends have been looking for you," he said. *Not very hard,* he thought, but maybe that wasn't fair. He hadn't been sure there was anything to be anxious about, either.

She said nothing. He wondered if she had even heard him. Then, after about ten yards of slow walking, she spoke:

"I could have come back sooner. The whole thing was probably over in a few minutes. But I sat for a while getting my breath back, and then I just didn't want to move."

"That's understandable," he said.

"I guess so," though she didn't sound so sure.

The anxiety in Fred's gut had let go, now that he knew Sophie was okay, and he walked beside her towards the hotel in slow, companionable silence until, suddenly, she stopped.

"This is not how I want it to be," she said.

"Sorry?" said Fred. Was she having some kind of emotional breakdown? He wondered if she was alright to walk the rest of the way, and was once more racked by indecision about what to do.

"When we get back, I'd like to book a single room for the rest of my stay please," she said, her voice sounding at once formal and childlike.

"Of course," he said, allowing his professional persona to take over. "That shouldn't be a problem. But perhaps the first thing to do would be to get you checked out by a doctor? There's a small clinic not far from here, although if you think you've broken something, you might need an x-ray, which would mean going into the city."

"I need to put my dress on," she said.

He handed her the dress, a loose, canary-yellow cotton shift that she pulled on from the bottom up to avoid lifting her arms. Still, she winced as she put her right arm through the armhole.

"Maybe you could take me to the clinic?" she said.

He was silent for a moment.

"I'd have to let them know at the hotel. I'm supposed to be working the afternoon shift."

"That's alright," she said. "I mean if you can spare the time."

Fred felt his indecision vanish. It was a slow day at the hotel. The thought of leaving work early for a good reason gave him a giddy sense of freedom.

"Tell you what," he said, "my car's parked in the lower parking lot. We can go there and you won't have to climb the steps. Then we'll drive to the front entrance and I can let them know. And you'll need to get some ID from your room if you're going to be seen by a doctor."

"Okay," she said.

When they arrived at the car park, Fred opened the passenger door for her then settled himself behind the wheel. The sun-drenched upholstery felt hot through his black trousers. They got out together at the front entrance and he took a moment to rehearse what he was going to say at the desk, while she headed down the corridor towards the suite she shared with the two men. He wondered what she was planning to say to them.

At the front desk, they accepted his gesture of good Samaritanism without question. He was normally so reliable that he figured this afternoon was long overdue. He went back to the car to wait for Sophie. When she came out, she was moving a bit more quickly than she had when she'd gone in. Though they drove to the clinic in almost complete silence, he felt freed from his shyness around her.

He noticed the summer foliage and the stately houses with their colourful gardens with the pleasure and openness of a child or tourist.

When was the last time he had been a tourist, worry-free? He couldn't count the trip to Bermuda with Jamie. There had been too much baggage, both literally and figuratively, too many times when he found himself second-guessing Jamie's motives for wanting to go out alone, too many times when he was awoken by Jamie's body slipping between the covers at unpredictable hours of the night. Too many times when he found himself watching Jamie's averted profile for signs of an impending crisis.

A few months after he and Jamie had first started dating, they'd gone skiing. When Jamie hurt his back, he'd done the same thing that he was doing for this woman now. He'd driven him to the hospital, sat patiently in the waiting room, filled his prescription. He'd often wondered if the painkillers from that ski accident had been what set Jamie off again. Jamie admitted soon after they met that he'd used cocaine in the past, but said he was clean now, and Fred had believed him. Who knew for sure, though. Maybe he'd always been subconsciously looking for an opportunity to start again.

"This is beautiful," said Sophie, lightly touching the cross that hung from his rear-view mirror. "Did someone give it to you?"

"My parents, after I was confirmed. When I moved a couple of years ago I found it in a box of stuff I hadn't opened since I left for college. It's not something I'd wear, but I like it hung here. Reminds me of my childhood I guess."

"Are you Catholic?"

"No, far from it. I grew up in one of those forward-thinking Protestant denominations that Catholics despise.

They performed gay marriages before any other church did. Saw Jesus as a radical social reformer and emphasized the "Judge not and thou shalt not be judged" part of scripture."

"Lucky you," she said.

Jamie, who'd been raised in, and escaped from, a small Baptist community, had scoffed at Fred's religious background, calling Fred's hometown congregation a bunch of politically correct "wolves in sheep's clothing." He hadn't seen the irony in his choice of a biblical metaphor. Some things you couldn't escape from, no matter how hard you tried.

Fred surprised himself by praying the night Jamie almost died. He prayed now on occasion, even though the content of his prayers was gradually starting to change. For months after he left, he prayed for Jamie's recovery. For a while Fred's prayers had included the possibility of reconciliation, but not anymore. He told himself leaving Jamie was both a personal survival tactic and altruistic, not the premeditated, easy desertion Jamie had accused him of. Fred had done his share of reading about co-dependence and enabling.

They had arrived at the clinic parking lot.

The waiting room was the same as the one at the city hospital after Jamie's suicide attempt, when Fred had felt numb exhaustion take the place of love. The same bolted-down furniture, the same hand-sanitizer dispensers on the wall, the copies of *Chatelaine* on the table.

It seemed a long wait, but Fred was content to drink a juice from the vending machine and stare out the window at the green summer day. When Sophie came out, she definitely seemed more are ease, although she told Fred that she might have a small fracture. She only needed to book an x-ray if there were complications, like more shortness of breath than she had now, or pain in a new place in her chest. She had been given a prescription for painkillers, which she filled out at the drug store downstairs. Her sophistication and poise had returned. But there was also something different about her, Fred thought; a slow, thoughtful quality. He supposed nearly drowning would be a sobering, life-changing event. He realized he no longer thought she looked like Catherine Deneuve. But he thought she was lovely anyway.

Afterwards, as she got back in the car, she turned and, for the first time, gave him a smile that was uncomplicated, friendly, and open, as though she saw him without the shadow of her own thoughts getting in the way.

"Thanks for helping me out, Fred," she said. "It's been quite a day."

"It certainly has," he said.

He had the bizarre sensation, briefly, that he was an actor in one of her movies and that this was an improvised scene on which they were collaborating. Still, he felt at ease in her presence, as though they were colleagues or creative allies, not too close, but comfortable with each other. He wondered why she told him on the beach that she wanted to book a separate room, but only briefly. He no longer wanted to know the details of her life, to take part in her world. He realized that, despite his interest in with her, he would probably never know her more than he knew her now. He would take her back to the hotel, work what was left of his shift. For the rest of her stay he would be slightly friendlier with her than with the average guest, because of this shared experience, his hand under her arm at the beach, their brief moments of quiet in the sunbaked car, the way she had touched the cross dangling from his rear-view mirror. Already he could feel himself retreating into his own life, and despite what had happened to her on the beach, despite the fact that she would soon be leaving for who knows where, while he would stay and keep working at his uncomplicated job, returning nightly to his comfortable apartment, his blessed solitude, despite all of this, he felt as though an ocean current were pulling him farther away from the shore, just as she found her footing on dry land.

NEXT OF KIN

ANNE MARIE TODKILL

I N OUR first house, the city house, there was a cold storage in the space under the front steps. This used to be the coal cellar; a hatch opened from the outside, revealing a chute through which deliveries for the old octopus furnace were poured. Not that I remember anything about it. And not that I could ever picture someone dumping coal into our house, or the fact that milk was still delivered on our street by horse wagon when my sister Ruth was very small. One day, she climbed up into the milkman's seat when he was at someone else's door, and the horse took this as a signal to advance. This would have been in the summer of 1952, two years before I was born. Ruth was barely three years old. My mother used to tell the story whenever she wanted to portray—well, I don't know what. The innocence of the past, maybe. Or its remoteness. Or Ruth's fearless will. She would act out the milkman's outrage as he ran down the street, leapt into the wagon, and came pelting back with a screaming toddler in his arms. "My goodness, he was *mad!*" She mimed his shouting, his indignation, his waving arms, as if she were re-enacting a scene from a silent movie. This used to be the defining anecdote, trotted out at social

gatherings, to sum Ruth up in the teasing way that families
have of summing one another up. *That was Ruthie for you,
my God what a handful.* I've realized only recently, thinking
how my mother used to tell it, that the wrong part of the
story impressed me when I was young. The part about it
being a bad idea to run away with a milk wagon. The part
about it being unwise to be like Ruth.

Ruth met me at the bus with her boyfriend. She had a terrific haircut, aggressively short. She recognized my suitcase
(it used to be hers) from the line of bags unloaded by the
driver and pointed it out to Russell, silently.

"What do you want to do when you're here?"

"Anything."

"I've got classes, you know."

"I know."

"I suppose it was Mom's idea."

"Not really."

"Do you get how messed up that is?"

"She didn't *send* me," I replied, mortified to be put on
the defensive so soon.

Russell, the cause of our mother's anguish, was already
ahead of us by a few paces with my suitcase.

Ruth called to him. "Are we going for lunch?"

"Wasn't that the plan?" he asked, turning around. He
shot a bright smile at me.

"That was the plan."

"Or do you want to go home first?"

"No, let's just go have lunch."

The unspoken phrase "and get it over with" floated like
an itchy veil around my overheated face.

"It's crazy how much you two look alike," Russell said,
leading the way to the car.

We sat on the patio. Russell ordered a carafe of the house white, without consultation. Ruth ignored the menu and asked about the specials. They were chummy with the waitress, who gave me a long look as she set the wine glasses down. I expected her to ask for ID, but that wasn't it. "God, do you two ever look alike. Imagine if you both had short hair."

"Imagine," said Ruth.

Russell poured the wine when it arrived and lifted his glass. "Welcome, Marian," he said.

"Contrarian," Ruth said.

"Ruth. Less."

"Been at this for years, I see," Russell said.

"Not lately," I said. "There was nowhere to go after Carrion."

"Nice."

I could tell I was impressing him, and this gave me the courage to turn to Ruth and say "So how is your work going?" At any other time I would have said "your courses" or "school," but now, aware that Russell was looking at me, I managed to produce the vague and important phrase *your work*, as if to signal that I knew she considered herself— having just finished third year, and already planning for grad school—not merely a student, but an *academic*, and through my awareness of that fact to include myself in her sophistication. The word felt in my mouth like sweet, chilled wine (incredible that I hadn't been carded), like the taste of the life that was suddenly spread out before me, all the cafés and smoky bars where one day I would meet with edgy friends to talk about *our work*. And at the same time I was thinking how surprising it was that Ruth, who had never in her life made an effort to charm anyone, had attracted this man, who was not only significantly older but disconcertingly gorgeous.

Ruth went straight for the slap-down. "Which *work* do you mean?"

Russell bailed me out, perhaps without realizing.

"She's just finished an amazing paper on Yourcenar."

"Oh," I said. "That's terrific."

He was looking at me intently. Was it obvious I'd never heard this name before? But no, it was the usual thing.

"I've got it now," he said to Ruth. "It's like she's a time-lapsed twin. Truly uncanny."

"Jesus," Ruth said.

And Russell smiled at me.

"Vera's got cancer," I said to Ruth.

"Oh. That's too bad."

"Who's Vera?" Russell said.

"A neighbour," I said.

"A crazy bird," Ruth said. Then: "What kind?"

"Stomach."

"Really. I'd have figured lung."

"She says she'll be fine. Vera the lion."

I felt guilty, invoking Vera's illness to decoy the conversation. As if sensing this, Russell moved on.

"So, what will you be writing about in your 'How I spent my summer holidays' theme?" He said this broadly, effusively, so there'd be no mistaking his irony, and leaned back in his chair, as if he would be pleased to indulge whatever performance I might come up with.

"She'll be writing the first chapter of her spy novel," Ruth said.

"Hey now," Russell said, and stroked her arm.

A tactical error, as I saw it. But Ruth ignored the gesture and kept her dark gaze on me. I leaned into the table, toward Russell. "I'm selling teacups to old ladies. At Ogilvy's—downtown, on Rideau Street."

"Tell me about that," Russell said. "Tell me about your old ladies."

"Here we go," said Ruth.

"They buy wedding gifts," I said to Russell. "They don't have much to spend, but they have to buy something. So they get a piece of Czechoslovakian crystal. A covered butter dish. Or a vase. They always ask if it's full lead crystal, and I point to the little blue sticker that says it is. And I hold the piece up to the light to show them the bubbles, which means it isn't perfect, it's handmade, so it's special. They know all that already, but they want me to know they're choosy. And then they dither about it. And I keep them happy by finding the piece that has the fewest bubbles, so it's almost perfect but you can still tell it's real. And I tap it with a pencil to make it ring. And then they start to dither about whether they should get a piece of china instead. But that's no good if the bride doesn't have a gift registry. So I check on that. And if there's no gift registry I give them my speech."

"Oh God," Ruth said, into her wine glass.

"Go on," Russell said. "Give us your speech."

I knew that if I glanced at Ruth even for second I would lose my nerve. So I kept looking straight at Russell and launched in. "Well, *Ma'am*," I said, "it's always nice to have a good piece of crystal to put on the table. It never goes out of style, and even if the bride thinks it's a little old-fashioned now she'll be glad she has it as the years go by. She'll get tired sooner or later of her china pattern, but she'll always keep the crystal, and it will always go with her dishes, whether she changes the pattern or not. One day she'll have her china cabinet with glass doors and she'll have her crystal on display. All the toasters and clocks and linens will wear out. But she'll always have the crystal that her aunt gave her. You can't go wrong with crystal."

"Amazing," Russell said, without lifting his eyes from my face.

"Bridal registries," Ruth said. "For fuck's sake."

When Vera Lyon entered a room, my father once said, sex came with her. My mother retorted that he could leave that kind of comment in the garage but, as far as I could see, it hit the nail. Sex swelled under Vera's bright polyester blouses, gaping at the bustline. It rounded out her pencil skirts, which she no longer had the figure for. It was implied by her blowsy hair, which always seemed to be falling out of a previous evening's up-do. Vera was raspy-voiced, loud, and always on the brink of an unsuitable remark. I used to find it odd that my mother overlooked these deficiencies. "She's had troubles in the past," she said once. "Disappointments."

"How do you know that?" I had asked.

"Some things show."

Whereas my mother was careful not to let things show. She was of that postwar brand of women who would be described at their retirement parties and funerals as ground breakers and, therefore, feminists—pushing ahead with careers in business, independent and apparently fearless. But she was as hard on other women and as unforgiving in her double standards as any man in her day. So it was strange that she never said anything critical about Vera. Perhaps this had to do with Vera's larger-than-life persona, which made her not like someone real, someone you might have a real affection for, a real opinion of, but a spectacle that you watched. Vera carried with her the air—the scent, really— of an alien life (there was always a waft of cigarettes, for one thing, and occasionally booze), suggesting, vaguely, an era now made distant and harmless by the permanence of our middle-class lives. The *outré* Vera Lyon—*But you can call me Vera Lynn, I don't mind, ha haha—We'll meet againnnnn, don't know where, don't know whennnnn*—would blow up against our side door and plaster herself to the screen like a sheet of soggy newspaper—*Liz, you home? Queen Lilibet! Halloo!*—and sit in the kitchen with my mother, making raucous confidences, presuming the rest of us to be out of earshot, which of course we contrived not to be.

"Vera Lynn," my father scoffed, at one point. "She's dreaming."

"Well, she's better-looking than Vera Lynn ever was," my mother said.

Before supper, Ruth and Russell worked in the kitchen like they'd been together for a million years. I offered to help; Russell handed me a bag of carrots and a knife. "Don't peel, just scrape." I complied, worrying about microbes. They discussed the herbs for the soup, passing the spoon back and forth. This made me feel dispirited. So did my ignorance of the world, which was pointed out to me by newspaper clippings posted on their fridge about Pollution Probe and DDT. They ate fish but not meat. One day soon, Ruth said, they were going to stop eating fish. Ruth launched into a description of our mother's culinary habits. Cooking the last drop of juice out of every chuck roast. Eating white bread. Taking the skin off everything. Scalding peaches and tomatoes in a bowl of boiling water so they could be peeled.

"But not nectarines," I said.

"Who would scald a nectarine?" Russell said.

"Who would scald a tomato?" I said. And Ruth and I said in unison, *Mother*. It was an odd little moment. It broke an unspoken rule of ours, which was never to criticize our mother at the same time, never to let our separate tinder-boxes of resentment spark together, never to let ourselves become, in that convergence of emotion, true allies.

And then Ruth said, "I think she hates food."

It was a mean comment, but it struck me just then as true. And I wondered why I'd never reflected on this fundamental fact before. I wondered what other basic points I'd been missing while I sat with Mom in the kitchen of our third-floor walk-up on Friday nights, after my evening shift, eating grocery-store baking while Ruth and this elegant stranger were scrubbing the dirt off their political carrots in his fine brick house with bay windows and old wood that had an arousing smell, like varnish and honey and lemons.

"Do you ever break things?" Russell asked me after supper, when we were sitting on the porch. Ruth was inside reading for a seminar.

"*Break* things?"

"In your china department."

"*Oh.* Yeah, every once in a while."

"I suppose they deduct it from your pay."

"Actually, no. They expect a certain amount of breakage."

"'A certain amount of breakage.' How resonant."

"It's resonant all right. The other day I was taking a glass serving bowl down from a display and somehow I knocked it against the edge of the shelf. It felt like just a tap, but the bowl went to smithereens. You wouldn't have believed the sound. The whole floor went quiet. Everyone stood there thinking 'I'm glad it wasn't me.'"

"Were you embarrassed?"

"More exhilarated, really." This was only very slightly true.

Ruth came out; the porch door swung shut behind her. "I bet you peed yourself," she said, sitting down.

Russell ignored this. "Why don't we go for a drive to-morrow? We could pop up to Westport. Say hi to Dan and Janice."

"I think I've had enough for now of Dan and Janice."

"So we'll take a drive to Westport and not see Dan and Janice."

"It's impossible to go to Westport and not see Dan and Janice. Dan and Janice are ubiquitous in Westport."

"Who are Dan and Janice?" I said.

"Janice is an old friend of mine. Dan's her husband. Ruth thinks he drinks too much."

"I think he *talks* too much. Whilst drunk."

"Ah, Ruthie," Russell said. There must have been some quarrel, I figured. Maybe some problem about whatever there used to be between Russell and Janice—since there could be no such thing in the known universe as a woman content to be merely Russell's friend. Ruth was staring, expressionless, into the feathery shadows of the twin ash trees that flanked the porch. Russell reached over in the dark and put his hand on her arm. "We'll think of something else to do. C'mon, Ruth, your sister's made this trip just to see you."

"She has made this trip because my mother is hoping that the demure face of Maid Marian will shame me into renouncing my life of sin." And she cracked a slight, worldly smile at him.

It was at rare moments that I saw, or thought I saw, my sister's face the way other people did, the face she wore, confidently, with friends, with professors (as Russell had been, first professor, then "friend"; our mother caught the whiff of danger the first time Ruth mentioned him); and I imagined that, to strangers, her face—intellectual, *garçonne,* unapologetic—would carry no overlay of family resemblance and so would be hers and hers alone, an original face sprung into being, ready-made, not as someone's daughter, sister, expectation, but belonging only to herself. There was more definition in her features than in mine. More maturity. "Your problem," she once said to me, "is you lack *tone*. You should exercise more." Whereas Ruth, thinner and finer-boned than me, always looked more snappy. A stranger might imagine her going home at Thanksgiving or Christmas to an urbane family, a sophisticated and well-connected bunch. Instead, she had me, our defeated, widowed mother, and a couch to sleep on if she wanted to go back to what was left of home.

Ruth had taken me upstairs to a spare room after we arrived. I dumped my bag on the bed and started to unpack. "I brought a dress, for some reason. I guess I should hang it up."

"You won't need a dress," Ruth said flatly, but she opened the tall wardrobe beside the bed and took out a hanger. I looked around. Everything in the room was antique. "You have some beautiful stuff," I said.

"It's Russell's. He's been collecting for years. Everything I had looked like it belonged in a dorm. I got rid of it."

"Got *rid* of it?" I protested. "Maybe I could have used it."

"At university, you mean? That's two years from now." She hesitated for a moment. "You'll probably have to stay in Ottawa, you know."

Perhaps she saw how this stung. "But anyway if you do go away you'll be in res in first year. After that you can pick up stuff for free; people leave furniture on the sidewalk when they move out. Although we had a yard sale, come to think of it. Russell off-loaded some stuff his wife left behind."

"Doesn't she mind?"

Ruth gave me a slow, warning look. "No. She doesn't mind. She doesn't *know*. She took off two years ago and Russell doesn't even know where she is."

"What do you mean, took off?"

"She left. Decamped. Vamoosed. Buggered off."

"There must have been some reason."

"Sure there was a reason. She's a head case."

"So how does Russell know she's okay?"

"She's never had trouble looking after herself."

"This is so weird."

"She's done this to him before." In her voice I heard, for the first and only time, her allegiance to Russell, her protectiveness, her tenderness. And in that moment, too, I could have become her ally; I could have sympathized; could have dissed the unseen, crazy wife I knew nothing about and would never meet; I could have made her feel less lonely (not that it occurred to me that my sister, in her magnificent transgression, was lonely), but instead I summoned our mother into the room. I did this by saying, "So what happens if his wife comes back?"

"She won't. But, if she ever did, Russell would tell her he's done."

"It's so weird."

"Christ, Mare, is that your message from her? 'It's so weird?'"

"I don't have a message from Mom."

"Bullshit. *You* are the message."

The truth was, I had been given an earful. As in, "I hope you don't do anything so foolish yourself one day" and "He must be some smooth talker" and "Ruth can't be the first to have fallen for that liar" and "I didn't send my daughter to university so she could ruin her life" and "Maybe you can talk some sense into her; she's never once listened to me." And there were ugly words, disloyal words, as if Ruth had merely confirmed Mom's doubts about her all along. If she can run off with the milk wagon at the age of three, it stands to reason that she'd be off with some milkman or other by the time she was twenty-one.

At the time, I don't think I could have explained why I took the bus to Kingston to visit my sister and her married lover. I guess I wanted to see what it looked like up close—I mean, making a mess of one's life and not giving a damn what anyone thought. And I think, in some screwed-up way, I wanted to claim status. To make it clear that I was not the fuck-up in the family.

What I didn't expect was for this thing with Russell to become a non-issue almost right away. I didn't expect things to seem so normal. I thought that, face to face with the real situation, I would feel shocked. Shocked enough to snap my sister out of it and bring her back into my small universe. To our mother's small universe.

Vera was sitting at the kitchen table with Mom the night I got back from Kingston.

"What happened to *you?*" she said, as soon as I came in the door.

"Vera, don't razz her, it always shows in her face when she's tired."

"Raccoon eyes," I said, rubbing them with the heel of my hands to mask the tears that sprang up with Vera's opening line. "I'm fine. It was good. I'm going to have a shower."

"Right, luvvy," Vera said. "I'm heading off now. I've just brought over my keys, for when I'm in hospital."

"Oh right. Sorry. When?"

"Wednesday. It's going to do wonders for my figure.

Here, let me give you a hug. Come and see me if you can. But not right away, I guess. I'll be at the Civic."

"Sure, sure," I said, and Vera called me a darling and tucked my hair behind my ears. "Go have your shower."

I sat in the bathtub, quietly sobbing, a warm rain pouring over me. I tried to plan what to tell my mother about Russell when her interrogation began: *Stop worrying about it. I'm sure he really loves Ruth. She's old enough to know what she's doing. He's a nice guy. His wife is nuts; that's why he can't divorce her. There's some complication. I didn't pry. You owe it to Ruth just to trust her on this.* Or maybe this: *If you want the real story you just need to ask her yourself. Ask her like you really want to know.*

While we were still in the house in Ottawa, and Ruth was in high school, our mother cooked up a scheme that we should all live in some pretty town in the country and that the way to do this was to be entrepreneurial. She'd get her real estate licence and sell cottage properties. Dad would quit his job as a mechanic and set up a shop of his own. That's what people in the country do, she said, they have their own businesses and they're resourceful and they build their lives the way they want to, from the ground up. *Yes, from the very ground up.* She leaned into that phrase in the self-congratulatory, theatrical way she used to have, as if she'd hit upon some brilliant insight that less interesting people would miss. And so for the next few years she kept dragging us all out on country drives, scouting for property. This was decades before the days of Internet listings, and so her method was based on maps and time-wasting hunches and impulsive detours down side roads. She kept a notebook of mechanics' shops between Kingston and Gananoque, Smiths Falls and Brockville. Once in a blue moon there'd be a place with a for sale sign. And that's how she found the place Dad was eventually persuaded to buy. A small acreage, with a small house, a small gas station and a small store, and a small mechanic's garage to one side. The land of small, Ruth called it. It fronted a secondary highway that anyone could have told us had been losing traffic for years. To the back was a septic field; beyond that, cedar woods; beyond that, a marsh. Across the road old fields sloped up to a low rise of hills. It was quietly pretty on that side. On our side, not at all. But this way, as Mom said, *we* had the nice view. The people we bought from lived across the road in a new bungalow, on a ten-acre severance from their own property. They'd given the rest to their son, who now lived in Oshawa but still took off two cuts of hay every year, they told us. The son wasn't interested in the store, the gas station, or the garage shop, so he sold them, and the land they were on, to us. They would show us the ropes until we knew what we were doing.

"We'll be living in a fish bowl," my father said. "They'll take offence if we change anything."

"Well, what do you know about running a country store?" my mother said. "We're lucky they're willing to help us."

It was a maddeningly circular argument. Ruth and I couldn't fathom the weakness, or the apathy, that let our father go along with it.

We took possession at the beginning of the summer of 1968. "It's perfect," Mom said. "You don't need summer jobs. We've got ourselves a *family business.*" I was the one who learned to run the store. Ruth pumped gas and cleaned windshields and checked oil and talked diffidently to boys and as little as possible to girls. She spent every moment between customers with her nose in a book. Mrs. Curran sat in the store with me for hours at a time, ostensibly to tell me where to find things when people asked for them, showing me how to work the cash and to fill out order lists and sales-tax returns. Most people who came in knew where things were already. Cheap dog food in a brand I'd never seen. Instant coffee. Cream. Barbecue starter. They'd say, Hi there Joan and look at me and nod and say to her I see you got yourself some help, I thought you and Frank were selling, and she'd say Well we have but somebody's got to help keep it all straight haven't they—which made me feel invisible and ashamed of my absentee mother, the unreasonable one, darting off to the city every morning to a real estate class and breezing back at some useless hour to make a lame attempt to help me with the inventory.

It was a starting point, our mother would say. A toehold. Once she got her business established we could buy a nicer acreage, a bigger house, a garage with a gas station on a better road. In another six months she'd have her licence and we'd be off to the races, she said. Off to the races. Cooking with gas, ha ha.

Ruth frequently burst into foul-mouthed rants when we were alone. "For fuck's sake. There's more real estate to sell in the fucking city. She's out of her fucking mind."

"But she wants to sell cottages and stuff," I would say, trying to appease her.

"Oh, give me a fucking break."

The only thing that held Ruth back from mutiny was the fact that she'd be starting university in September. This would leave me in grade nine at the regional high school with a bunch of kids who'd known one another since, as Ruth put it, before birth. There'd be no point in making friends; I was going to clear out, like Ruth, as soon as I could. Although sometimes I wondered. Dad told Ruth he'd fix up a 1961 Beetle he'd bought off a customer so she could commute back and forth from classes. Mom said that would certainly burn up time as well as gas. She should know, with her fucking commute to fucking Ottawa, Ruth said to me, but what she said to Mom's face was that the only reason she was pumping gas was to pay for residence. I kept my mouth shut, harbouring two thoughts I couldn't admit to anyone. The first, that I was jealous as hell that Ruth was offered a car of her own. The second, that it was gratifying to be in charge of an enterprise. So I put up with the musty odour of Mrs. Curran's cardigans and worked the till at the store, restocking candy bars, soup cans, ant traps, ticking everything off on the packing list when a shipment came in, making lists of damaged goods and short orders. Mrs. Curran sat on a vinyl-and-chrome chair behind the counter, not saying much and sucking her teeth as if she were testing her dentures or else mulling over some dark speculation about me. She always had an expression like she was looking at you from a distance, like you were from somewhere far off, somewhere strange. I used to invent scenes in which Vera would blow in and give her something to think about. The problem was that she and Mrs. Curran didn't belong to the same plot. There was no plausible event I could imagine that would put them in the same room together. They didn't belong to the same lifetime.

I tried to make myself feel better about my summer in purgatory by giving the store a scrub-down. I took bottles of Mr. Clean from the inventory, along with a pail and packages of J Cloths and some rubber gloves and went to town, shelf by shelf, washing every surface. I put iffy-looking packages and dented tins in cardboard boxes labelled "Free" near the door. Nobody ever took anything. They glanced down and pretended the discards weren't there and bought what they'd come in to buy. A week later, when my mother finally noticed the freebies, she started going on hysterically about how they amounted to a quarter of the grocery inventory. Mrs. Curran piped up and said as long as a can wasn't bulging it was fine and besides older stock was useful to make the shelves look full, you just had to keep it at the back where people didn't pick from, and Dad said nothing much could go wrong with a box of macaroni anyway, but Ruth said to me afterward that she sure as hell wouldn't want to eat anything from Mrs. Mothball's old tin cans. The next day she helped me put the stale-dated stuff in green plastic bags, also from the inventory, and we drove it to the township dump. Nobody asked about the inventory after that. I suppose my mother thought I'd put everything back in stock like Mrs. Curran said, and Mrs. Curran decided to stay out of it. And in the meantime Dad wasn't up to much. Something was off with him. He was complaining of migraines and my mother was saying it was the stress of the move. That forgiving tone alternated with frustrated rants, in which she complained that he had no initiative, that he'd never had the nerve to go out on a limb. To which, to my knowledge, he responded in anger only once. "You never considered the girls," he said. "Not with your whole heart. You have never considered the girls." He said this, shockingly, in front of all of us. I sometimes think that my father, a man who always went along to get along, would never have said this devastating thing, accusing her, apologizing to us, unless he had a sense of what was coming.

At any rate, he helped me with the mousetraps. My cleaning frenzy had turned up piles of mouse turds, stuck to mouse urine, in various mouse runways on the floor behind the dry-goods shelves. "Dad, I need to show you something," I had said, after Mrs. Curran had left for the day, and the look on my face brought him straight out of the garage and into the store. "What am I supposed to do about *this*?"

So we took every mousetrap we had out of inventory along with a jar of peanut butter and he showed me how to set the traps. "I'll check them every morning until the problem is solved," he said. "You don't have to look." But I did look, curious to see what destruction I had caused. After a while I didn't mind the look of their surprisingly clean white bellies when I released the stiff little corpses into a garbage pail. When I found one that was still alive I considered whether it would be better to hit it with some object, to get the suffering over with. But I worried that I might do this clumsily and have to strike more than once. Or that there'd be mouse guts, and then what would I do about that? So I left it alone to die. I left it to suffer for my crappy life. I was prepared to let everyone suffer in whatever trap they'd wound up in until I could see a way out of mine.

The next time someone came in looking for mousetraps I told them we were all out. Mrs. Curran rolled her tongue over her teeth and said we used to have a good stock of them and I said maybe so but they're all gone now. I used to think up Vera-isms for situations like that. *Make the cow a peanut butter sandwich,* she might have said. *Glue the old girl's dentures shut.* In fact, I knew Vera would never say anything so crude as that, so unkind, to anyone's face. But she'd let you indulge your worst thoughts in private, in therapeutic gossip sessions. It would have been a great luxury, having her around.

But we didn't see Vera until November, at Dad's funeral. He got up one morning complaining of a pain behind his eyes; at noon my mother found him dead on the garage floor. It was five months almost to the day after the move to the new place. Ruth was at university. Mom was working on her seller's licence and was still clinging to the idea of setting up a rural office. We had the funeral in Ottawa. My homeroom teacher drove a van load of students into the city for the wake. My mother and Ruth and I formed a little receiving line at a discreet distance from the coffin; the kids from my class shuffled past and shook our hands in turn and said *Sorry for your loss.* A couple of the girls were crying. This wasn't for me, I understood, but in response to whatever drama they were making up in their minds about what it would be like if it happened to them. But afterward a few made an honest effort to be friends. I made up excuses about having to work at the store and tried to think of something that would persuade Ruth to move back home. Especially since Queen Liz had no clue what to do next. Vera drove out to see us about a month after the funeral and sat beside Mom in the living room, patting her knee. "You can't stay out here on your own, Lilibet my dear. It's too much. You don't have anyone to run things. Sell the place, make a little profit, and get an apartment in Ottawa that you can manage. Once you get established with the real estate thing you can start over somewhere that takes your fancy. But it's too sad to stay here."

"I'm too tired," my mother said to Vera. "I'm too tired to think about this now." It took her four months to finally list the property, another four to close the deal. Vera's make-a-little-profit idea was a fantasy. People like my mother, people willing to buy a house with mice in the walls, a grocery store with stale goods and a garage in serious need of a retrofit on a nondescript stretch of highway were, as Ruth put it, already in an asylum. Mom lost money on the deal. A great deal of money, as far as Ruth and I could tell. Ruth was ticked; Mom's ideas, she said, were as useless as a firecracker in the rain. There was no money set aside for my tuition. If I didn't work my ass off for the next few years, or for God knows how long, I'd never get to university. I pretended I didn't care.

It was Mrs. Curran's son who bought the property back from us, for a song—since, as he put it, the store and garage were no longer a going concern. But he wanted to help us out, he said. Mom found this galling. He'd wait for the next sucker to come along, she told Ruth and me, and flip the property again.

We thought about moving to Kingston, to be near Ruth, but she said there wouldn't be any point in us being there after she finished her degree. Besides, she was thinking about taking a year off before grad school to travel around in France. She wanted to polish her French; she could tutor English. Mom and I should go back to where we knew people already, she said, where we had friends. It was hard to argue. Mom said she wasn't sure about anything but she agreed to rent a place in Ottawa until I'd finished high school. So that's what we did, taking a lease in a six-unit walk-up in Centretown. The neighbourhood, she kept saying, had potential; who knows, if she could scrape the money together maybe she could eventually buy the building, renovate, and sell it again. Other people make a killing doing that, she said. I doubted we would ever be like other people. On Thursday and Friday nights and all day Saturday I worked at Ogilvy's. A year went by, and then another, and it wasn't so bad, mainly because no one expected anything particular of me. Not my friends from school; not the other sales staff at work, who were almost all considerably older; and not my mother, who had no energy left after she'd spent all day and half the evening running after clients.

When I worked the evening shift, if Mom was finished with clients and paperwork she'd wait at the kitchen table for me. She'd put two cinnamon buns on a plate and set out fancy teacups and silver coffee spoons, as a little joke, a pleasantry between us. The kettle would be steaming; she'd bring the water to the boil, switch the kettle off, and then start it up again as soon as I got in the door. On summer nights I'd lock my bicycle to the wooden stairs at the back of the building; if I could see the kitchen light was on, I'd climb up the stairs to the back door. Otherwise I'd go in at the front, use the inside staircase, and turn on the lights as I entered, all of them, room by room. But I remember the typical nights as those when Mom was waiting in the kitchen, sitting sideways at the table with her arm draped over the edge, like she was holding on, braced for a jolt that never came. Sometimes Vera drove over from the old neighbourhood and would be at the kitchen table with Mom when I got home. I always had the impression that they'd been sitting there for a long time, talking, while the dark filled in around them. I can't imagine how Vera got any conversation, any disclosures, out of Lonely Liz, but she must have garnered something, because as soon as I turned up Vera would seem all breezy and relieved. And I was relieved to see Vera. She was someone you could tell a story to, who'd let you play-act your life as if it were unusual and amusing. I'd imitate customers for her, or the department manager— stupid stuff, like being chewed out for not wearing nylons. *In heat like this!* Vera would say. *You should've asked the bitch if her girdle was too tight.* Even Mom would laugh. I think it helped us both to have someone encouraging me to make my small life a half size bigger than it was.

After my sister's accident, Vera said, to comfort me, that some people are destined to get most of their tragedies over with at a particular stage in their lives. Years later, I thought of her saying this when the Queen made that speech about her own *annus horribilis*. It occurs to me now that when the Queen used that phrase Princess Diana was still alive. So you never do know, really, when the worst calamities are over. But it seemed obvious to me, at Ruth's funeral, that the worst for Vera wasn't over. And that's what made her remark so sweet and unassuming—because it was clear that she wasn't including herself. Despite her pallor, her frailty, despite the fact that she needed more surgery, she didn't count herself among my reasons to grieve. Vera talked about how terrible Ruth's death was for my mother, and for me; how we'd hardly had a chance to get over the first loss, how you expect your children, and your siblings, to go on forever, and not to be taken before they'd barely got started with their lives.

And I remember wondering as she spoke, despite myself, whether Vera would have preferred to trade places with Ruth and not see the end coming, to never see the motorcyclist that knocked her down on a rainy April night in Montmartre, or whether she thought it was better to know, as I was sure Vera knew by then, that the end was coming and that one day soon there would be no point in trying to hold on.

Holding on was all I was doing, it's clear to me now, with respect to my state of mind. There was no muscle that didn't ache, but my mind was numb, like it had been beaten flat by a board. I heard someone comment in a low voice behind me: *She's always been strong for her mother. It was the same at her father's funeral, and she was so young. She's always had that poise.* This was a word I'd never have thought of applying to myself. And so it gave me a character to play, a way to hold myself, a sense of what to do, and that word, drifting on someone's whisper past my ear, is probably the

reason I showed no emotion when I saw Russell on the other side of the room—Russell, whom I hadn't seen in—well,
it seemed like a lifetime, but it was barely two years—and
why I walked so calmly to where he stood and lifted my
hand toward him while I said that it was kind of him to
have come.

"It's unbelievable, unbelievable," he kept saying, looking at me like a man I met once who'd had a stroke and
seemed to be talking from far down a well. And so I murmured whatever I'd been murmuring to people all afternoon about it being very hard for everyone. I felt it was my
job to preside over my sister's funeral, to be the one who
dispensed comfort and reassurance.

"Tell me—how is your mother bearing up?" he said.
It was perfect, familiar, a statement of sympathy and allegiance. Even though he knew and I knew that my mother
had always resented the very fact of his existence.

"I think she's still in shock. Whatever that means.
There's some technical definition. She carries on as nor-
mal but then she loses her words. She's completely tied up.
Maybe that's shock."

"Maybe it is," he said softly. "But how about you? How
are you bearing up?" And his voice was brimming with tear-
fulness, a most beautiful empathy.

"I'm coping," I said.

"Yes. Yes," he said. "You're coping."

The one good thing about Vera being in and out of hospital for the rest of that spring, in 1973, and then through
the summer and fall—for me, I mean, since things never
improved for her—was that keeping an eye on her there
gave me a sense of having something real to do. I did not
want to go to Paris with my mother. I did not want to see

the road where Ruth died, or the arrondissement where she had stayed, or anything about the life she'd been living. The life she had barely started. The life that she had planned out, resolutely, in her mind, and that I didn't know anything much about, because I'd never asked her, and that she had never tried to describe to me. I did not want to meet her friends, to be given any more versions of her that I would feel excluded from. I wanted to feel what I used to feel when Ruth was away at university. A placid kind of forgetting, or ignorance. An understanding that she was doing her thing, and I was doing mine; that there was little point of connection, but nothing to be preoccupied or regretful about.

For the first while during her last stay in hospital, Vera talked about my mother more than anything else. "She's still draining the swamp," she said to me. "You need to get her onto higher ground. You need to get her to look around a little."

"She did the Paris trip, you know."

"That was looking around a graveyard."

"I know. That's why I didn't go. It was pointless."

"I wouldn't say pointless. But you needed to stay with your dad. How is he doing now?"

"Dad passed away, Vera, remember? Before Ruth."

"Yes. Yes I remember now. That's when Liz's depression started."

"Depression? I never used to think of her as depressed. Just dissatisfied."

"When is she coming back from Paris?"

"She's been back for a while now, Vera. Would you like to see her?"

"Yes, I'd like that. I've always liked your mother. She was always friendly to me."

The next morning I told Mom she needed to pull herself together and see Vera before it was too late.

"All right," she said—and then, with a helplessness I could barely stand, "Can you take me today?"

"You can't just go and spend some time with her by yourself?"

"I don't think I can deal with it. I don't have the jam. I really don't."

"Mom. You're not the only person in the world with a sad story."

It was as if she didn't hear me say this. She fiddled with something on the table and then said, "Has she mentioned her daughter?" She looked up at me, straight, level, and I remember thinking that she'd never spoken to me like that before, as if to an equal, maturely, woman to woman.

"Her *daughter*?"

"She had a daughter. Out of wedlock. I guess people don't say that anymore."

"*When?*"

"During the war."

"But..."

"I think she lives out west somewhere. I wonder if Vera wants to see her. I don't know if she's *ever* seen her. I know she tried. She wanted to know her own daughter." And those words made Vera's grief indistinguishable to my mother from her own, and she started to weep.

I left her at the kitchen table and went to the hospital.

That day was one of Vera's lucid days. I asked whether there was anyone she wanted me to call. Anyone she'd like to see. Anyone at all.

"So your mother told you."

"She meant well."

"Your mother was so lucky," she said. "So lucky to know her daughters. So lucky to still have you. She'd be lost without you, you know."

"Tell me about your daughter, Vera."

She told me the story—how she met someone while her husband was posted overseas. You could blame it on loneliness, she said, but by golly she fell for him. Then she got pregnant and that was that. She gave up the baby, but when her husband came back he found out about it and then he left her. It was all because she was so young, she said. She had married in the panic that swept over young people during the war, overcommitting because they would soon be separated. Girls desperate to think that all of the men were leaving and they might never have husbands and they might never have sex. And terrified that they might get pregnant, and that their men might be killed or sent home maimed. Even at the time she knew she was marrying the wrong man. But there was, oh, such urgency. To feel like you belonged to someone. To show your girlfriends the ring. To be entitled to womanhood. Even before her husband shipped out she knew it was a mistake. But the baby's father was the wrong man, too. So 1945 was Vera's *annus horribilis*, the year she lost everything and had to start over. She got a job waitressing and took classes in shorthand. Got a job in an office, and a divorce. Married her boss's brother. "Another mistake. God, that was a doozy. But you know, you could put all of it in a TV show now and nobody would blink an eye. Nobody would see what the fuss was about. Take your mother and Ruth now," she added. "That whole thing never made any sense. I mean, really, what did they have to fight about? But I guess your mother had her ideas about how things should go and you girls were supposed to stick to the script."

"Maybe that's where Ruth got it," I said then. "Her grand plans. But she always blamed Mom's schemes for getting in her way."

"We resent the people who love us the most."

"Do you know where your daughter is, Vera?"

"Yes, I know. She's a pharmacist. She's married. I don't know what he does. She has two children. I promised not to contact her. I signed the adoption papers and promised to stay out of her life. Can you imagine? I mean, what kind of rubbish was that? I don't think I really believed I would never know her. I mean, how could that be possible? But I tracked her down. Lord, it took me years. I found her—she was grown up by then, you know, and had her own family—but she wasn't interested. I can understand that. I mean, I was a stranger to her. She didn't owe me anything. But I carry her address in my wallet. As if I might end up in Edmonton by chance one day. You know, and just drop in. Just knock at her door. 'Surprise! Guess who?'"

And she started to laugh a little.

"I'm sure she's lovely," I said. "Lovely and happy. You did your best for her, Vera."

"Give that address to my lawyer when the time comes, okay?"

A few days later Vera started off talking about my mother and Ruth, as if she needed to sort it out, to get it clear in her mind. She preferred this to talking about her daughter, and I preferred it to talking about myself. But after a while she looked at me hard and said, "You look like you're having bad sex."

"Vera!"

"You have a hollowed-out look, my girl. Who's messing you around?"

"No one is messing me around."

"I bet I can guess."

There was a long pause.

"I saw the way he latched onto you at the funeral. It can't be good, Marian. He's sleeping with a ghost."

I thought for a while before I said, "I'm not so sure about that."

"Well, whatever he's doing, it's too strange. He left you for your sister, remember."

"No Vera, it was the opposite." And as soon as I said this I realized that I had it all twisted up, too. Russell had never left my sister for me. Strange, that in some way, deep down, I'd felt that was true, that he had chosen me instead of Ruth. That he was, in the present, betraying her. And that of course I was, too.

"He's a vampire, that's what he is. How many bite marks have you got on your neck?"

"Baudelaire, is it?" Russell had said on the last night of my visit, the night I'd deliberately missed my bus and Ruth was holed up in the university library and I'd made myself a sandwich and sat in his study, looking at his books, until he came home. He was smiling that smile of his, openly, serenely, ready to say some mocking thing that flatters with the assumption that you will be equally sardonic, sophisticated, that you won't mind.

I felt exquisitely happy, all of a sudden. I felt like laughing at myself, confidingly, confidently.

"No," I said. "A history of the Rideau Canal."

"Christ, you're a nerd," he said. And we both laughed.

"I'm not sure why I have this," he said as I handed the book to him, "but I'm sure I've read it." He sat down beside me and started fanning through the pages.

"Ah yes, with the engineering drawings. Feats hitherto unattempted in the Americas. Inventive fellow, our Colonel By. All for nought. Those poor Irish bastards, thrashing around in malaria-infested swamps so we can putter up to Ottawa in houseboats. In some places the woods were so dense they did the surveying at night, in winter, lighting flames in the dark."

"Really? Neat."

"They sometimes set tall pines on fire, if I remember."

"Well, I've only just started."

"Keep going. I think it will interest you."

"It does interest me," I said. "To a point."

"A lot of things interest you, to a point."

"What do you mean?"

"You spend your time observing. Old ladies. Sisters in disgrace. Crazy neighbours."

Detachment, a quality I never knew I had, suddenly seemed like my most desirable asset. Wasn't it true, how powerfully aloof I was.

"You and Ruthie are amazingly alike."

I was grateful even for this.

"You're both so stubborn. And so critical of yourselves."

Oh, it was wonderful how this man perceived the truth. How it was all a mistake, what people said about my sister and me, that I was the practical one, she the brain; that I would be the homebody, Ruth the adventuress; that Ruth would look after herself; that I would look after everyone else. It was marvellous that he saw it so clearly: my powerful, selfish self.

He looked at me, his eyes warm, wrinkling at the corners, as if he were savouring an amusing detail. Surveying with a flame held against the dark. A simple idea. He pushed my hair back and held it up behind my ear.

"Do you ever wear it up?"

"Sometimes," I said. The truth was, never.

"You and Ruth have the same neck. But you're the one with the square chin."

When he started to kiss me, on the neck, the temple, the mouth, it was like something I'd made up in my own mind. I suppose I had imagined his tenderness, his slow, inflaming deliberation, his sweet melancholy, his appraising, aching remoteness all along. This is the formula for seduction, the accumulation of anticipation, imagination, into a kind of inevitability that becomes, or so it seems, its own justification. In retrospect, of course, it all flattens out into a tawdry plotline: my sister's lover kissed and half-undressed me when I was seventeen and did not stop until it was confirmed for me that I was right to desire sex more than anything, that sex was what I was missing, the only thing I was missing, and he knew it—although he would not, as he put it, dream of hurting me. He would not satisfy that burning, would not do anything unsafe. And I was grateful, and flattered, to be shown and denied with such apparent tenderness what I knew but could not have admitted I was looking for. It was clear then to me that I had come to Kingston not as a spy, or an ambassador, but as a thief.

When Vera was in hospital I used her as a way to talk about Russell. I wanted to say Russell's name out loud to people, and I suppose it seemed safe enough to let it slip while talking to a dying woman in her hospital room. As in: Remember Ruth's old boyfriend? The married guy who caused such trouble? He's a visiting professor at Ottawa U now. Or, remember Ruth's old boyfriend? He's just published a book.

Russell had come looking for me at Ogilvy's a few weeks after Ruth's funeral. He found me in the men's department and came up to the cash with a pair of briefs. "I need a wed-ding present for my niece," he said. "Do you think these will do?" and I said "You can't go wrong with underwear" and he said "This is the last department I expected to find you in" and I said "It's always in the last place you look" and we went on like that for a while until we arranged to meet for something to eat after my shift.

The sex started that night. I told Russell I would go on the pill. The sex carried on. I lied to my mother about the hours I was working. There was nothing I wanted to do more than to be with Russell. Meaning, to be in bed with Russell in his sublet in Sandy Hill. We had desperate, unro-mantic, lustful sex that left both of us disquieted, and for which the only remedy was more sex. Although sometimes as we stood together in the shower, leaning together under the water, I felt a kind of relief in his body, as if perhaps this tenderness was what he had wanted, after all. These encounters went on for, I don't know, three or four months, at every opportunity, at any hour I could plausibly be away from home or work and he from the university, and the lovemaking was always tense and sorrowful, as if we were trying to unlock something, to clear away some obstacle, to break one another into love. At the time, though, I thought that this was as close as anyone as unlucky as me would ever get to love.

"I want to ask you something," I said to him one day when were staring in parallel at the ceiling.

"Okay," he said.

"What happened between you and Ruth?"

I expected a long pause. A reluctance. But he said, so matter of fact, barely missing a beat, "My wife came back."

"Oh."

There was a long silence then. I considered not filling

it. I considered not asking for anything more. But I kept going, despite myself. "Ruth thought you were done with her. With your wife."

"That's what I thought, too."

"So what about Ruth?"

"You could say she left. Or you could say I didn't follow her. She wanted her adventure in Paris. I wasn't in a position to leave."

"Where is she now?"

For a moment the question, bizarrely, sounded like "Where is Ruth?"

"My wife moved back to Kingston. She has her own place. We stay in touch."

"Is it sexual?"

"Sometimes," he said. "When that's what she wants."

"How obliging of you."

"Nothing, absolutely nothing, is as simple as you insist on making it seem."

"Is it because you feel guilty?"

"Maybe I feel guilty. But I don't think so. We're no good living together. It never worked. For no good reason, really. Sometimes I think for no reason at all."

"Do you think you'll know when you find what you're looking for?"

"I'm not *looking* for anything," he said.

And so I wrapped myself around him, fervently, desperately, as if I could erase all of his desires and rebuild them, remake them, as me and only me.

"This isn't fair to you," he said, when we were finished.

Dracula's gone, I told Vera the last time I saw her, whispering close, and her eyes looked sad and concerned and confused, as if she was sorry for me but couldn't remember why.

I went to the public library and photocopied the page with the name Jessop in the Edmonton phone book. Then I went home and started dialling. I got to number five.

"I'm looking for an Amy Jessop, formerly of Toronto?"

"That might be me."

"Um, well, I'm looking for an Amy Jessop who is related to a Vera Lyon."

"What's this about?"

"Well, I'm a friend of Vera's, and I'm looking for her daughter."

Silence.

"I'm sorry to say that Vera passed away a few days ago. She had cancer. And so I'm trying to locate her next of kin."

"Who did you say you were?"

"A friend—well, actually, Vera was my mother's next-door neighbour at one point. She mentioned you in the last weeks of her illness."

Silence.

"It *is* you? You're Amy?"

"You're talking about a Vera Lyon who was born in Kitchener?"

"Kitchener. Yes, I think that's right. In 1923. Her daughter was born in 1945."

"What date."

"January 11."

Silence.

"I'm very sorry to break this news so out of the blue but I wanted to put you in touch with the lawyer who is handling your mother's estate."

"Why are you doing this, rather than the lawyer?"

"I was very fond of your mother. I just felt that I wanted to find you."

"To find me."

"I mean I want you to know that your mother was thinking of you. She thought about you a lot over the years."

"I'm sure."

"She was a wonderful woman, really."

"Well, the lawyer can reach me at this number, the same as you did."

And then she hung up.

I stared at the phone for at least ten minutes before I redialled. She didn't pick up. After six rings the answering machine clicked on. So I said this, to the machine.

"Amy, I apologize for having intruded, and it is none of my business, but your mother was always kind to me and I wanted you to know that it seemed clear to me that she did not want things to have happened as they did. She felt she had no choice but to give you up, since she had no way to give you a decent life. I think she did her best. Times have changed and so it's hard to imagine how a mother could be separated from her child like that. I think everyone was doing what they thought was best. I don't know. She said to me that if it had been in this day and age no one would have batted an eye. I'm just trying to say that she was never indifferent. You probably never want to hear from me again but if you want to ask me anything I will certainly tell you what I can. Not that it's much, but maybe it would be of some help. I'm very sorry for your loss. I mean, your loss now and before. I'm sorry if I've said the wrong things. I wish you all the best." And then I left my name and number.

A couple of months passed. And then, after I'd given up any thought of ever hearing from Amy, I found this message on my line one day when I got home from work.

"Hello Marian. I just wanted to say you meant well but there really is no need to stir things up. When I was small I was told I was adopted and that my natural parents had died. So when she tried to contact me it was difficult. I'm sorry if she thought I was indifferent but it really was very hard for me. But she's gone now and so there's really no difference from the way it was before. Maybe one day I'll feel like getting more of a story about her but I don't think I can deal with that right now. There's a lot going on and I really didn't need this, you know? Anyway I told the lawyer I don't want any of her effects. If there's anything of hers you'd like to keep I've told the lawyer you can just let him know. He'll be putting the estate in a trust fund for my kids. Not that it's much. But it looks like they might need it. My husband and I split up a few years ago and now I'm not well myself. So I'd prefer you didn't call me back but maybe when things have settled I'll get in touch. But probably not. So I guess that's it. Okay. Goodbye."

There was a second message, left a few minutes later.

"I meant to say thank you for the kindness you showed to my mother when she had her cancer. The lawyer told me about that. I meant to say thank you in my earlier message. Goodbye again."

I told my mother about the messages, and we spent almost as much time analyzing the second one as the first. Imagine thanking a stranger, we said, on behalf of a mother you never knew. How odd that must have felt, and yet it seemed fitting for her, as a daughter, to do.

MISS CHARLOTTE

MARTIN WEST

MISS CHARLOTTE opened her front gate and saw the young boy on the curb. His shirt was covered with blood and his arms were covered with blood and his cheeks were too. So why was it true that all young men who came to the city these days had blood on them? The boy looked up at her in the same vagrant way all vagrants looked; lazy and confused that the world had not given them precisely what they had asked for. What bothered Miss Charlotte most was that the boy's fingernails were dirty and it was already mid-morning.

"I have done something terrible," he said to her.

"The only thing you have done is failed to wash today."

"I don't have a sink."

"Where is your home?"

"I'm not ever going back there."

Miss Charlotte walked around the boy and her new pumps crunched the pebbles on the concrete. She liked the sound of things crunching beneath her feet. It was the sound of strength and cruelty. Of things being ground into place through cold Vancouver days when the clouds swept across the concrete buildings and the labour unions were on strike and the busses weren't running, either.

"I suppose you expect everyone else to look after you," she said. "To give you food and soap and probably a new car too, if you are old enough to drive."

"I'm old enough," he said

Maybe he was. Maybe a stretch. He was a churlish animal who had probably scurried in off one of the valley farms after his father had beat him or the grocer abused him. Charlotte felt a quiver down her spine, then her thumb tightened around the strap on her purse.

"I don't suppose you'll work, will you?"

"I'll work."

"I'll only pay you five dollars a day."

"I'm fine with that."

She wasn't sure if she was fine with that. She had half expected him to say no. It would have given her more satisfaction if he had said no. She liked to read in the newspapers how hippies said no and the protesters said no, and the social workers had said no and after she'd thrown the paper into the fireplace and watched it burn she turned on an old Lana Turner movie and watched her say yes.

"What is your name?"

"Gerald."

"All right then, Gerald. You shall do my shopping. You shall carry it home for me. You shall clean my garage and my house. I even have some wood in the shed that needs splitting. I shall not pay you until everything is done. But the first thing you must do is wash your hands."

"Where?"

"Where do you think?"

A steady stream of water ran down the street into a drain. With it went leaves, Popsicle sticks and the last regurgitation the wet winter had to offer. He gazed into the gutter, unbelieving, but she remained resolute and so he knelt before the ditch and rubbed his hands in the crystal current. When his mendicant eyes inched up to meet her gaze the whitecaps broke in the waters of False Creek and the wind pushed seagulls around in tight circles.

"Now come over here," she said.

Gerald stood, but of course there was nowhere to dry his hands so he let them drip on the broken concrete until they tingled. He limped a little and looked concussed some but then she wasn't exactly hiring him for his mathematical aptitude.

"What should I call you?"

"You may call me Miss Charlotte. Not Charlotte. Not Miss. And never Mrs. Do you understand?"

"Yes Miss Charlotte."

"Can you follow orders?"

"Very well. I want to get into the Navy."

The Navy. Of course. A militarist. The other reason the world had become the way it was. "Then I will ask you one question before I make up my mind. Do you think I'm pretty?"

Gerald thought a very long while. A glacially long while. Then the logjams in his brain moved over and rolled downstream. "I haven't seen anyone so pretty in this town yet."

"You are smarter than you look."

Hiromi's Sweet Coiffures used to be a confectionary but now it was only a boarded shop that smelled of linseed and bottled aerosols. The windows were soaped and advertised Persian movie stars from the Middle East. Charlotte had always wanted to go to Persia before they changed the name.

The front door was boarded shut. Clients had to gain entrance through a side door using a key kept hidden under a potted plant. Charlotte couldn't get the door to open with the mauled tool, so she lit a cigarette, stepped back and glared at the offence.

"Fix that."

Gerald looked puzzled, but then he was a country boy so he got down on his knees and twisted the bolt into the dirty socket with a strand of wire. That was a clicking Charlotte particularly liked so she exhaled the tobacco fumes with satisfaction that shot right up to the eaves.

"Do you smoke?"

"Oh, yes Miss, Charlotte."

"And would you like one right now?"

"If you don't mind."

"I do mind. You may have one later. An entire package—if you must—after you come back from the grocer's with list fulfilled. You must bring me the bill and the receipt."

The boy shrugged. Before them lay a long hallway with doors that could have been cupboards and windows that might have been mirrors. At last there was an orange waiting room decorated after Shanghai 1920 with sticks of incense burning and Madam Butterfly on the stereo. Past a curtain of glass beads a row of women with beehive hairdos smoked and waited under dryers.

Mrs. Peabody was a greying oriental woman who, despite having been interned during the war never seemed to be angry at anything occidental and always hurried to meet her patrons. She managed the shop and called all the women by their favoured name, be it Charlotte or Natalie or Alana and never spoke about the outside world because none of that ever really mattered.

"Mrs. Peabody," Charlotte said. "My new boy has had a dreadful mishap."

"Is he safe?"

"He just needs a place to clean up."

"Of course my dear."

"He'll be all right once he's washed."

"He's a little cutie," Mrs. Peabody said and curled open a lace apron in the air while she prepared the shampooing basin.

Gerald stared at the woman on the far side of the beads under their maelstroms of hot air and dissatisfaction. His eyes darted to their fingers and laboured lips and then up to a chandelier that had a string of rotating glass peacocks hanging from its hub.

"Then go ahead little cutie," Mrs. Peabody said and gestured to the sink. "Go and wash up."

The boy hesitated dutifully, stuck his thumbs under his belt and waited for royal assent. Charlotte at last knew how beautiful this moment of Madam Butterfly really was so she waited until the crescendo had finished and then gave him the wave to proceed. Hiromi showed Gerald to the sink. He washed the red from his fingers and the blackened parts ran like crabs into the drain.

"I didn't mean for it to happen this way," he said.

"You are too young to mean anything," Hiromi said and dried his hands with a towel.

"Young Gerald shall be doing chores for me today," Charlotte said. "Or as long as he needs to until he ships out."

She reached down and flicked a few curls of red sawdust off the young boy's shoulder. She didn't want to think of where he might have picked them up. A mill. A dumpster. God forbid an abattoir. Her hand waited on his collarbone long enough to feel what youthful abeyance might be. His body felt much more muscular than she expected from a boy his age, much more like a panther ready to pounce than a puppy set to be pampered, and so she led him into the setting room to meet his new public.

The chatterbox stopped. The nail filing ceased. The chamber fell into silence except for a leaking faucet that dripped water into a bowl every other second.

"He's too young," the blonde woman said.

"You're too old," Charlotte said.

"No, he's far too young."

"He looks like my grandson," Mrs. Kind said from the corner.

Charlotte was half ready to let the boy flee. But he did not flinch, did not flare out. Instead, he smiled and gave a faint bow to his new hosts.

"He's going to have us all put in prison," Natalie said.

"Nobody is going to prison," Charlotte said.

"Mrs. Peabody, you cannot possibly allow this. There's blood on him. We have rules. There is the Vice Squad."

"This poor young man has suffered a mishap and was left alone," Mrs. Peabody said. She folded her black sequinned gloves together and smiled in a way she seldom had to. "And we cannot turn him away from our shop any more than you or I."

A flick of newspapers rose across the room. Faces disappeared. Any mutiny on board was obscured by the thin rustle of air print flown in weekly from New York.

But Natalie was not to be obscured. She smoked slowly in a way she thought aristocratic and gazed at the boy in disdain.

"Do you mind if I ask your charge a few questions?" she said.

"Not at all," Charlotte said. She didn't care. Or wouldn't show that she did.

There was the sound of breath held nasally, the way people do when they are trying hard to listen without being heard.

"Where do you come from?"

"From out on a farm."

"Why did you leave?"

"It was a cruel life."

Natalie examined her fingernail and her eyes then lingered on the boy's torso for what Charlotte thought was far too long a time. "And what do you hope to get here?"

"To join the Navy."

"What and go out and sink ships and drown people?"

"To serve my country."

"What kind of country is this that keeps people oppressed and stifled in their own homes, in their own bodies?" Natalie said, and her voice shot up a semi-tone.

"It is a good country."

Natalie pitched her half-smoked cigarette into the waste bin and leaned toward the boy. "Do you know what evil is?"

"Oh yes, ma'am, I do."

"And what is that?"

"Evil is ugly. It is unnatural."

"And you don't see anything evil in the Navy?"

"No ma'am I don't."

Natalie gazed up at the chandelier and some of the makeup on her face flaked off. She consulted her pocket mirror to repair the damage then crossed her legs to show off her bony knees. "And do you see anything unnatural here?"

Gerald gazed at the rows of heavily padded brassieres, the towering wigs and the smouldering ashes in the waste bin and shook his head.

"There, do you see?" Charlotte said. "You have about as much to fear from the boy as a tulip."

She took Gerald into the coffee room that doubled as a laundry for the salon's linens. Two dryers tumbled in opposite directions, which Charlotte always thought was wrong. She leaned against the soiled chute that went to the basement and let the smoke from her cigarette drift between her fingers.

"Don't pay any mind to them," she said. "They are savage, cruel creatures. Each and every one of them."

Gerald stared at the floor and his jaw trembled. His fingers fluttered down his dirty jeans and Charlotte feared he might collapse back into adolescence right in Hiromi's salon, which would be trouble, trouble indeed.

"Did Natalie humiliate you?" Charlotte said. "That little shrew. Her real name isn't even Natalie, you know. She just calls herself that because she thinks she looks like Natalie Wood. If I thought they weren't going to smoke themselves to death inside the year, I'd have them all burned alive as witches."

Gerald pondered the weight of those words and said; "I've got to tell someone about last night."

"Last night doesn't matter."

But one more look at the blood on his shirt and his face quivered then exploded. Despite herself, or maybe just to shut him up, Charlotte pulled him into her chiffon dress, which was supposed to stay pristine until Sunday morning.

"I was in this stranger's room," he said.

"Shush."

"What is going on in there?" Alana called from beneath her dryer.

"Listen to me," Charlotte said. She held the boy at arm's length and shook him. "Shut up. Never mind about what has happened. It's over. And of no relevance here."

"Madam?" Hiromi called. "Shall I fetch a doctor?"

"No," Charlotte said. And then to Gerald: "For god's sake have a brandy."

Charlotte stuffed a chrome flask in the boy's face and he seemed remarkably adept at sucking the liquor back. Then she produced a roll of her favourite French cigarettes and lit two up. After puffing in his backwoods style, he held the cigarette up to his eyes and stared deep into its embers.

"Do you hate them here all that much?" he said.

"Maybe I hate this place and maybe I don't. But you're not going to see me spending my whole life crying about it."

Gerald nodded, his attention drifting over to the garbage chute, which was cluttered with cleaning fluids and aerosol bottles. Suddenly Charlotte didn't feel so sorry for him anymore. In fact, she wasn't so sure if she could trust him with the grocery money. But she held the chute open for him and on cue he pitched his butt into the hole. Then she filled out the grocery list and gave him the cash.

"The grocer's is down on the corner. If you tell him my name he'll show you the right brands and give you credit if we're any short."

"Are my smokes on there too?"

"You're a fast learner," she said.

They walked out past the setting room and Alana lifted the dryer from her skull. "Are the eyes all dry now?" she said.

Gerald didn't bother to answer. He was out the door with the list and the cash before anyone had a chance to point the way.

"There's the last you'll see of that money," Natalie said. She flipped through a Hollywood magazine half interestedly.

"What do you have against the boy?"

"He's fourteen."

"He's old enough to join the Navy."

"He's not old enough to understand the likes of you," Natalie said. "You're just looking for a young churl that you can crush under your foot and fetch your groceries for you."

"At least I can find someone to crush and fetch."

"Peace my good friends," Hiromi said and stuttered a needle on a wobbly stereo that stood on a brass podium. After a few scratchy seconds the music from Carmen filled the room.

"You like to speak of peace, do you Mrs. Peabody?" Natalie said.

"Of course I do."

"Do you bring up Singapore, Hong Kong or Pearl Harbour?"

"My dear, I do not bring up anything."

Hiromi concocted the mixtures of resins and dyes in her beautician's cauldron and hummed with the melody. "You want light or dark tonight, Miss Charlotte?"

"Almost blonde," Charlotte said, leaning back into the ivory sink. On the ceiling there were murals of lotus flowers, pandas and a curious interpretation of Parliament Hill. "I want the Monroe look tonight."

"Do you have a date?" Mrs. Kind said.

"We were thinking of going to The Cave."

"I've heard it's frequented by the police."

"Then Charlotte certainly doesn't want to be there," Natalie said. She ground her cigarette out into the ashtray and when she saw the ashtray itself was filled she turned it upside-down into a waste basket.

Charlotte thought of ashes and then of embers and then of amber licks of fire twisting up dry wood towards a grey sky. When Natalie checked her watch every other minute, Charlotte calculated how long it would take a human body to combust if it were filled with aerosol.

"I don't think he's coming back," Natalie said.

Charlotte felt the dye and warm water settle onto her skull and she thought of waterskiing on Cultus Lake in the warm summer sun when life had been simpler and she might have fallen asleep. Then the key slid into the lock and the side door opened. There was the rustle of bags and Gerald appeared in the room groceries stacked in front of his face and his fingers entwined with bills.

"Go ahead and put them on the counter," Charlotte said.

He did as he was told and carefully counted out the change into her hand along with the receipt. Then he vanished to the kitchen only to return with a tray of chocolate that he served to the ladies. Mrs. Kind took three and smiled. Alana took four and blushed. Gerald was especially proper with Natalie, offering to fetch her a dark chocolate if the light wasn't to her liking.

"Why on earth would you want to go into the Navy when you'd have such a fine career in pampering," she said and took the time to undo the boy's top button.

"When you have serviced all of my friends," Charlotte said. "Would you be kind enough to empty the other ashtrays? The soot is hurting my eyes."

Gerald collected the sum of butts, lipstick-smeared filters, and matches into the wastebasket. Then he turned and went into the laundry room. Charlotte saw the boy's reflection in one of the mirrors as he glanced over his shoulder. Instead of choosing the trash can, he emptied the smouldering mess down the laundry chute.

"Perhaps I shall take him to The Cave tonight," she said out loud and was rather proud that she had.

"They would never let him in," Natalie said. "There's no chance he could pass for nineteen. They keep much stricter rules in the clubs than Hiromi does here."

"The Cave is no place for a boy like that," Mrs. Kind said.

Despite being pampered, Natalie remained unsettled. She was like that, Charlotte knew, unable to move forward in life until every scab had been picked back to blood, every imperfection exposed and infected. "How old are you, anyway?" she said finally to Gerald. "I have to tell you now your presence is making me, and I believe many others in this room, uncomfortable. So speak up right now. And don't look to Charlotte for help. A real man doesn't need his mother to look after him."

The boy held up three fists and several fingers as if he were afraid to say.

"Then that's too young," Mrs. Kind said.

"Well, I hardly believe that," Natalie said. "And even if I did, that's not old enough to get you into the Navy. So you may as well take whatever it is Charlotte has promised you and go back to your barn."

Mrs. Peabody straightened her back and stared at a delicate glass dragon her relatives had sent her when she had opened her first business importing cosmetics from the East. "That age is old enough if a relative signs for you," she said. She massaged a rinse through Mrs. Kind's hair, her fingers kneading through a simple fact that was lighter than air.

"My parents aren't here," Gerald said.

Hiromi only raised her eyebrows in silence the way she did when everyone knew she was right about a basic world fact, be it the finest shade of a dye or the town councillor that would be most sympathetic to their cause.

"Then we shall do it," Charlotte said.

"What, you shall go as his mother or his father?" Natalie said.

"I shall go in either case." Charlotte stood up. She felt angry for the way things were and what she had made them. "We can go directly if you wish, Gerald."

"You stupid tart." Natalie stood up as well. "You self-centered egotistic stupid tart using this stupid young man for your ridiculous crusades. And you'll take us all down with you. Everything that Hiromi has worked for."

"The naval office is open until three on Saturday," Hiromi said.

Charlotte tucked Gerald close to protect him from an evil no one else but the two of them could see. Then she walked with him through the glass beads and into the hallway.

"Would you like me to split the wood?" Gerald said.

"After we get to the naval office."

"Did you want me to take the trash out for Hiromi's sake?"

Charlotte pushed open the door and a cold ocean breeze washed her face. She wondered if trash ought be taken out or at least left to flavour the harbour with a twinge of melancholy smoke.

CLEAN

MARTHA WILSON

A FTER STOKES gently tugged off the condom, balled it inside a tissue, put it down on the floor by the bed to throw away later, and said how great that had been, he added, "I know it's still a long time away, but it'll be nice when we can stop using condoms." Liz, now nestled in the crook of his arm, didn't answer, though in her imagination her eyes shot open and she said, "Whoa; hang on now." She had no plans to stop using condoms, and it was news to her that Stokes had such an idea.

Still, they didn't intend to try for a baby for quite a while. No rush.

Liz and Stokes were living in Brockville ("near the Dollarama"); she worked for an insurance firm and was thinking of studying accounting. Stokes worked at a farm museum, letting school groups help with shearing, or teaching interested people to handle a scythe—he'd established an annual scythe-mowing contest that was turning into one of the museum's most popular summer events.

Their small postwar house was sunny and quiet. One morning the cat, alert even in her sound sleep, heard a car in the driveway and popped her head up from her basket. "Someone here?" Liz asked her, and went to the kitchen door and looked out. "It's Mom," she said, and Stokes jumped up and made a quick sweep through the rooms, gathering up evidence of slovenliness, indulgence, or questionable taste, sweeping his hand over flat surfaces to dust them as he went by.

Liz stood on the tiny front porch to greet her mother, who wasn't supposed to be there and whom she'd be seeing on the weekend anyway. "Is something up with Dad?"

"No, he's all right this morning," her mother said, stepping inside and working her sandals off. "He's got another few days of feeling pretty good before the next round. He was sleeping when I left, but he has that new Henning Mankell book you brought him, and that yogurt he likes. I told him I'd be back before lunchtime."

"Is his mouth any better?"

"A little bit. That mouthwash helps with the sores."

"That's good. Come on in. You want some coffee?"

Stokes came into the kitchen, having hidden the gathered pile in their bedroom. "Hi, Rena," he said. "How's Calvin feeling this morning?"

"Oh, it's so hard on him. It just decimates him. It's very tough to watch."

Liz said, "Mom, you said he was all right today."

"I meant he's feeling better than he was last week. He's not doing better than he was a year ago."

Stokes put an arm around Rena and gave her a side hug. "Nearly halfway through chemo, right?"

"Almost halfway," she agreed. "If we make it. Here, Liz; did I bring my tote bag in?"

"I'll check the car."

"Friends have been bringing us food and so on, and your dad wanted to send you some of the peanut butter cookies. He could only eat one."

Liz had gone to Calvin's chemotherapy training with him and Rena, before the treatment started, to learn what to expect and how to take care of him. It was alarming but sober, and set the tone for the dogged family culture they would need over the next few months. There was a plan for the mental part, the physical, for the logistics of hospital visits. Parking. Costs. Dealing with middle-of-the-night medical emergencies; side effects; toxicity. It was all just some form or other of head-down coping.

They were given housekeeping regimens for handling bodily fluids after chemo treatments. His laundry had to be done separately; vomit would need to be cleaned up with great care; the toilet, after he used it, should be flushed an extra time, with the lid down; family members, remember not to touch pills with your bare hands. Calvin's body would be metabolizing what was pumped into him. Rena was in charge of all the systems. Liz was the helper.

Liz drove them back to their house in Peterborough afterwards. Her mom gazed out the car window, holding a Kleenex, while her dad rested on the back seat with his eyes closed. He wasn't feeling sick or weak yet, but the narrative of what lay ahead seemed to have punctured him internally, so the energy and courage he would need were already leaking out of him. "It's not the cancer that makes you feel so awful; it's the treatment," they'd been told by a couple in the waiting room, when they struck up a cautious, genial conversation. That sentence kept running through Liz's head now, and she wondered whether it was the same thought her dad was having. How strange for the cure to be the worst part.

Two deer picked their way along the ditch by the road. Liz slowed down to give them time to panic and bolt. They stared at the vehicle and passengers for a long moment. Then the panic seemed to come out of nowhere, like a wave that scooped them up, anticipated by the humans but not by the deer themselves. They managed to flee away from the car rather than into it. Liz wondered whether this was new to them every few days, as if they'd never experienced it before.

"Close," Rena said.

"Do you think they saw us, sitting inside here?" Liz asked.

"I'm not sure how good their eyesight is," he father said from the backseat, laying his head down again. "I saw an eagle in a tree last year, and I pulled over, and we stared at each other for a good long time. I remember thinking, it can see my face a lot more clearly than I can see it. It could have been looking at the backs of my retinas, the way it was searching me."

One thing she had always appreciated about her dad, Liz thought, was that he clearly had an interior life that he enjoyed, didn't mind sharing, and yet kept mostly private. He seemed to her to be a person who liked his own company.

"What kind of expression did it seem to have?" Liz asked.

He considered this. "Assessing," he said.

After her father had been gone for more than a year, Liz and her mom planned a trip to Calgary, just the two of them. Her mom had apparently "always wanted to see the Stampede," though Liz couldn't remember her ever mentioning this before. It wasn't the kind of spectacle that interested Liz, though her experience with such prejudgments was that the event always turned out to be far better staged and more worthwhile than she anticipated.

Her trip came just before a pivot. Liz had turned thirty-two that spring and Stokes turned thirty, and they decided to start trying to get pregnant. In the fall, they said. A small gap; a couple of months to finish painting the basement, in case she got pregnant right away. It had been four years since the morning Stokes mentioned that someday they would throw out the condoms.

Liz had always been a person who was careful about germs, a cautious person, with the conversations about handwashing and potential cutting-board contamination in the kitchen and the proper temperature meat should reach. All of that. But in recent years she'd also heard countless mentions of various forms of disease transmission, of MRSA on hospital countertops and paper towel dispensers, staph bacteria on doctors' stethoscopes, the many elements contributing to a separate area of concern. Don't ever listen to the damn CBC, she kept thinking. Or pick up an *Oprah* magazine.

Moreover, there was HPV, the human papilloma virus, spread through contact and linked to cervical cancer. Even, lately, found on doctors' exam tables; *what the fuck*. And the women from Stokes's past—what were their stories?

And chlamydia, so easily transmitted, so often asymptomatic until you wound up infertile. Liz could still hear her health teacher preaching, "No matter what, even if you're on the Pill, you want to always use a condom to protect those delicate, delicate fallopian tubes."

And she had become so used to condoms. How clean they were. How separate and conclusive.

She left Stokes behind and flew with her mother to Calgary for four days.

As they bumped their wheeled carry-ons behind them in the airport, Liz studied her mother. By the expansive windows of the terminal, a new slackness in Rena's skin showed clearly.

"We could get a coffee here, if you want, before we go to the hotel," Rena said. Liz often had trouble figuring out whether her mom's innocuous statements held a message. She had never become skilled at it, but now she seemed to hear a tremor or something wistful, like the curled, shy tendril of a vine, trying to reach.

"Sure," she answered. "Let's find a coffee place."

They found a Starbucks and sat at the tiny table, so close to each other. "How are you holding up?" Liz asked. She took a cautious sip of her foam. Her mother's lower eyelids reddened, even before tears appeared, as if the crying began with her skin rather than her tear ducts.

"You know what I was thinking, flying here," Rena said. "Looking down at all those towns, neighbourhoods, houses. That every family is like a machine. It's like some intricate device, some kind of fiddly tool with gauges and gears that you'd see in the Lee Valley catalogue."

"A family's like that?"

"Yes. All these moving parts that make up the motor, and the motor is the family. And it's encased in its house."

Liz saw the rows of Monopoly houses again, from high above. Indistinguishable from one another, yet distinct.

Her mom went on. "And the job of that engine, that family, is to protect itself and keep humming along. He took care of me, and I took care of him. I think it's the only way a society can function. All this work, this caretaking, goes on invisibly inside the walls of these houses."

"It's not public? Is that what you mean?" Liz asked. "It's concealed?"

"Well, not that it's hidden; but unexposed, uncounted. All this practical daily work of caretaking, caregiving. It's like, I don't know, you can tell how many dogs live in Canada because you can find out how much dog food is sold. But in the days when people fed their dogs table scraps, there was no way to count them. Does that make sense? All this family work—it's not being measured, but it's vast."

"Yes," Liz said.

"But if we were trying to pay for it, trying to quantify it, trying to hire hospitals and aides to handle all of it for the whole country, it would be unaffordable."

"Oh, I see what you mean. It's a form of savings. An efficiency."

"Right. And I thought—well, that's what a family *is*. Not only that, obviously. I loved him so much. But partly, yes, the simple fact of having a person to depend on. And it's important. We're these self-contained little units that handle our own business, clean up after one another, deal with the vomit even when it's literally toxic waste, flush the toilet twice because a drop of the urine is poisonous, keep going, do for your family, and so the larger society is able to get far more done."

"Mom, you're so philosophical," Liz said.

"Well. You know me," Rena said. She fell silent and sipped her black coffee. The reddened eyelids reappeared.

"What is it?" Liz asked.

"Now there's just me. No other half of my machine. I'm like a wrecked helicopter in a shed."

Liz covered her mother's hand with her own. Rena said, "There's the problem with the tidy system. One person is left over, after the end."

It made Liz think of the apprehension she'd felt before her own wedding, when she tried to focus on the gravity of marriage. It was meant to last so long—decades longer than any project, relationship, contract, or loyalty she had ever entered into before. Daunting, but also heartening.

And, of course, there was that future waiting, as a downed and busted helicopter.

Long before she ever met Stokes and had to think about what decades of marriage might involve, Liz had once found herself standing in a bookstore reading about fisting, which she had never heard of or imagined. Putting your hand, wrist, possibly forearm inside someone. She read with fascination that it was uniquely intimate, requiring new levels of trust and caution. Her clearest takeaway from the book, though, was that once you got your hand far enough up there, in the neighbourhood of the sigmoid colon, it was actually possible to feel the feathery villi lining the intestinal wall.

For years, this extraordinary scenario came back to her from time to time. It would be, she imagined, like running your palm and then fingertips across the underside of the starfish and the sea anemones in the Tidal Touch Pool at the aquarium—the very creatures those stern admonitions posted on the low glass sides of the exhibition were warning visitors not to handle. As if anyone coming to the touch pool longed to pick up rocks or seaweed. It was so obviously the anemones that offered up their tempting brush ability; why were they there, if you weren't allowed to stroke them? The notion that expansive areas of a similar waving, velvety, living nap could reside, hidden, deep inside people had not exactly surprised Liz—she'd taken Human Biology in grade 10—but never had she considered sex as a kind of interior petting. It might feel, she thought, like touching a washcloth underneath the surface of the bathwater, but even softer, and tight around your wrist—a muscular cuff. Holding an octopus that grabbed you back in a fearsome, unchosen hug.

She forgot the book for a few years. Sometime before her wedding that passage came back to her, with its idea that this was another definition of closeness. It still struck her as odd, the notion of having someone on your arm like a glove puppet. Intimate, obviously. *Intimate.*

At that time, Liz seemed to have reached a backstop in the level of closeness she foresaw in her marriage. She thought this was perhaps not the most hopeful sign, right beforehand. Getting ready to spend decades together, presumably through corporeal events like childbirth, accidents, illnesses (food poisoning; surgery; whatever else might come along), aging, infirmity, death; and already she had made up her mind: Beyond this I will not look, so don't ask me. I won't be going inside you.

Not, she believed then, pre-wedding, that she ought to feel guilty about her uninterest in massaging the epithelial lining of Stokes's colon. Just that maybe it would be prudent not to have her lifelong decisions made before the ceremony even took place. That it sounded wise to head into a marriage aware that there might be visceral things to attend to, someday. Growing old or dying, either way, would mean blood, mess, getting closer than you thought you could. Being willing to delve in there.

Liz got back to Ontario late on Tuesday, spent the night at her mother's hushed house, where she had left her car, and drove the next morning to the farm museum. Stokes was in his work clothes in the shingled office attached to the barn, making notes for the unstructured playground they'd received a grant to build.

"There he is," she said. He felt so firm when she hugged him. Like a trout. "I missed you."

"Hey, I missed you more. It was boring here."

"I brought you some waffles Mom made this morning." She handed him a margarine container of warm waffle sticks and a mini jar of maple syrup, sticky on the outside. While he ate, she told him about the chuck-wagon racing; the beef jerky competition they went to, one of many; the mechanical bull in the hotel lobby that she'd urged Rena to ride, osteoporosis notwithstanding. Rena refused but seemed to like being asked.

"Mom kept saying, 'It's just so different, everything's different.' She acted old, but we stayed busy."

"I'm glad," Stokes said. "She needed something like that."

"And what did you get up to? No affair while I was gone?"

He shook his head. "No affair. Netflix and potato chips."

"Well, that's a relief."

After years of never having semen inside her, she needed now to want it, desire it as wholesome. No squeamishness about stickiness, dampness. Years of containing had to be switched off. Receptiveness and welcome.

Sharing the Calgary hotel room with her mother, Liz had thought about Rena's words in the airport. Her mom's legs had gotten so skinny and blue; her buttocks drooped down, without her floppy underpants, like unbaked biscuits. It had been so long since Liz had seen Rena change clothes. Her little breasts bagged down the front of her bony chest. All over, she was blotchy, discoloured, knobby, loose. And she wasn't even sick.

Liz would take care of Rena when she was dying, of course, but it was different from what Calvin had been lucky enough to have. One goes; one remains: math.

She thought of all the things she had known and forgotten, remembered again and forgotten again—all the weird facts and discoveries that kept disappearing and then washing ashore again. A few weeks before her father died, she was sitting in the room with him, keeping him company and not talking much.

"Wasn't I telling you about the eagle that watched me one time?" he asked. His voice was roughened but faint.

Liz nodded. "You were in the car, and the eagle was in a tree. And you stared at each other."

He said, "I was thinking, that's probably the most clearly I've ever been seen in my life."

Though it was far from the last time he spoke to her, that was the last story he told her. A story could be so short, she thought. Just a sentence, a line.

As she grows older, there seems to be more confusion inside her head about events from the past. She'll ask herself, *How long ago was that? Three years, ten years?* They seem equally plausible. The future, too, with the baby, the aging, the dying. Her or Stokes; fifty-fifty.

The mess is okay, she thinks. The blood not so bad.

Lisa Alward was born in Halifax and lives in Fredericton. Her story "Old Growth" won *The New Quarterly's* Peter Hinchcliffe Short Fiction Award in 2016 and was featured in *The Journey Prize Stories 2017*. She won *The Fiddlehead* Short Fiction Prize in 2015 and was recently long listed for *PRISM International's* Jacob Zilber Prize for Short Fiction. Her work has appeared in *16: Best Canadian Stories* as well as *The Fiddlehead*, *The New Quarterly*, and *The Dalhousie Review*.

Frankie Barnet is the author of *An Indoor Kind of Girl* (Metatron Press 2016). She is a graduate of Concordia University's English and Creative Writing and currently pursuing her MFA in fiction at Syracuse University.

Grant Buday has published ten books. His new novel, *Atomic Road*, is based on a concept by writer and curator John O'Brian of UBC. It follows Clement Greenberg and Louis Althusser on a road trip from New York City to Weyburn, Saskaktchewan, for LSD therapy, and is set against the backdrop of the Cuban Missile Crisis. It will be published in the spring of 2018 by Anvil Press.

Jowita Bydlowska was born in Warsaw, Poland, and moved to Canada as a teenager. She wrote a bestselling memoir, *Drunk Mom* (2013), and a critically acclaimed novel, *Guy* (2016). Her short stories have appeared in *Hazlitt*, *The Literary Review*, *Numéro Cinq*, and more. She currently lives in Toronto. She doesn't play any instruments and doesn't run. She's funnier in person.

Paige Cooper's short fiction has most recently appeared in *West Branch*, *The Fiddlehead*, *Canadian Notes & Queries*, *CAROUSEL*, and *The New Quarterly*, and has been anthologized in *The Journey Prize Stories* and *Best Canadian Stories*. Her first book, *Zolitude*, is out Spring 2018 with Biblioasis.

Tamas Dobozy is a professor in the Department of English and Film Studies at Wilfrid Laurier University. He lives in Kitchener, Ontario, Canada. He has published three books of short fiction, *When X Equals Marylou*, *Last Notes and Other Stories*, and, most recently, *Siege 13: Stories*, which won the 2012 Rogers Writers Trust of Canada Fiction Prize, and was shortlisted for both the Governor General's Award: Fiction, and the 2013 Frank O'Connor International Short Story Award. He has published over seventy short stories in journals such as *One Story*, *Fiction*, *Agni*, and *Granta*, and won an O. Henry Prize in 2011, and the Gold Medal for Fiction at the National Magazine Awards in 2014.

Cynthia Flood's fifth collection of short stories, *What Can You Do*, appeared from Biblioasis in 2017. Her previous book, *Red Girl Rat Boy* (Biblioasis 2013), was shortlisted for the BC Book Prizes fiction award and long-listed for the Frank O'Connor International Short Story Award. She has published widely in magazines and anthologies, most recently in *Making Room*, a 40th anniversary book publication of *Room Of One's Own* magazine (2017). "Calm" is her seventh appearance in BCS. Cynthia Flood lives in Vancouver.

David Huebert grew up in Halifax, Nova Scotia, and lives in London, Ontario. His stories have appeared in magazines such as *enRoute*, *EVENT*, *The Puritan*, *The Fiddlehead*, and *Canadian Notes & Queries*, and received awards such as the Sheldon Currie Fiction Prize and the CBC Short Story

Prize. David is also the winner of *The Walrus'* 2016 Poetry Prize and the author of the poetry collection *We Are No Longer the Smart Kids in Class.*

John Metcalf has been one of the leading editors in Canada for more than five decades, editing more than 200 books over this time, including 18 volumes of the *Best Canadian Stories* series. He is also the author of more than a dozen works of fiction and nonfiction, including *Standing Stones: Selected Stories, Vital Signs: Collected Novellas, An Aesthetic Underground: A Literary Memoir,* and *The Museum at the End of the World.* Senior Fiction Editor at Biblioasis, he lives in Ottawa with his wife, Myrna.

K.D. Miller's stories and essays have appeared in Canadian literary magazines, and her work has been broadcast by CBC. Her fourth story collection, *All Saints,* was short-listed for the 2014 Rogers Writers' Trust Award and named as one of the year's best by the *Globe and Mail.* Her forthcoming story collection, *Late Breaking,* was inspired by the paintings of Alex Colville and will be published by Biblioasis in 2018. Visit her website at: www.dawnwriter.com

Lisa Moore has written four novels, *Alligator, February, Caught,* and *Flannery* for young adults. She has written two collections of stories, *Degrees of Nakedness* and *Open.* Lisa has adapted her novel *February* for the stage. Her third collection of stories will be published Fall, 2018. She teaches at Memorial University.

Alex Pugsley is a writer and filmmaker originally from Nova Scotia. He won the 2012 Writers' Trust McClelland & Stewart Journey Prize and recently wrote and directed the feature film *Dirty Singles*, nominated for Best Canadian Feature at the 2014 Vancouver International Film Festival.

Beverley Shaw lives and writes on the South Shore of Nova Scotia. Her short story "Currents", which appears in this anthology, and another story called "New Shoes", appearing in an upcoming edition of *The New Quarterly*, are both part of a novel which she is currently writing, tentatively entitled *Undertow*. Other short fiction and poetry have previously appeared in various North American publications, including *Grain*, *Event*, *The Antigonish Review*, *Existere*, and *The Nightshade Short Story Reader*.

Anne Marie Todkill divides her time between Ottawa and North Hastings, Ontario. Her short fiction, essays, and poems have appeared in various Canadian literary magazines.

Martin West has been published in magazines across the nation and twice anthologized in the Journey Prize. His collection of stories *Cretacea* won the gold from the Independent Publishers Award and his novel *Long Ride Yellow* was released this autumn from Anvil Press.

Martha Wilson has pieces forthcoming in *The New Quarterly* and *Canadian Notes & Queries*. Her first fiction collection, to be published next year by Biblioasis, will include the story anthologized here.

"Old Growth" by Lisa Alward first appeared in *The New Quarterly*

"Cherry Sun" by Frankie Barnet first appeared in *An Indoor Kind of Girl*. Metatron Press.

"Beasts" by Grant Buday first appeared in *The Fiddlehead*

"Funny Hat" by Jowita Bydlowska first appeared in *Numéro Cinq*

"Ryan & Irene, Irene & Ryan" by Paige Cooper first appeared in *The New Quarterly*

"No. 10" by Tamas Dobozy first appeared in *Canadian Notes & Queries*

"Calm" by Cynthia Flood first appeared in *Numéro Cinq*

"Suture" by David Huebert first appeared in *The Puritan*

"The Last Trumpet" by K.D. Miller first appeared in *Canadian Notes & Queries*

"The Shoe Emporium" by Lisa Moore first appeared in *The Walrus*

"Shimmer" by Alex Pugsley first appeared in *SubTerrain*

"Currents" by Beverley Shaw first appeared in *Grain*

"Next of Kin" by Anne Marie Todkill first appeared in *The Malahat Review*

"Miss Charlotte" by Martin West first appeared in *The Fiddlehead*

"Clean" by Martha Wilson first appeared in *The New Quarterly*

The following magazines were consulted: *The Antigonish Review, The Capellano Review, Event, Exile, The Fiddlehead, Geist, Grain, The Malahat Review, Matrix, The New Quarterly, Canadian Notes & Queries, Prarie Fire, PRISM international, SubTerrain, The Puritan, Numéro Cinq,* and *The Walrus*